The Slithy Toves

Ryan Scoville

For Amy

ACKNOWLEDGMENTS

I would like to thank my mother for instilling in me the power of a story, and my father for giving me the confidence to give it a try.

I am thankful of my wife for many things, but here will just mention her continual support and encouragement. On the other hand, my three children delayed this book's completion by almost nine years due to sleepless nights, stinky diapers, crying fits and a million other things, all of which I am thankful for.

Since we do judge a book by its cover, I am in debt to Shari Glickman for the beautiful cover.

Finally, thanks to my English teacher Mr. Beato for showing me how to think critically about a story, including the question, "Does the character grow?" And yes, the first line is telling, not showing.

JABBERWOCKY

Lewis Carroll
(from *Through the Looking-Glass, and What Alice Found There*, 1872)

'Twas brillig, and the slithy toves
Did gyre and gimble in the wabe:
All mimsy were the borogoves,
And the mome raths outgrabe.

PROLOGUE

The villain's depravity is easily recognized. Wearing tattered overalls and a worn flannel shirt, he slinks through the forest, peering out from a dirt-speckled face, making sure that he is alone. His teeth are rotting and his pale flesh crusts over into pink spots. People have always turned away from him, ignoring his existence, as he lay curled up in a building entrance or pacing ravenously beneath an overpass.

Beyond appearance, loathsome desires hold sway of the thoughts behind his squinty eyes and snarled mouth. Only a few times has he given in to them, but only with stunted action and little relief. But this time is different. Realizing this strained existence can only continue for so long, that his every breath and every thought has been consumed by restraining these primal urges, he finally gives in. And completely at that.

The man frets that the barren trees don't provide enough protection, while the fallen leaves whorl around his footsteps. He has lived out here for many years now and has yet to see another person. There is no reason for today to be different. These are his woods, he reassures himself, and he is safe here.

He makes his way to the top of a ridge and shuffles into the next ravine, marked by a large white stone that lies solemnly at the bottom. The stone is distinct, separate from the hundreds of others that pockmark the forest floor, and he identifies this as the one he wants, the one that signifies fulfillment. As he nears the bottom, he slows down, bends over and carefully searches for what he knows is there. Against the uneven forest layers, the man makes out three mounds that are visible only to him. They lay haphazardly, two with maple-colored protrusions, carefully wrapped towels, extending from one end. The man walks to his favorite pile and eyes it excitedly. He no longer has to restrain himself, and the freedom alone is exhilarating. He reaches down and touches a towel. It flinches and his guilty

1

heart races faster.

The man carefully unwraps a towel to reveal a small foot underneath, soft and pink, ending in five beautiful, brightly painted toes. Each nail has been meticulously coated in Siren Red nail polish and then outlined by a thin black line. The man can hardly contain himself and lets a guttural noise escape. He unravels the second towel, revealing the matching foot, and feels giddy about the two perfect specimens before him. He holds them in complete disregard to the slender legs they are attached to, legs that jut out from an oval mound of leaves. He is ever so careful that the feet don't come into contact with the filth of the forest floor, careful to rest them on the unraveled towels, ensuring they remain clean and pure. Regardless, when he is finished, he will wash them again.

The man caresses the left foot, but as he does it jerks, and a whimpering noise rises from beneath the leaves. "It's all right," he says, petting more harshly, troubled that his appreciation for these perfect little feet is causing distress. "It's all right," he repeats, his voice echoing with uncertainty. The whimpering turns to a gentle sob and the feet, those beautiful, beautiful feet, wrench with contractions. He centers both feet on the towels and folds the sides over them. He stands and walks to the other side of the leaf pile and brushes away a handful of leaves, revealing the face of a sobbing girl beneath the foliage. Metal wires cover her face, part of the cage that holds her down. "Please don't..." he pleads, but she only cries more, cries at the sight of his grotesque features. Her tears make rivulets across her grimy face. She tries to wipe them away but can't raise her arms inside the wire cage.

Built out of necessity, the cages serve the man's needs perfectly. After laying down tarps, he wrapped each child in galvanized chicken wire. Like a spider's prey, he lugged these bound masses onto the tarps and unrolled another sheet of chicken wire across them, as if tucking them into bed. He then secured these sheets to the ground with tent spikes, ensuring the children would not be going anywhere. With his prey pinned down, he camouflaged them with a layer of leaves. This was not only to hide them from anyone passing by, but the leaves hid them from his view, allowing him to focus on the objects of his desire. With wire cutters, he freed the girl's feet from the cage and then resealed it with tape and more wire. Once finished, the mounds were almost imperceptible, leaving their unbound feet in sight, his delicate lovelies alone in the forest, waiting for him, creatures in their own right.

But the feet are still attached. And when the girl cries, they cry. His angels cry. A situation he cannot accept.

The man replaces the leaves over the girl's face, muffling her sobs, and looks around. He makes his way to another pile, the one without any protrusions, and scoops the leaves away from one end. A young boy's face, fearful but resolute, looks back at him. He kneels down and places his face directly in front of the boy's, filling the hole in the leaves with thick, rotting breath. He whispers a plea, "I need you to do something." The boy turns his head as far as he can and closes his eyes. He shakes forcefully, trying to somehow escape, but the cage is too tight. "Stop your crying," the man whispers angrily, but the boy only convulses more violently, writhing in protest, rubbing his already raw skin against the wires.

The man reaches into a pocket and pulls out a switchblade. With purpose, he slowly opens it over the boy's face, twirling it in the light. "See this?" he asks. The boy stops and studies it with widening eyes. "Feel this?" the man asks, as he puts the blade against the center of the leaf pile and pushes downward, cutting lightly into the boy's chest. He now has the boy's attention.

"So nice," the man smiles, exposing teeth in their final stage of decay. "I want you to talk to your friend, the blonde. Go ahead, say something! Say her name."

The knife scrapes along the boy's chest, as he gasps, "Sue!"

The man waits, but there is no response. "Say it again, but nice like."

"Sue."

"Andy?" comes trembling from the nearby pile, between sobs.

"Answer her," the man whispers.

"Hi. It's me."

"Help me, Andy?"

The boy looks to the man for guidance.

"Tell her everything is all right," he instructs. "Tell her to stop crying, because everything is all right."

"Stop crying. Everything is all right."

"It's not," Sue replies. "I want to go home."

"Tell her not to cry," the man whispers, more emphatically.

"Don't cry, Sue."

"I want to go home," she repeats, but with a steadier voice. Her sobs are subsiding.

The man contemplates what should be said next, glad the children seem calmer, when another girl's voice, farther down the ravine, calls out, "Help me!"

"You shut the fuck up!" the man yells, standing tall and storming toward the pile that just spoke. "Just shut the fuck up!" A mousy squeal comes from the pile and then silence, and he is certain she will not talk again. But as he turns, he hears sobs from Sue's pile, and he is back to where he started.

The man returns to the boy's pile, kneels over his face and talks to him. "Now I want you to know everything's going to be all right. Okay? Everything's going to be fine."

The boy says nothing, trapped in the shadow of his jailor.

"Now that Sue, she's all afraid and all. I don't know why. I haven't done anything to her; she just is. But you're a big boy. I need you to tell her everything will be all right. I need you to comfort her. As long as she stops crying, everything will be all right. You go and tell her that." The man tries to smile innocently, but the boy winces, knowing he doesn't want to find out what lies behind that smile.

"Sue," the boy says, trying to sound confident, "this is Andy again."

"I miss my mom," she responds.

"I know, but you need to stop crying. The less you cry, the more likely it is we can go home."

"Good, good," the man whispers to the boy.

"Do you hear me, Sue?"

"Yes."

"Can you keep calm for me?" There's no response, and the boy asks again, "Can you do that for me, Sue? Keep calm?"

"I think so."

"Good, Sue. If you can do that, everything is going to be all right. We just have to keep calm. Okay?"

"Okay, Andy."

"Get her to say it," the man whispers. "Get her to say she won't cry anymore."

"Can you say it, Sue? Can you tell me you won't cry?"

"I'll try."

The boy looks at the man, who shakes his head. "That won't be enough," the boy says. "I need you to tell me you won't cry anymore. You need to be strong, Sue. Can you do that?"

"I think I can."

"And you won't cry anymore?"

"No, I won't."

"You won't what?"

"I won't cry anymore."

With that, the man smiles and whispers, "Good boy," before replacing the leaves over the boy's face, plunging him back into darkness.

For a moment, the boy feels all right, distracted by thinking about someone other than himself. Asking Sue to calm down helped him as much as it helped her. That is until the noises start.

At first, there is just heavy breathing and incoherent muttering, which the boy tries to ignore. But the forest seems silent against the backdrop of the man's noises. "Oh such beautiful... so soft... angels... yes... little perfect angels..." The breathing gets heavier, and through it all, the boy keeps his fists clenched. He hears no one besides the man. He thinks of anything and everything but the man and Sue, then settles on thinking about nothing at all, listening to nothing, interpreting nothing. All things eventually pass. He hears some final movements, and eventually the man trudges off across the forest floor, leaving only silence.

They know not to speak. They have already experienced the consequences of talking. And they never know when the man is listening. But as the boy breathes in his cage, the freshly-cut wound across his chest stings, and with it, a new hope. He works his right hand, pressed against the side of his body, upward across his emaciated stomach and chest. His arm snugly squeezes between the wire cage and his rib cage, where he finds the switchblade, still open. He grabs it firmly, knowing if it falls, he'll never reach it again. He works his arm back to his side and begins the laborious process of rubbing the knife-edge against one of the metal wires. His arm tires and he wonders if the blade is sharp enough, when he finally feels it snap through.

The boy prays no one is around, that the man doesn't come back, as he slowly cuts through two more wires. The second one frees his elbow and allows him to swing his arm out and work at a better angle.

Many of the wires still pull tight across his body, and so he must awkwardly manipulate the knife between them and his flesh, pushing outward. The back of the blade rubs new cuts into his skin, while the pointed end jabs open fresh wounds. He works through the pain, discovering extra resolve each time a wire snaps free.

He brushes the leaves away from his face to reveal a sliver of moon illuminating the desolate tree limbs reaching above him. He works the strand that holds his neck and chin down, until a final slice allows him to squeeze down out of the trap and then sit up. His muscles stretch with freedom as he looks around, but no one is there. He works his legs out, pulling back with his elbows along the forest floor, writhing out from the hole he has made and eventually flopping over as he breaks free. He lies there momentarily, expecting the man to pounce on him, but when nothing happens, the boy rises.

He stands slowly, reacquainting himself with a posture other than lying down, his muscles bracing to hold balance. He looks around in the darkness, unable to see either of the other girl's mounds, not comprehending how well they have been hidden. He cannot call out, afraid the man may be nearby, and sees only the black trees around him and the muted glow of moonlight on the leaf-strewn ground. He would help the girls if he could, but as far as he knows, he is alone. Not wanting to be there a moment longer, the boy chooses a direction and starts running, running as fast as he can. He moves blindly, clipping himself against trees and tripping along the craggy ground. Each time he stumbles, he regains his footing and resumes his sprint, his only thought being escape.

After what feels like an endless distance, the boy comes over an embankment and discovers a road below. He mindlessly chooses a direction for his escape, sprinting until his side explodes in pain, forcing him to walk, crying softly as he pushes his fingers into his abdomen. Once the pain subsides, he runs again, but the pain returns and he reverts to walking, wondering how he will ever make it home.

Near exhaustion, lost and desperate, the boy realizes light is making its way into the forest. The moon has disappeared behind the tree line, and a smoky haze fills everything around him, signaling the coming day. A low rumbling noise grows in the distance; the sound of a car approaching. He leaps into a ditch and cautiously watches as a station wagon approaches, its yellow headlights piercing the dawn light. As the car passes, the boy sees a lone woman driving the car.

He rushes to the road behind her waving his arms. The car almost disappears from sight when the brake lights flash and the car squeals to a halt. The driver's door opens and the woman steps out. "Hello?" she calls out, studying the hunched shadow down the road, unsure what she is looking at. "Who's there?" She cautiously approaches, squinting through the morning light until she can make out the young boy's figure, until he comes into focus, when she stops and mutters, "God in heaven."

The man hardly sleeps that night as his mind bounces between fits of guilt and pleasure. He tells himself he is too far in, there is no point in feeling guilty. This does not help. He tells himself it is not his fault, that the lovelies called him, seduced him into these acts, but this does not help either. He convinces himself he is not hurting anyone, not really, not like he's been hurt, and this helps a little. Only when he thinks of his perfect little angels, only when he concentrates on them and nothing else, when he remembers the way they look and feel, their perfect juncture of curves and lines, the maturity of the Siren Red polish softened by the youth of their soft, pink underside, their smooth arch stretching into delicate indices, only then does he fall into an anticipatory sleep.

He rises well after sunrise and pulls a loaf of stale bread from the cupboard of the dingy one-room shack. He can't find his switchblade, vaguely remembers leaving it with the children, and finds a serrated knife to cut the loaf in half. He consumes his half, puts the knife in his back pocket and tucks the other half under his arm. Grabbing a jug of water with a long straw, he heads out for the children.

Crossing over the last hill and into the ravine, he immediately sees what has happened. The broken cage and tussled leaves lay open like a ruptured organ. The man looks around the empty forest, certain the boy is long gone. Fear screams in his head. What to do? What to do? He runs to the broken cage and inspects it, examines the sawed edges of frayed wire. His switchblade! In his ecstasy, he left it with the boy, within the boy's grasp!

He runs to a set of towel-wrapped legs, the ones he revered yesterday, and unwraps them, finding the same, perfectly manicured feet. The girls are still here, but what about the boy? How far has he gotten? He has to be found. All he can do is stare at those feet, those tiny little toes painted in that perfect Siren Red and outlined with black eyeliner. His little angels. He runs to the top of the hill and looks out, around, but sees nothing. He runs to the next ravine and then the next, teeth clenched as he holds his breath. Birds chirp in the distance. The forest is too large. The boy is gone.

He walks back to Sue's mound, contemplating what to do next, fear and anger rising inside. When he arrives, he looks at the ankles, those ugly connections protruding from the pile of leaves, leading to his angels. One foot jerks, a subtle side movement before returning to its resting position. This gesture confirms what he knows, a quick wink of acknowledgement, mockery. They made him do this. They made him do everything. It wasn't his fault. He just listened, listened to their commands and obeyed. They are the cause of everything.

Anger wells up inside the man as he realizes that they have conspired against him all along. They've set him up. Those little toes, those little spies. They devised this. They are to blame. All those years, calling him, seducing him, only to now betray him. He looks at the little creatures, no longer his angels, no longer his lovelies, and wonders how things have come to this. The man wretches as he realizes what must be done, but simultaneously commits to the task. He steps over the girl's feet and sits across her ankles, pinning the spies before him. He reaches into his back pocket and grasps the handle of the knife, ready to make its serrated edge, the blade's tiny toes, go to war with his lovelies. He holds her right foot securely in his left hand, questioning one last time how it could be unfaithful, and places the blade against the outside of the smallest toe, sawing inward.

The wailing starts immediately and the feet writhe. The man almost falls over, steadying himself again and putting all of his weight on the girl's ankles. The leaves piled behind him shake as the girl struggles. The man's thoughts drown, mixing his anger with her screams, as if she were yelling with him, encouraging his rage. Dark red splatters across the toes, defiling their intrinsic beauty, and for the first time the man senses his control over them. Feeling empowered, he clenches his teeth and saws faster.

"You betrayed me!" His voice echoes through the forest. "But I know, now I know, you are not my angels, you are lying spies!"

The knife has trouble cutting through the bone, scraping back and forth but not breaking through. He pulls it around and wedges it between the adjoining toe, working from the other side, determined to take it off, still oblivious to the girl's screams.

"Spies!" he cries at the toes, "You fucking spies! There'll be no more!

No more spying!"

And then it is done. The angel slices off, landing delicately in the leaves, with one coat of Siren Red polish glistening beneath another coat of blood red. The girl momentarily stops screaming, wiggling her still-connected toes as the full weight of what just happened dawns on her. The man looks at his bloody hands, the bloody foot, and grins.

The girl's realization breaks the silence with even more intense screams and shakes. The man replies, "Spies! Spies! Spies!" He settles into a repetitive mantra, yelling, "No more spying toes!" over and over.

The other girl is now screaming too, and he needs to silence them. He needs to concentrate on the spying toes.

He looks around and spots the ravine's marker, the pallid white stone, its chalky surface mocking the purity of his devotion. He hunches around it, braces it in his arms, and lifts the stone up into his chest, his bloody palms leaving handprints as he adjusts the stone. He lumbers back to the edge of the pile from where the covered screams emanate.

"No more spies! No more spying toes!"

The man stands resolutely over the mound of leaves, knowing the girl cannot see him, unaware of her impending fate. He raises the stone higher, balances it against his shoulder and prepares for the finishing motion. He pulls up onto the balls of his feet and gathers his will, when a shot rings out and a force rips through his side.

The man stumbles and the stone's weight pulls him down, like clutching an anchor thrown overboard. Instead of wondering what happened, or even acknowledging the hollow pain in his side, he feels only the single-minded determination to finish the act. He must end his lovelies' screams. The man pulls himself up onto the stone and sees blood gathering across its pitted surface. He hunches over and heaves the stone up one more time. He steps toward the pile when another shot rings out and a pressure explodes through the side of his head. The rock thuds to the ground, followed by the man's limp body.

The villain is dead.

1

Routine is a friend to Jim Hughes. It always has been. He wakes at the same time each morning, never hitting the snooze button, and jogs for twenty minutes. He showers, eats breakfast while reading the news on his iPad, and goes to work. Day in and day out, year after year. Up at 6:30, breakfast at 7:30, lunch at noon, dinner at 6. He reads for a half hour before going to bed. He cleans the house on Saturdays. Every six months he goes to the dentist, changes the furnace filter, and partakes in the semi-annual Hughes Big House Clean, more commonly known as spring and fall cleaning.

Jim takes pride in his routines, but he also takes pride that he isn't compulsive. When need be, he can move or skip part of his daily rituals without a worry, just as long as he gets back on track as soon as possible.

He appreciates the benefits of being habitual. Those tiny questions that fester in peoples' minds can usually be satisfied with a few minutes of routine each day, every day. Did I pay my bills? Am I gaining weight? Do I know what's going on in the world? Pay your bills on a schedule. Jog twenty minutes in the morning. Read the paper. Done, done and done.

Jim also gains security from his schedule. No matter what's going on in his life, no matter the ups and downs at work or home, his routines provide the taut stability of tent ropes in the wind.

Which is why he feels disorientated when he realizes he has run too far. Rather than turning right on Old Tavern Road, he continued jogging up Blackhawk until it ended at Ogden. He jogs in place, staring at the red light, aware there are no red lights on his route. 'How did I get here?' he questions before turning around and getting back on his usual route. He picks up the pace, makes only one trip around the park instead of the usual two, and is home and in the shower by 7:00. Back on track, back on schedule. Nothing to worry about.

Showered and dressed, Jim sits before a plate of scrambled eggs, two strips of bacon, and a glass of orange juice. "Morning," he calls out, perching his iPad above his plate. He swipes through a few headlines and reads the first paragraph or two of a few business articles when he notices the mumbling across the table. Jim looks at his daughter across from him, schoolbook open, with her head turned at an awkward angle as she mumbles something into the air.

"What are you doing?"

Emily's lips stop moving and she traces her finger along a line of text. "Stupid poem," she mutters.

"What?"

"I have to memorize a stupid poem."

"Which poem?"

"It's called 'The Jabberwocky.' It's so stupid."

"Really."

"Everyone in class has to memorize a poem, and I got stuck with the hardest one. Arielle got that two-roads-in-the-woods one. That's so easy." Emily looks at the book again, mouths a line, and then closes her eyes and mouths it again, this time taking a lock of chestnut hair and curling it in her fingers.

"You're doing it again," Jim points out.

"I don't care. This poem is so stupid. It doesn't even use real words."

"'Twas brillig and the slithy toves?" Jim asks, reciting the first line in the poem.

Emily looks up, more annoyed than impressed. This means her teacher didn't pick the most ridiculous, most obscure poem possible. "How did you know that?"

"College. For some reason I always remembered that one. *Alice in Wonderland*, right?"

"I think so, but it's not fair. The words are just made up. How am I supposed to memorize..," she looks back down and points at a line, "All mimsy were the borogoves?"

Jim worries this will not diminish Emily's long-standing notion that all her teachers are out to get her. It is an extremely hard poem to memorize. "Let me see," Jim says, standing up and walking behind his daughter.

Carrie Hughes, wife and mother, watches them from the adjoining kitchen, completely overlooked. She won't sit, instead standing all morning with a glass of orange juice, nibbling a strip of bacon, silently observing. Her eyes are tired, bloodshot, and sagging, and she watches her family as if they're an exhibit behind a glass partition.

"It's so stupid, it doesn't even mean anything," Emily complains again. "Why did you have to learn it in college?"

"It was a philosophy class. We were learning about meaning, how things don't really have meaning until we give it to them. Like the words in this poem."

"That doesn't make sense."

"Yeah it does," Jim replies. "It did."

"Then what does this mean?"

"Well that's the thing. It's using regular grammar: nouns, verbs, and what not. It has lots of little real words to make a sentence, but it also has made-up words that almost sound real. I mean, what's a slithy tove? They're not real words, so you have to provide the meaning. You can read it however you like, whether you want it to be scary or happy, funny or dramatic. Let me see..." Leaning over Emily's shoulder, Jim begins reading in a deep, thunderous voice, holding out his hand as if orating Shakespeare.

"'Twas brillig and the slithy toves,
Did gyre and gimble in the wabe:
All mimsy, were the borogoves,
And the mome raths outgrabe."

"What are you doing?" Emily squeals.

"That was a dramatic reading."

"It was?"

"Yes. Or how about this?" Jim rereads the first two lines, this time in a quick squeaky falsetto.

"What was that?"

"That was comedic."

"How was that comedic, Dad?"

"You're laughing."

"No I'm not."

With that, Jim makes a quick movement toward his daughter's side, not touching her, but enough to make her squeeze her arms into her sides. There's little she can do, as Jim only has to pretend to tickle her to send her into fits of giddy laughter. "You really didn't think that was comedic?" Jim asks, poking her armpits as she bites her lip, holding back. "Cause it sure seems like you thought it was funny."

"Mm-mm," Emily disagrees, her lips clenched.

"But you see what I mean?" Jim says, returning to his seat, "It doesn't have meaning until you provide it."

"Whatever."

Jim lets it go, realizing he's repeated the words from some professor he heard years ago, a lecture he probably mouthed 'whatever' at too.

They finish breakfast and put their plates in the sink. Emily approaches her mom, who bends over without looking, and gives her a kiss on the cheek. "'Bye, mom."

"Be careful," Carrie says out of habit.

"Can I sleep over at Arielle's tonight?" Emily asks, halfway out the door.

"Sure," her mother says reflexively.

Jim pauses and adds, "I may be late tonight too. We have some clients in town..."

"Sure."

"Have a good day," Jim says, closing the door.

He throws his briefcase into the backseat of the old blue Porsche while Emily holds her backpack in her lap. He starts the car, they buckle up, and Emily puts the stick shift into reverse. He backs out onto the street and she puts it into first, while Jim holds his hand in the air above hers, ready to take control and put it into second, father and daughter following their daily routine.

2

Steve Cardell opens his laptop and begins the presentation one more time. "The semiconductor industry has been riding the exponential growth of Moore's Law for almost fifty years. But as process geometries shrink into the deep sub-micron…"

Too wordy. Too polished. Too much trade jargon. He has never flubbed a presentation before, a fact that should instill confidence, but his mind keeps thinking – it has to happen someday. The words just weren't coming out right.

And as always, this is the worst possible time. This presentation is important.

The sun is coming up, but the shades are drawn in Steve's home office, and he stares in the darkness at his laptop. There's a knock on the door.

"Yes."

"Hey dad."

"Morning Arielle. What's up?"

"Can I sleep over at Emily's tonight?"

"Yes."

Arielle stands at the door until Steve realizes he needs to say something else. "You're not missing anything?"

"No. Soccer's at eleven tomorrow. I'll bring my bag and we'll get a ride with Emily's dad."

Steve grabs his phone, pulls up his calendar and confirms. "Okay. Sounds good." Arielle continues to stand in the doorway, staring at Steve, while he stares at his presentation, aware he should say something. There are just a few more bullets in the slide deck he wants to clean up.

"Do you want breakfast, Dad?"

"No thanks, I'm not hungry."

"It's the most important meal."

"That's what I keep hearing." They've covered this many times before. "What are you having for breakfast?"

"Apple Jacks."

"Sounds like a nutritious start."

"Apple, Dad. It's like eating an apple for breakfast." Steve smiles. They've covered this before too, and he wonders where Arielle got her dry sense of humor. He enjoys it, but feels it makes her seem older. Too old. He glances over, and she's all angles and elbows in her jeans and t-shirt, a slightly awkward eleven-year-old, not far from twelve and then a teen. Her frame looks barely able to support her wild curls, her mother's curls, as she leans against the doorframe. He can imagine how she'll learn to maintain those frizzy locks, grow into them and make them her own, just like her mother did. He turns back to his presentation and tries to concentrate.

"Do you want coffee?"

"Yes, please," he thinks, wondering again how she was becoming so old. Not long ago she would wrinkle her nose at the smell of coffee. Now she can make a pot, probably from watching him, and he's sure she'll someday be a coffee drinker, making him buy expensive flavored coffees instead of his tub of Folgers. He used to buy the expensive brands, for Arielle's mother, and he wonders if he's really envisioning the woman she'll grow into, or just re-imagining who her mother was. He looks to the doorway to tell Arielle something, but she is gone.

3

Carrie notices the leaves have changed color, hanging loosely overhead in oranges and reds, and wonders if this happened overnight. She wonders if everything changes overnight. This had once been her neighborhood, their neighborhood. They were one of the first families to move in almost eleven years ago. She was pregnant, and it seemed like every block had young parents moving in, swing sets going up in the back yards, miniature basketball hoops in the driveways, and the chaotic clustering of front lawn toys throughout the summer.

Most of the houses were still being built back then, filling the neighborhood with large trucks and construction crews, land-moving vehicles embedding dirt tracks along the streets. The worry back then, with kids chasing errant baseballs, was that the streets just weren't safe. Neighbors gossiped about how somebody saw a construction crew speed in, roll through a stop sign, and careen into a work site. This was a minor scandal and as bad as things got.

Within two years, most of the homes were complete. Their lawns had merged over the lines of freshly unrolled sod, and the parkway saplings had outgrown the strings holding them. These little trees grew few leaves, provided little shade, and weren't thick enough for the children to hide behind, let alone climb. Men would stand around during the block parties, a beer in one hand and a spatula in the other, and discuss how those trees would be giant pillars someday, secretly thinking how they might provide shade for their children's children. Everyone would nod and smile, admiring the straight, simple line through time, and how easy it would be to go from here to there.

Carrie walks past the neighbors' houses and thinks about their first

Easter egg hunt, when Emily was not much more than a year old. The trees were just starting to look like they belonged, fences were going up, porches were being built, and the neighborhood was showing character.

Jim and Carrie had a bag of multi-colored, plastic Easter eggs and took great pleasure in hiding them. They laughed as they walked around their open yard, dropping an egg in plain sight, bright oranges, greens and blues scattered across the lawn, and asking each other, "Do you think she'll find this one?" They then hovered over Emily, one with a basket for holding the eggs and the other with the camera.

"Go get that one!" they exclaimed, pointing to an egg only a few feet away, allowing Emily to amble over, giggle as she picked it up and held it high, eliciting clapping and praise. She would place it in the basket and wait for them to point out the next egg for her to find. Even after she "found" them all, they spent most of the afternoon re-hiding the eggs so she could chase them down again.

That day seems forever ago. Carrie is certain that it was not only a different time but a different place. She has these memories of happiness, but nothing recent. The joy is gone. Their youthfulness disappeared in the night, taking the warmth and sunshine of summer with it, leaving only the consolation prize of these brightly colored leaves, portraits of past sunlight.

Carrie walks to the north end of Tate Park and steps over a low hanging chain to enter Busey Woods. These trees are old, remnants of the forest that once covered most of the state. They were here long before she moved in, and will be here long after. She wonders what they're thinking, if they have a better perspective on the vastness of time, if they have a secret method for staying strong.

When she returns home, she will wander from room to room with nothing to do, determined to do nothing. She refuses to give in to television, sedating her day with distractions, preferring to wander aimlessly, sit for long periods of insatiable silence, and wait.

But for now, her morning walk through the woods makes her life seem almost bearable.

4

Natalya Collini lines up sandwiches across the kitchen counter, each one next to the brown bag it will end up in, her ingredients gathered to the side. She takes inventory. Two peanut butter and jelly sandwiches, one ham and cheese, and one crunchy peanut butter with Miracle Whip, which of course is for Alex. He claims he likes it, but also likes the attention of being different. She plays along with his requests and hopes it will pass. "Gross," his sister says, watching Natalya spread Miracle Whip on an empty piece of bread and slap it together with the crunchy peanut butter.

The children are all around her, although there is too much commotion to look after them. As long as she knows baby Vincenzo is all right, then she assumes the rest are all right until one screams above the din. In the Collini house, screams are what it takes to get any attention. The difficulty for Natalya is subduing one child's meltdown before another starts up. Sometimes motherhood is just keeping the plates spinning.

The bread lies open in pairs and Natalya meticulously continues assembling. Jab, scoop, spread. Place, ply, fold. Repeat. Repeat. Repeat. Four sandwiches placed into four bags, an apple in three of the bags and a banana in the last. Antonio's bag also gets a snack bar, as he will probably work late, this being the start of the busy holiday season.

Of course, Antonio would never complain about what she put in his lunch. She wonders what keeps him going, how he remains so enthusiastic when their lives are so chaotic. How, after putting in so much over-time, did he still summon the energy to come home and play with the children? On those nights when he is visibly exhausted, when he should go straight to bed, he instead takes a deep breath, puts on a smile and charges into the children's rooms as the tickle monster, riling them into screams of delight, while Natalya waits down the hall and worries about how much more difficult it will be to get them to sleep. "If I can't play with my children…?"

he replies to her disapproving looks, never completing the alternative, just flashing his misaligned grin and romping off after the kids.

Natalya marvels at how he can carry on like this with the knowledge that bills are not being paid. Perhaps it's because he doesn't spend all day in the presence of the mail holder full of late notices and overdue slips, and he's never repeatedly run the calculator over the same numbers, watching their meager savings dwindle away. This is why she tells him to be careful, although he just laughs it off. "Careful of what?" he asks, and she doesn't think he really knows. "Just be careful," she repeats, to which he embraces her tightly and says, "Yes, mio amore."

But they aren't careful enough, and here she stands over four bagged lunches, waiting for her husband and children to scoop them up, leaving her at home with Katya, baby Vincenzo, and the new Collini just starting to form in her belly, assuming the test was right. That will make six kids.

Natalya picks up Katya, who likes to stand in the doorway of the open fridge and look up at all the things she dare not touch. She carries Katya by her armpits, her curly hair bouncing, and places her by the kitchen table, out of the way but not out of sight. To Natalya's continual dismay, the girl begins undressing, taking her shirt off first. Natalya closes her eyes and shakes her head, not because her little girl is a streaker, but because she sees the thick scar across her still bloated tummy, the last visible sign of the disease that almost took Katya away. Natalya hates Katya's scar, yet views her own scar, the one from which doctors took out part of her liver and put into Katya, with great pride. She cherishes her own scar. Natalya picks a stuffed animal off the floor, hands it to Katya as a distraction, and redresses her, lost in thought once again about the procedure.

Even though Natalya provided Katya with part of her liver, and the family provided all the love and support a family could, they could not afford the procedure. Or to be more precise, their insurance thought they could afford it, forcing them into monthly payments that took just enough out of the paychecks to keep ends from meeting.

So rather than declare bankruptcy, Antonio's paycheck has just enough taken out each month that they slip a little further behind, until years from now they will find themselves in the same predicament. Bankrupt. Every day she is thankful for the procedure, and will do whatever it takes to pay their share, but she knows that right now they are just not doing enough. Another child will only make it harder.

She has not told Antonio yet. He won't see the downside. He'll claim she worries too much and ignore the medical costs of having another baby, the costs of another mouth to feed, the costs of another delay in her returning to work.

And what if something else goes wrong? What if the car breaks down, or the refrigerator makes one of those ominous sputtering noises and peters out for good? Or what if something happens to another one of the children? That is her deepest fear, that Katya might one day reject her transplanted liver or this new child will be born with its own special disease. She doesn't want to concentrate on these possibilities, yet can't keep them out of her mind. Only during the rush of activity can she let it go, which luckily, is most of the day. She watches Alex dump his cereal bowl into the sink, grab the wrong lunch, and start for the door.

"Alex, whose name is on that bag?"

"I don't know, Momma," he answers, suspecting that it's not his, but not willing to look.

"That's your sister's."

Gemma gives him a stern glare as she marches over and takes the bag out of his hand. She peers inside and asks, "What'd you do to this?"

"Nothing."

Gemma assumes otherwise.

"He didn't do anything," Natalya assures her.

"What did you do?" Gemma repeats.

"He didn't do anything, Gemma."

"Who didn't do what?" Antonio asks, entering the room with baby Vincenzo in his arms. Gregor, quietly in the middle, grabs his lunch, and now all three children are rummaging through their brown bags, taking inventory of the meager contents. Complaints are soon to follow. The day's turmoil gets underway, and Natalya's worries are put on hold.

5

Jim calls home a little after five. Nobody answers. He doubts Carrie is out, and the thought that she is sitting somewhere in the house, listening to the phone ring without responding, chills him. Another reason not to go home. "Hey," he says into the answering machine, "I do have to take out those clients, so I won't be home until later." He waits, glad she is not answering, but at the same time strangely perturbed.

He arrives at the apartment complex at six. For some reason he has gotten into the habit of parking in front of the wrong building, as if this little trickery will let him deny ever being here. The blue Porsche stands out wherever he parks it, and he ends up conspicuously walking two blocks with a bottle of Bordeaux in hand. On other trips he's carried flowers. Very discreet.

He punches the code to enter the main hallway and finds door 5B slightly ajar. After stepping in, closing the door, and taking off his jacket, Reagan leaps around the corner into his arms, almost knocking the wine out of his hand. She presses her lips hard against his, exclaiming between kisses, "I've been wanting to do that all day."

"Glad to be of assistance."

At work, Reagan wears modest outfits, keeping her auburn hair up and away from her face, which is always framed in narrow black glasses. Yet inexplicably beyond her conservative dress, she exudes a sex appeal that makes every male at the office wonder what she looks like when she lets her hair down. Jim knows, surveying the chocolate-colored skirt and jacket she wore all day, but now with her pressed white shirt midway unbuttoned. Reagan's thick hair bounces at her shoulders, accentuating the soft patches of freckles on her nose and cheeks. She's applied new makeup, a darker eye shadow and crimson lipstick, which Jim will have to thoroughly check himself for before heading home.

"Oh how thoughtful," Reagan exclaims, taking the bottle and reading the label, "This is French, right?" She stumbled miserably the last time he brought a French label, pronouncing every vowel and consonant in Languedoc Roussillon. Jim thought it was cute, watching her finish with squinting eyes, then mutter "whatever," and change the subject. He hopes she attempts this one, Chateau La Boutignane, but she hands it to him saying, "Someday I'm going to learn all about these."

"I can help, if you'd like. It's hard to learn about wine from books," he says, reflecting on the frivolous period he went through in trying to become a better oenophile. He wonders how much he can remember from the hours spent memorizing labels and vintages, trying to discern the perfect adjective for each wine before recording it into his wine journal. He finds the plastic corkscrew in a drawer of ladles and wooden spoons, matchbooks sprinkled throughout. The handle has Fat City Saloon written across it in bubble letters.

"Exactly. I don't want to learn them at the store or in some book," Reagan exclaims. "I want to go there and visit all the vineyards. I want to make a trip of it."

"That's probably the best way to do it."

"Do you want to go with me?"

She leans into him, her perfume filling his nostrils with the impulse to say yes. "We'll see," is the best he can do.

"You've been there before, right?"

"France? A few times."

"Well, that's it. I'm adding it to my list. Go to France and learn about French wines."

Jim wonders how big Reagan's list is, as she seems to be adding to it all the time. More importantly, he wonders if she ever crosses anything off.

"So you'll go with me?" she asks again.

"We'll see."

"What fun! I've never been to Europe. We can stay at cute little chateaus in the countryside, and you can show me all the places where the wines are made. Do you speak French?"

"Not really, a few phrases, but you can get by with English."

"Perfect. I can't wait."

"Me either," he says, avoiding eye contact.

She leans over and kisses him, then walks around and wraps herself in his arms.

Jim breaks one arm free to pour the wine, and tries in futility to think of the circumstances that would permit them to go to Europe together. The sheer impossibility makes him enjoy the idea more, but he knows better than to get Reagan's hopes up. "Do you have a passport?"

"Oh, no. I guess I need one?"

"Yep, they're pretty strict about that."

Reagan's lips pout, and with that one little obstacle, the trip to France may now be off the list, or at least pushed down far enough not to matter.

They carry the food and wine out to the living room coffee table, where Jim sits on the couch and Reagan sits across from him, on the floor. Candles flicker throughout the room and a DVD of a fireplace crackles on her flat screen, dimly lighting the main course. Reagan tears open a bag of salad, pouring the contents into their salad bowls. The main course is a quiche she poured and heated from a mix, and for dessert, they have the one thing she made herself, chocolate chip cookies.

"I hate that thing," Reagan says.

"What thing?"

"The fake fireplace."

Jim looks at the video of the fire and listens to the crackling and popping emanating from the TV's speakers. "It's nice. Easy to start, easy to clean up."

"But it's not real. It's a fake, and I'm tired of having fake things."

"What do you mean?"

"A fake fireplace. Fake leather couches. Fake china. Fake crystal. A fake glass table. I deserve better than this."

"I'm pretty sure this is real glass," Jim says, knocking on the coffee table.

"A fake relationship…"

"Yes, I'm certain this is real glass."

"Jim," Reagan pleads.

Jim straightens his smile and looks carefully around the room, not wanting to address the issue. He thinks of his apartment just out of college, when Carrie moved in with him. They didn't have much then, but he remembers it fondly. Now they have so much more, enough to trick a girl like Reagan into thinking she wants him and his lifestyle. If she only knew what his lifestyle is like.

"Well, however you feel about it, I enjoy coming over. I enjoy this place. You've got a real sense of style."

"Thank you."

And with that, he moves on. "What are your doing this weekend?"

"You're changing the subject."

"What? I want to know what you're doing this weekend. I'm interested."

"But you're changing the subject."

"What subject?"

"Never mind," Reagan concedes. "I've got a bunch of errands to do tomorrow, then maybe some shopping. I'm going out with the girls tomorrow night; there's this new club they want to try."

"Sounds fun."

"I'll miss you."

"Oh, don't miss me. I'm doing work around the house, taking Emily to soccer practice, and probably staying in to read. Not exactly glamorous."

"That sounds fun to me. Nice and relaxing."

"Really?"

"Really. I would love to spend a nice and relaxing day with you."

"Mmm-hmm," Jim grunts with a smile. "You'd be bored in a minute."

"No I wouldn't."

"Then we can relax right now."

"Maybe," Reagan says, as she runs her fingers across the open buttons of her blouse, revealing the tract of skin beneath her neck.

"Maybe later," Jim says as he stands and circles the coffee table, lowering himself onto the pillow next to her, glad the uncomfortable need for discourse has passed.

6

Jim wakes with a slow drowsiness. The sheets are mostly off him, and he gives a reflexive tug, finding them wrapped around Carrie, clutching tight. This is one of the few interactions they still have. He thinks about where he was the previous night and decides to let Carrie have the covers. It's time to get up. He changes into jogging clothes and stretches in the foyer. He does a quick morning run, drinks a Gatorade, showers, and dresses for the day. On the way downstairs, Jim checks Emily's room to find her bed still made, and remembers that she spent the night at Arielle's house.

He makes a large pot of coffee, and halfway through the first cup, gains his resolve for the day, mentally checking off everything he needs to do and how long it will take. The only unknown is Emily. Will he have to drive her to soccer practice? What will she do afterwards? Where will she want to go tonight? Jim might not finish everything he wants to today, but doesn't mind chauffeuring Emily around, glad that she still needs him. Soccer practice doesn't start until eleven, so he has some time.

He goes to the garage, pulls out both cars, unravels the garden hose and fills a bucket with water. The air is crisp, football weather, and the soapy water prickles his skin every time he sticks his arm into the bucket. Carrie's Lexus hasn't left the garage since he last washed it, but he still sponges it down, part of his Saturday routine. He extends the wipers like fractured joints, and works across the windshield. A Volkswagen Jetta passes but Jim pays no attention. He doesn't see Reagan drive by, doesn't comprehend her need to see the house he lives in, and is completely oblivious to the pounding excitement she experiences from catching a glimpse of him. Instead, he finishes and steps back, admiring a completed chore, parks the cars in the garage, and goes inside, opening and closing his fingers to warm them up.

It's almost ten, and Emily's practice starts at eleven. Jim knows Arielle's dad well enough that he may not remember their soccer practice. He sits down at the kitchen table and dials Steve Cardell's number. As it rings, he wonders if Carrie is up yet. Yesterday's breakfast dishes sit in the sink, and he wonders what she did all day. He wonders if she even ate. He makes a mental note to wash them after this call.

"Hello?"

"Hi Steve, this is Jim," Jim starts, and adds for good measure, "Emily's dad."

"Hi Jim."

"I'm just calling because the girls have soccer at eleven."

"They do? Oh right, let me check my phone…, yes, eleven o'clock, Arielle's soccer practice. Got it."

Jim waits, wondering how little this guy knows or cares about what is going on with his daughter. It worries him that Emily spends so much time there.

"So?" Steve asks.

Jim closes his eyes with annoyance, "I was just calling to remind Emily, see if she needed anything."

"Hmm?"

"See if she has her cleats and uniform. Or if she needs a ride. Could I speak to her?"

"She's not here."

"What?"

"She's not here. They spent the night at your house."

Jim rubs his still-closed eyes, certain Steve is making a mistake. He wonders if he's going to have to make Steve search his own house for their daughters. He is also annoyed at the tinge of worry he feels, picturing her still-made bed this morning. "Are you sure?"

"Positive."

"Are the girls there?"

"No, definitely not." Jim thinks, wondering what he's missing. Maybe they slept in the basement. "Hold on." Jim mutes his phone and yells, "Carrie!" He leaps up the stairs to their bedroom, where Carrie still lies on her side, one pillow wrapped between her legs, another over her head. "Carrie, where did Emily stay last night?"

She does not move, but after a long pause asks, "Why?"

"Where did she stay?"

"At Arielle's house."

"She's not there," Jim says, leaving the room. He checks Emily's room one more time, but the bed is still made, just like last night and just like this morning. He goes down the stairs two at a time, into the basement, but the lights are out, and it's clear no one is down there. He walks back upstairs, gathers his thoughts, and begins, "They're not here. Emily told us she was spending the night at your house. You're a hundred percent sure they're not there?"

"Positive. Arielle said they were spending the night at yours."

"Shit," Jim mutters.

"What?"

"They're probably trying to pull one over on us. Maybe there was a party or whatever that they wanted to go to, or something like that, so they lied, saying they were sleeping over at the other's house."

"Arielle wouldn't do that," Steve states assuredly.

"Neither would Emily, but where are they? They're kids. That's what kids do, no matter how good they are."

"So then how do we find them?"

"Start calling their friends' parents. Something will come out pretty quickly."

"Arielle's friends' parents? Like who?" Steve asks. "I'm not sure who to call."

Jim is not surprised. He could name a dozen of Emily's friends, maybe two dozen, and has most of their parents' numbers saved in his phone's contacts, while Arielle's dad is on the other line, unable to name a single friend they hang out with. The girls are inseparable, but that doesn't mean they don't have other friends. "I'll do it. I'll call you back when I'm done."

Jim spends the next half hour making phone calls, starting with the most likely friends he can remember, but eventually scrolling through his contacts for anyone Emily knows. He calls each one, calmly explains the situation, and listens to each parent say they have no idea where Emily is, asking if there's anything they can do. He has to repeat that he's sure everything is fine, just some misunderstanding, while his gut tells him otherwise. He is most comforted by thinking about what he'll say when he finds her, how mad he'll be at her for lying, and what sort of punishment she'll receive. But he needs to find her before he can punish her.

Jim calls Steve back and explains the situation.

"So what should we do?" Steve asks.

"I didn't get ahold of everyone. They probably stayed somewhere else and got a ride to soccer. Look, you stay at your house, in case they call or show up, and Carrie will be here. I'll drive over to the Community Center and find their field. Practice doesn't start for another twenty minutes…"

"That makes sense. I'm sure they'll be there. Arielle wouldn't miss soccer."

"Good." Jim hangs up, wondering how worried he should be. He stands and turns to find Carrie leaning against the fridge, head down, staring through the tile floor.

"Emily didn't spend the night at Arielle's," he says.

"I know."

"You know? Where is she?"

"No, I mean, I know she's missing."

"I'm going to head over to the Community Center…"

"I called the police."

She doesn't look up when she says this, and Jim wonders if she's kidding, but he sees the cell phone in her hand and knows she doesn't kid about anything anymore. "What? Why would you call the police? We don't know anything's wrong. I'm sure Emily's fine."

"Then where is she?"

Jim exhales deeply, shaking his head at his wife.

"They said they'd be right over," she continues, "They sounded concerned."

Jim squints, unsure of the messenger more than the message. "Concerned?"

But Carrie doesn't explain, doesn't even look up, just stands there until the doorbell rings, and Jim shakes his head again, passing by her as he heads to the foyer.

Jim is surprised to find two men at the door. The taller one wears a long tan jacket with wrinkled slacks. His dress shoes are old and scuffed, and have probably never been polished. He looks Jim's age, maybe a little older, with a serious face beneath a crop of thinning brown hair. He could be selling life insurance or religion, about to go into his spiel, if it weren't for the police officer beside him, a younger kid with dishwater blonde hair and distracted eyes.

"Hello," the taller man says, extending his hand, "I'm Detective Terrence Kruthers and this is Officer Ed Baumgardner."

Jim wonders if they're overreacting, if somehow the act of calling the police could turn this into a situation where the police are actually needed. He wonders if he just ignores the two officers and doesn't shake hands, if he walks right by them and drives straight to the Community Center, could he somehow will the girls into being there, dressed in cleats and shin guards, chasing a ball?

"You probably get this sort of thing all the time," Jim starts, shaking hands. He doesn't like that Detective Kruthers feels the need to pull out a pen and notepad, while the police officer stands to the side, oblivious to the sound of the keys he's turning in his pocket.

"Enough," Detective Kruthers says, looking at his notebook, "but let's get started. When was the last time you saw…"

"Emily, " Jim finishes.

"Yes, Emily, when was the last time you saw Emily?"

"Yesterday morning. She was supposed to be staying at a friend's house. Arielle Cardell. But Arielle told her dad she was staying here. I'm guessing they spent the night somewhere they weren't supposed to be."

"Where does this other girl live?"

"Over on Emerald Street."

"Do you know the address?"

"No. I know which house it is, just not the number. I can give you the phone number. It's just Arielle and her dad, Steve Cardell, and I just got off the phone with him. They're about four blocks down from Stephen Street."

The Detective takes everything down and looks over his notes.

"Is that by Busey Park?"

"Yeah, about there. Why?"

"Do you know the Collinis? I think they have a girl about the same age as Emily. Her name is Gemma, Gemma Collini?"

"No, that doesn't sound familiar. What grade?"

"Fifth."

"Yeah, Emily is in sixth."

"What about her brother? He's a little younger, named Alex. Alex Collini."

"No, never."

"They live on the other side of Busey Woods. Off of CR 24."

"Never heard of them. What does this have to do with Emily?"

"You know something." Carrie states to the detective, never looking up, never stirring.

Detective Kruthers glances at Officer Baumgardner, who continues twirling his keys, oblivious to the rattling they make.

"You know something," Carrie repeats. "Tell us what it is."

"Mrs. Hughes…" Detective Kruthers starts.

"Our daughter is missing," Carrie says looking Detective Kruthers in the eye, "Our daughter is not the type of girl to stay out late, to lie to her parents. She's not the type of girl to go missing out of some misunderstanding. There are two police officers in our foyer asking questions, and they know something. I don't want any more questions until you tell us what you know."

Detective Kruthers looks at his notepad again, listening to Baumgardner manipulate his keys in his pocket, and then looks up at Carrie, who has not wavered. "Their son Alex, he's eight years old. He was playing in the woods out past their house. A section of Busey woods not too far from Emerald Street."

"And?"

"Alex never came home last night."

With that, Officer Baumgardner stops twirling his keys.

7

Terrence Kruthers watches the flurry of activity within the Edgebrook Police Station from his desk, knowing with all the commotion, he is in charge of this case. Phones are ringing, people are scurrying, and everyone knows to look busy.

"So why aren't we issuing an Amber Alert?" Baumgardner asks.

"I told you," Terry repeats, "there's not enough evidence. Are they all missing together, or are they separate cases? Are they lost or were they abducted? If they were abducted, we don't know anything about who took them. What are we supposed to say, keep an eye out for three kids?"

"I know, but it seems like we should do something."

"No," Terry corrects, "we need to do the right thing, the thing most likely to find those children." The problem is that Terry doesn't quite know what the correct thing is. He does know it's not worth explaining to Baumgardner how Amber Alerts are more often than not part of the so-called "Theater of Crime." For the truly brutal abductions, when the children are killed, it's usually done before an Amber Alert can even be issued. For the more common scenarios, when the wrong parent or guardian takes the kids, they're usually not in danger to begin with, and just as likely to be found through a normal investigation. Terry wouldn't say Amber Alerts are useless, but they must be used carefully, rather than the knee-jerk answer to, "We have to do something."

Terry's cell rings and after reading "Collini" on the caller ID, he takes a deep inhale, watching the station's commotion, and wishing it counted for something. "Hello, this is Detective Kruthers."

"Hello Detective, this is Natalya Collini, Alex's mother."

"Hello, Mrs. Collini."

"Detective, I was wondering if you've done an Amber Alert? I was trying to find one on-line, but don't think you have?"

"We haven't. Not yet."

"Why not?"

"There isn't enough evidence."

"My son's missing. Those two other girls are missing. You do believe they're missing?"

"Yes, of course."

"Then what else is there?"

"The problem," Terry starts, "well, we just don't know what happened. We don't know if they got lost in the woods or if someone took them. An Amber Alert needs specific information for people to look for. A type of car, a license plate."

"What about three missing children, Detective?"

That's another problem, Terry thinks to himself. Although each Amber Alert has a website with full details, most people don't see anything more than the quick update flashed along the highway, and how do you describe three missing kids to cars traveling sixty-five miles per hour? "There needs to be more than that. We don't even know if they were together or not. Should people be looking for a boy and also two girls, or all three together?"

There is a pause on the other end. "I don't know. Why can't they all be missing?"

"Because if someone is looking for three children but only sees Alex or only sees the girls, they'll immediately assume they're not the missing children."

"But what if they look distressed?"

"If they're distressed, then the witness should help them regardless, and the Amber Alert doesn't really do anything."

"So when are you going to issue an Amber Alert?"

"When we have something concrete. When we have something actionable. When we have something that can help find your son."

"Okay," Natalya says, accepting this answer with her head, but not her heart.

"Natalya," Terry says, "we're doing everything we can. Everyone in the police station knows what is going on. In a way they're all on this case, and they're all spreading the word."

"I know."

"Now if you don't mind, I need to get back to work."

"Yes, sorry. Thank you. Sorry."

"It's all right, Mrs. Collini," says Terry, and before he can stop himself, finishes with, "I understand." He hates saying that, hates when other people say that, when they really don't understand. And Terry doesn't. He doesn't have kids, doesn't have nieces or nephews, and knows he can't come close to understanding the horror of having your child go missing. But then again, he doesn't need to understand. He just needs to find the children.

This is not a typical case where somebody witnessed a young girl being pulled into a van, or a custody case where the "wrong parent" picked up his child from school. There is no description of the perpetrator. There isn't even evidence that somebody took the children. They were just as likely to have gotten lost in the woods, and were now eating cookies in some kindly woman's farmhouse, as they were to be tied up in the back of a van. Yet without any witnesses, he has no idea where they might be.

The majority of missing children cases are runaways. Yet after questioning the parents, Terry doesn't believe that to be the case. There were no fights, no signs of despair or depression in the children, no signs of wanting to get away. One of the girls was a straight-A student, the other close behind. The boy had a classmate's birthday party today that he had been looking forward to for weeks. Maybe one of them could be a runaway, but not all three. So next on the list is abduction.

Almost 80 percent of child abductions are committed by relatives. But the children are not related, and so far, there does not seem to be any connection that would point to a common third party. That leaves a stranger. Terry looks at the information scribbled before him. Two girls, both age 11. A boy, age 7. He has their pictures on his desk, and he studies their smiling faces, searching for a connection. Why would someone abduct all three children? How could someone abduct all three children?

Terry notices Officer Baumgardner standing against the next desk, watching him with curiosity, waiting for acknowledgement. "Yes?"

"So what do you think's going on?" Baumgardner picks a pencil off Terry's desk, distracting himself by bouncing the eraser against a stack of papers.

"I have no idea."

"Yeah, this really sucks."

"Three kids are missing. It's been almost twenty-four hours since they got off the school bus, twenty-four hours since they were last seen. You know what I think?"

Baumgardner looks up for a glimpse of hope.

"I think we've got this wrong. I think we're going to get a phone call shortly, saying either the girls or the Collini boy just showed up at home and there's some explanation to where they've been. If we can cross out some of these kids as not missing, then it begins to make a little sense."

"That would be good."

"It would be something. I mean, nobody abducts three children at once."

"It's not common," Baumgardner says, "but with Busey Woods and all…"

"That's what worries me. Those damn woods go on forever."

Busey Woods edge up against the east side of town, trickling in here and there as a village park or the entrance to a hiking trail. It is one of these parks that separate the girls' subdivision from where the Collinis live. About a half-mile on the map, this area consists of well-worn paths with a spattering of clearings used by young kids to camp out with their parents, or older kids to meet and drink beer. But heading east, these trails are part of a much larger wooded area, extending across the Ohio border into Pennsylvania, where they join with the Allegheny Mountains which reach out into a dozen other states. Thousands upon thousands of acres of dense forest without a soul in sight. Thousands upon thousands of acres to take an abducted child. But three children? Terry looks at their pictures again, imagining the near impossibility of one person forcing three children into the woods. Every passing second worries him more, knowing Busey Woods also provides thousands and thousands of acres to dump a body.

Or two.

Or three.

"Those woods just worry me," Terry repeats, "too much space without a witness."

"I hadn't thought of that."

"That's why I called in the canine unit. We can search town from end to end and put up checkpoints across the state, but it's those damn woods."

Baumgardner tries standing the pencil on its eraser, catching it as it falls over, distracting himself from what he says. "You know Terry, there's another possibility."

"What?"

"Two boys and a girl. Just like before."

"Don't go there."

"It's been thirty years."

"Don't say it."

"It's exactly like *The Spying Toes*."

"Shit. I told you not to say it."

"It's not just me, Terry. Everyone's saying it."

"Shit, shit, shit."

8

"Where's Alex?" asks Katya, hugging her stuffed Barney doll, too young to know she shouldn't ask. After hearing her parents say his name all day, she decides it is her duty to ask over and over, "Momma, where's Alex?"

"Please Katya," Natalya says, hunching over and holding her daughter's shoulders, "please stop asking that."

But Katya doesn't know any better. She doesn't understand what's going on, doesn't understand what "missing" really means, and she likes the attention she's getting. Standing there in a sweatshirt that goes to her knees and a diaper underneath, she pulls her thumb out of her mouth and asks again, "Where's Alex?"

Natalya sent the oldest children, Gemma and Gregor, over to friends' houses. She instructed them to call all of their friends and ask if they had seen Alex. Next, Natalya called all of Alex's classmates herself, but no one knew anything

Antonio called his mother in New Jersey. She deserves to know, he claimed, which was true, but Natalya knew she would tell all his relatives. Now they were getting calls from up and down the East Coast; brothers, sisters, aunts and uncles, all calling to say what they heard or thought but not really knowing anything, treating Alex's disappearance like it were gossip. Natalya is waiting for a call with real news and so she demands that Antonio get off the phone as quickly as possible. "What if Alex calls?"

"I'll switch over," Antonio says.

"No," Natalya demands, not trusting such a simple feature when it comes to news about her son, "It might not work."

But when the phone isn't being used, just resting silently on the kitchen counter, those are the worst moments. Each minute is another one with Alex missing and nothing being done. The afternoon sun is setting, which means the start of another night without him. Natalya doesn't think she can handle that, another night like last night. And of course, she's supposed to get her sleep; she is supposed to keep calm now with a baby growing in her belly.

She grabs Vincenzo out of Antonio's arms and smells his diapers. "I think he needs changing."

"I don't smell anything."

"He needs changing." She puts her nose against the bottom of his diaper and inhales deeply. "There's definitely something there."

"Okay."

Antonio doesn't question her. He switches positions with her on the couch, sitting by Katya, who changes her tactics by asking him, "Where's Alex?"

"Want to watch Barney?" he offers up, "Barney's Christmas?"

"Barney Christmas? Barney Christmas!" Katya leans forward, falls onto the floor, and crawls over to the small television, staring up into the blank screen. "Where's Barney?"

Antonio begins digging through the VHS tapes when the phone rings. He walks over and picks it up while Natalya watches him intently. "Hello?"

"Who is it?" she asks.

"Hi Chuck," he says aloud, more to her than the person on the phone. Chuck Lattrell, from two houses down.

"Uh-huh... yes... we don't know... yes, two other girls... older, Gemma's age... the police are already... really... thank you... no, thank you Chuck... bye."

"What was that about?"

"Barney Christmas! Where's Barney Christmas?"

"Chuck heard what's going on. He said he's going to go around the neighborhood, door-to-door, asking people if they've seen anything."

"How nice," Natalya says. She knows other neighbors will start calling, to see how they're doing, if there's anything they need. She would do the same. They're going to get phone calls all night, from all sorts of people, while the only one she wants is the one that says Alex is safe and healthy.

Antonio unwraps Vincenzo's diaper to find it clean, but now Vincenzo is awake and working up a good cry. "Where's Barney Christmas?" Katya asks, standing by the still-blank television.

Natalya looks outside, clutching the front drape with one hand and the cross on her neck with the other, hoping to see Alex's form walking up the lawn, hoping to see a sign, hoping for anything. But the lawn is empty, the shadows are growing longer, and she wonders if she'll ever sleep again.

9

Steve's home office is a mess. It always has been and always will be. He enters oblivious to the long steps he takes over papers and around file folders, making his way to the desk chair. Stacks of paper encircle his chair like Stonehenge, allowing him to easily swivel and retrieve exactly what he wants. He knows what is in each stack, and that's all that matters. Market analysis, pricing, TMC notes, competitive bulletins, OI plans and org charts, all within his reach. His system works, and he has finally accepted he will never clean it up, having unwired the ceiling fan so that nobody can accidentally flip the wall switch and send his life into a whirlwind.

He sits down and turns on the monitor, just as he does every night, and waits patiently. The screen is still black and dimly reflects his image. In his early thirties, Steve's hair is mostly white, just as his father's and grandfather's were at that same age. A trait every Cardell was sentenced with, looking distinguished and dignified before being quite ready to act that way.

But the hollowness, the concave features that mark little more than a skull covered by a tight layer of skin, that is all his own. That is not an inheritance, but the result of a gradual erosion over the past six years.

His reflection mercifully disappears as the monitor comes up in Windows blue. He logs on, listens to his desktop go through its final booting stages, and stares at the empty screen. It is not uncommon for him to be here on a Saturday night, working away with a large coffee and a piece of carrot cake, typing way past midnight while taking occasional breaks to read trade magazines in his lazy-boy on the other side of the room. Tonight the house is empty, a condition he would normally savor. A quiet house would normally mean Arielle was at Emily's. That's what he thought it meant last night, when he was ultra-productive and finished his expense reports and most of the customer support slide deck. But tonight's house is empty because Arielle is missing, and he can only question what that means.

Steve opens a browser and glances over his homepage. He types, "missing children" into the search bar.

A link to the website for the National Center for Missing and Exploited Children heads the list and he clicks on it. Three pictures of little girls, all younger than Arielle, are posted along the top with the question, "Have you seen me?" They have all been missing for at least a month.

He clicks on the 'Frequently Asked Questions' link, and begins reading.

Aren't most missing kids a result of custodial disagreements?

Answer: The largest number of missing children are "runaways"; followed by "family abductions"; then "lost, injured, or otherwise missing children"; and finally, the smallest category, but the one in which the child is at greatest risk of injury or death, "nonfamily abductions."

The letters are in a small italic font, and yet the word "death" glares like it is flashing neon. Steve knows how large that little word is, how all-consuming it can be. He needs to keep reading, to distract himself from his thoughts, but he only manages to sink deeper.

How many missing children are found deceased? What hours are most critical when trying to locate a missing child?

Answer: According to the State of Washington's Office of the Attorney General "the murder of a child who is abducted ... is a rare event. There are estimated to be about 100 such incidents in the United States each year, less than one-half of one percent of the murders committed"; however, "74 percent of abducted children who are murdered are dead within three hours of the abduction."

So the odds are good that, no matter what is happening, Arielle will return safely. But if he is on the other side of those odds, then…

Then it is too late. Three hours. From the time she was last seen getting off the bus, three hours later would have been nearly seven o'clock last night. He was in this same chair, a beer next to the printer, and spent nearly an hour on the document's title, debating if "Service Level Agreement" was too strong, finally settling on "Service Level Understanding." The implications of having "Agreement" or "Understanding" in the title were his biggest concern, oblivious to the horrible things that were happening in the world, oblivious to the horrible things that might have been happening to his daughter.

Don't think that, he tells himself. The grandfather clock ticks away in the outside hall and minutes pass. The house is so empty. Steve looks away from the computer screen and stares at the framed picture on his desk. His eyes water as he holds his breath, holds back the convulsive choking in his throat. He is envious of the three grinning faces in the picture, envious of the full joy his family once had, the easy smiles of his deceased wife, his missing daughter, and even himself.

Please God, he thinks through the tears, please don't take Arielle too.

10

HOW R U

Jim reads the text message on his phone and deletes it. How do you think I am? Reagan called as soon as she heard, but he told her he couldn't talk; he had to keep the line open. A lie of convenience. As always, he could go to the den, shut the door, and talk to her for as long as he wanted. But it doesn't seem right now, seems like the last thing he wants to do. He says he can't talk, and so instead, Reagan sends him her distinct all-caps text messages throughout the night.

IM SO SORRY

ANYTHING I CAN DO????

IM PRAYING

CANT STOP CRYING FOR YOU

I LOVE YOU

The last one was ridiculous. Jim and Reagan had never spoken of love, had never spoken of a serious relationship at all. He knew she wanted more, but he truthfully told her he wasn't sure what he wanted. More importantly, he couldn't think about it now. Right now the relationship felt frivolous, less of an affair than passing notes in study hall, holding hands, or carving their initials into a tree, whimsical fancies that should be forgotten now that Emily is missing.

CALL ME WHEN U CAN.

He finally responds.

Keep praying.

Jim turns the TV on for a few minutes, watching the local news to see if they're reporting the case. Instead, they're airing a segment called "Tanorexia." Carrie drifts into the family room from somewhere and silently sits on the opposite end of the couch.

Jim watches the TV in disbelief as a platinum blonde with extremely dark skin like it was just pulled from the broiler sobs about her addiction to tanning beds. An addiction to tanning beds? Can this be real? He mutes the TV and just watches, wondering how tanning bed addiction can be the top news story when three children are missing. Emily is missing. For the first time in a long time, he senses Carrie's presence through the silence and wonders what she's thinking, if she's feeling his anguish and disbelief. He glances over at her and realizes that she isn't even looking at the TV. Instead she stares intently at an empty ornamental vase on the fireplace mantel. As usual, in the same room, but worlds away.

The afternoon had been long. Detective Kruthers told Jim and Carrie how every police officer in Ohio, as well as those in neighboring Pennsylvania and West Virginia, were now looking for Emily. Detective Kruthers answered their questions about missing children, the statistics of runaways, abductions by a relative and abductions by a stranger. They were both interviewed, but as Jim knew, it was a waste of time.

And now they sit here and wait. The house phone occasionally rings to life, but never with news. More questions from neighbors, more condolences from friends. Jim turns off the television as the early news ends. Nothing was said about Emily, and a Saturday night movie is coming on, some light comedy that sounds unbearable. How could anything be considered light comedy right now?

"So what do you want to do?" Jim asks into the space before him.

"Hmm."

"What should we be doing?"

"I don't know."

"I need something to take my mind off this."

Carrie puts her hand over her mouth to hide a smirk that never forms. Welcome to the hell of this house, the long beats of silence that form the rhythm of her every day. She has grown used to it. She could sit here all night, never flinching, never stirring. At times she wonders if she could just stop blinking. Would she turn to stone? "We're supposed to wait here."

"I know," Jim concedes, "but it doesn't feel right."

Carrie nods, wondering what "right" really feels like.

"Do you remember," Jim asks, rummaging through his thoughts, trying to remain positive, "when your mother was here and she needed to go to the drug store? Emily said she could get her there, and sat in the back seat giving her directions."

"Yes."

"She even took your mom on the freeway."

"Yes."

"They ended up at Toys 'R Us instead of the drug store."

"Yes."

"How old was she then?"

Carrie thinks back, trying to figure out how long that was before her Mom passed away. "Four? Almost five."

"She was so young, I didn't think she knew her way around the block, let alone how to get to the mall."

"Mom was not happy."

"Emily's such a smart girl. Such a strong girl. And Arielle too."

"They are."

"They're going to be all right. I'm sure of it. They have to be."

Carrie doesn't respond, wondering where Jim learned to believe that everything has to be alright. Or when she forgot.

Jim's cell phone vibrates and he grabs it off the coffee table. Another text message.

RU HOLDING UP?

It's Reagan again, to which Jim replies, Can't talk now.

The phone rattles again. I NOW KNOW HOW MUCH I REALLY LOVE YOU

Jim wants to turn the phone off, but Detective Kruthers has this number, and instead responds with, Stop texting, I can't talk now! He is embarrassed he is cheating on his wife with someone so delusional. He is sorry for hurting Carrie. His phone vibrates once again and he grabs it violently off the coffee table to find it's not a text message, but a notice that it's his move.

Words with Friends, Scrabble on their cell phones, has become the last strand of communication between Jim and Carrie. Moves are usually sent from different rooms, little reminders that there is another adult in the house. They never discuss the games, who's winning or losing, a good play or a complaint about bad letters. They're not even sure if they enjoy playing, but neither has yet had the courage to click No when asked to play again. Jim glances over from the couch to see Carrie put her phone down. He looks at her word, TEPID, and checks if it matches up with his letters.

They take turns for nearly an hour, and when Jim grows bored waiting for Carrie to play, he types out a message to Reagan, reads it to himself a few times, and deletes it. What the hell is he doing? Tears form in his eyes and they quickly swell to where he can't see anymore. He leans forward and presses his face into his hands, trying to wipe away the tears, but only finds himself sobbing loudly. His marriage is in shambles, and he can't imagine how it will ever come together again. His wife is hardly a glimmer of the woman he married. He's off cheating with the office floozy. None of this has ever had him close to tears. He's sobbing now for Emily, as he can't imagine life without her.

Jim tries not to cry with Carrie on the other end of the couch, but she says nothing, and for a good fifteen minutes he sobs. When he finally starts pulling himself together, his eyes have been rubbed raw and his stomach aches from convulsions. His phone vibrates again, pulling him the rest of the way from his episode, and he turns it on to see Carrie just played a word. It's his turn now.

11

Terry Kruthers sits at his desk, contemplating the day's strategy. He spent most of the previous night planning, but he wants to write everything down and look it over rather than trust the random thoughts that come before sleep. He is not an investigator in this case, at least not in the role to which he is accustomed. He has the entire police department, and probably the entire town of Edgebrook, at his disposal, and things will move much more quickly if he uses these resources to their fullest.

Terry knows he'd be better investigating instead of running the investigation. When questioning witnesses or suspects, he talks calmly and maintains a simple composure that says everything will be all right. A thin nose and pale blue eyes make up his modest face, which Terry uses to give full attention to whomever is talking, letting them know he cares about what they're saying and thereby allowing them to comfortably say more than they ever planned. Terry prefers being in the field and asking questions rather than giving orders and holding others accountable.

For the most part, he delegates from the station, studying information as soon as it comes in and redirecting personnel based on that. He will talk to the families again, after a full night to think in more detail, although Terry doubts he'll get any useful information out of them. The children disappeared without a trace, and with all three families corroborating that nothing suspicious occurred, he has to look elsewhere.

The neighbors are next, but other officers have to investigate them. They went door-to-door until almost ten last night and will start again this morning. Missing posters have to be printed and distributed. Word has to get out. And searches have to begin. There will be volunteers, and he needs to make sure they are coordinated and utilized in an effective manner.

The phone on his desk rings, resonating through the empty office, and Terry looks at his watch: 5:40 AM. Probably the parents. He can't blame them for being up already, wanting an update. "Hello?"

"Detective Kruthers?" asks a burly voice.

"Yes."

"This is Agent Samperson with the FBI, Columbus office. I'm calling about the missing children case you have on your hands. I have some questions."

Terry's brow wrinkles. "The FBI? What types of questions?"

"Let me be straightforward and start by saying we are by no means taking over this case."

"Taking over the case? Who authorized this?"

"Talk to Chief Mendelsohn when he gets in. He's approving right now."

"Approving what?"

"Like I said, we only want to help, provide whatever resources you need, and assist in whatever way that you see fit."

"Right now I don't see fit for any assistance," Terry replies, unsure if he phrased it right. "We don't need any help."

"Look Detective, you and your department know Edgebrook better than we ever could, both from the physical layout and, more importantly, the residents. You know who's who and I'm sure you know how to get information from them."

"Of course."

"But we'll send people who can help too, including child abduction experts, criminal psychologists, forensic and polygraph experts, basically whomever you need."

"Okay?"

"We'll also coordinate on a national level, getting the message out, searching databases for known sex offenders and coordinating the law enforcement in your region."

"I thought you were only helping if I asked for it?"

"Are you saying you don't want this help?"

"No, it's just…"

"Are you saying you want me to wait until you ask?"

"No, but…"

"But what?"

"But why? Why are you providing all this support? Children go missing every day, and they don't get this kind of attention from the FBI. Is there something I don't know?"

"Because this has national significance."

"National significance?"

"Detective Kruthers, check your email."

Terry looks at his screen, sorting through the junk emails he hasn't read, when a new one appears at the bottom from Agent Samperson. Terry opens it and sees a short message with a link that he clicks on.

It appears to be a blog, but Terry isn't quite sure if that's correct. There are ads and links to other stories, and Terry senses this is something more professional, although he has to admit he doesn't get much of his news from the internet.

"Go ahead and read it," Agent Samperson says, "I'll wait."

Terry sets the phone on his desk and reads.

CAN WE EVER REALLY BE SAVED?

By Christopher Heath

The feelings remain vivid. During my first job as a journalist working for the *Columbus Dispatch*, three kids disappeared from a small Southeastern Ohio town named Edgebrook. We did not cover their disappearance, but I was assigned to write a story after they were rescued. The children had been imprisoned in wire cages that were staked into the forest floor, and through the heroics of a boy who escaped, the other two girls were rescued moments before being killed. It was a story that would go mainstream, retold in the book and television movie *The Spying Toes*.

I visited Edgebrook shortly after their rescue. I walked down Main Street, which back then was a slice of small town Americana, and alongside the flags and flowers were signs proclaiming, "Welcome Home!" and "God Bless the Children." I sat in their coffee shop and talked to the locals, who turned handshakes into hugs as they retold the story over and over. Fathers breathed deeply, wiped their brows, and told everyone how blessed they were. Mothers who had spent the previous weeks grasping their children's hands in fear, now kissed their cheeks and basked in the gift of life, the power of love. I saw the quickly improvised parade. I listened to the mayor's speech in the town square, where people warmed each other with proximity, broke into cheers and tears as the mayor vowed, "We have come perilously close to losing our most sacred gift. We have seen the darkness and broken through to the light. Never again will we take for granted the beauty of the day, the wonderment of God's grace bestowed upon us, or the blessings of our town, our friendships and our families."

As an outsider, a reporter who mainly covered accidents and misfortunes, I remember experiencing a moment of skepticism. Checking into my room and going over the day's notes, fleshing out the thoughts I had transcribed, I asked myself, "Can this be real? How long can it last?" I then went down to the hotel bar, where I was invited to join a gathering of former Edgebrook residents who were visiting for the celebration, and found myself caught up in their newfound enthusiasm and appreciation.

I recently pulled out my journal from that day and found something I do not remember writing and cannot imagine ever thinking. Scratched in a margin was the conviction, "This is real."

Yesterday, three children were again reported missing from the town of Edgebrook. There are no clues as to their whereabouts. The people of Edgebrook have plunged back into darkness. The message of hope that once emanated from every townsperson is about to be tested once again. My resilient feeling of living in a changed world is long gone. I go over my old conviction, mesmerized by my own handwriting, and ask, "Can we really be saved?"

Terry rereads the last paragraph and picks up the phone. "I read it."

"Well?"

"Well what?" Terry asks. This is why he doesn't get his news from the internet. "There wasn't any news in that story."

"It's gone viral."

"Viral?"

"It's national. Everyone is reading that article or one like it. Everyone is watching this case."

"I know what viral means, but it doesn't change anything." He starts to make the case he's already made more often than he thought he'd have to, "Besides the number of children, there is absolutely nothing that relates this case back to the old one."

"They're the same gender and almost the same age. It's the same town in the same woods."

"Yes, but…"

Agent Samperson clears his throat. "Look, I agree. There is no substantial evidence linking the two cases, but there is no evidence at all. We have to keep all options open, and if there is public opinion that these cases are related, we have to objectively evaluate that scenario along with every other possibility. The entire nation will be watching the outcome of this case, and we need to do everything we can to make sure the outcome is successful."

"So you're getting involved because it's a public relations story?"

"Yes."

"Yes?"

"Look Detective, I know what you're thinking. The FBI has been called into this case just because it's in the newspaper and that when some poor child goes missing and it doesn't get the attention, no one cares. Yes, that's a shame, but the shameful part is that we're not able to help in those other cases, not that we're helping with this one."

"You're right, you're right. But that's not the only thing. It's more the…" Terry clears his throat, "I guess I'm worried about the direction of this investigation."

"Do you mean who's in charge? Like I said, I'm not here to take over the investigation, just provide support."

"No, it's not that. This will be in the papers, which will get us extra attention, and I'm thankful for that. But because it's in the media, that means we have someone else to answer to. We're not solving this case to answer the papers, to make a happy ending for a national story. We're trying to find three children."

"You don't think the media wants us to find the children?"

"Of course they do. But they also want to keep things interesting. I mean, the article you sent is digging up a thirty-year-old case where the lone perpetrator was killed. I feel like my hand is being forced to investigate that angle before going through the most likely culprits, like a relative, a local pedophile, or whatever."

"Detective, that's not the media's fault. Unless you have another lead, the case was going that way regardless."

Terry sighs. He sets aside his notes on where he wanted to investigate and replaces them with a blank sheet of paper. He is in charge, but he's already losing control.

12

Reagan places a washcloth of hot water against her face and inhales. She scrubs hard, attempting to wash away her headache. Last night she finished one and a half bottles of wine and fell asleep on the couch, still clutching her cell phone. While drinking, she kept re-reading her text messages, analyzing everything she wrote and trying to discern meaning from Jim's short replies. He was curt and emotionless, acting as if she were just anybody, which meant his wife was in the room, and Reagan hated her all the more for it. That woman has no idea how lucky she is, with the perfect husband, the perfect house, the perfect family. Reagan knows. Regan understands. She was so close to calling Jim's home phone last night, staring at all seven digits on her iPhone, talking herself into pushing the call button. She would then cancel, take a hearty sip of wine, and play out a pretend conversation in her head. It didn't matter who answered. She had words for both of them. She would set things straight. Jim needed her, and she would find a way to be there for him.

But now Reagan's head hurts and she feels less righteous, less indignant. It's Sunday morning and she just wants to get through the day, through another long weekend. She turns on her shower radio, undresses and steps inside. Standing in the spray of hot water, letting her pores absorb the heat, she feels the start of her hangover's eventual passing. Her head still feels distant from the cheap wine. She never gets headaches from Jim's wine. The disc jockey announces that a cold front is moving in this afternoon and temperatures will drop into the fifties. Fall is here and winter is not far behind. He goes on to announce that there is no new information on the missing children from Edgebrook, but anyone wanting to help can join the search parties at Tate Park, one of the entrance points to Busey Woods. As soon as she hears it, Reagan realizes the perfect way to show her love.

Reagan arrives at Tate Park just after 10:00 and finds the parking lot and surrounding streets filled with cars. Not wanting to park far away, she makes two laps and manages to park her Jetta so it covers only a few feet of yellow curb. No cop is going to ticket a volunteer searching for missing children.

She gets out of her car, careful not to spill the coffee in her leather-gloved hand, and feels proud to be doing something. She catches her reflection in the window and is happy with how her new mocha gloves and hat complement her sky-blue parka. She tells herself she is stylishly in control as she approaches the three tables that have been set out on a basketball court. People are lined up, collecting forms along the tables, gathering in a large group at the opposite end. A few have orange construction vests, which seem to signify their roles as coordinators. Reagan walks up to the closest person in a vest, a young man sitting behind the first table, and says, "I'm here to help find Emily Hughes."

"Great," the man responds, extending a hand to Reagan, who lets him shake the tips of her fingers. "Thanks for coming out. You can start here with this sign-up sheet and just go down the line. The sheets should have enough information to get started."

"Actually, I'd like to talk to who's in charge."

"Oh, okay," the volunteer starts, still smiling, "Um, let me see, is there a problem?"

"No, it's just that I'm a good friend of the Hughes, Jim Hughes specifically, and was wondering if there was anything special that needed to be done, anything significant?"

"Oh, well I'm sure they're grateful you're helping. Let me see though, there's nobody specifically in charge. Hold on." The young man walks halfway down the row of tables and calls out to someone.

An older man, also wearing an orange vest, with white hair creeping out beneath his baseball cap, walks slowly out of the pack and the two men talk quietly. The older man approaches Reagan and says, "Hello. My name is Gordon."

"It's very nice to meet you, Gordon. My name is Reagan."

"I understand you're looking for something special to do."

"I was just hoping, being friends with the Hughes...."

"That's very kind. Have you ever done anything like this before?"

"No, but I'm a quick learner."

"Good." Gordon has work gloves hanging from his jeans pocket and wears a thick button-down flannel. He maintains a genuine smile as he surveys Reagan. "Well for starters, you should sign in and collect all the material on the tables. Then review the rules of conducting a search, things to look for, what to do if you see anything suspicious, that sort of thing. We've also got pictures of all three children, a description of what they were wearing the day they went missing, and basically everything we know as of right now."

"Do they see the sign-in sheet?"

"Pardon?"

"Will they see the sign-in sheet?"

"Will who see it?"

"The Hughes. Will they see the list of everyone who's here today?"

"Oh. I don't know. I mean, I don't believe so, but I really don't know. It's not meant for them. We want to keep track of who's here, helping out, just for numbers' sake. I'm sure we'll submit it to the police department. That way, if something comes up and they need to question the people who searched a particular area, they'll have an easy list to go through."

"I see." Reagan bends over and prints her name in big letters, signs her name on the same line, and follows up with her address and phone number.

"You all seem quite organized."

"Thank you. That's good to hear considering how last-minute this is."

"Really?"

"We just found out about this yesterday afternoon. As soon as I heard, I went over to my grandson's in Tippington. He's a computer genius and found all sorts of information for organizing search parties. There were all sorts of logistics that never occurred to us. Most of these forms were already put together; we just needed to modify some of the information. And then he started putting together a Facebook page."

"Facebook?"

"So people can keep up to the minute on what's going on, how they can help, that sort of thing."

"Very nice."

"Now you say you're a good friend of the Hughes family?"

Reagan wonders if she had phrased it quite like that. "Yes."

"And you're looking for something special to do?"

"If there is anything."

"Well, we're running pretty solo here. I mean, there is a police officer we're in contact with, so information will go through him, but I was wondering if you would like to be our liaison with the parents?"

"What does that mean?"

"It just means calling them and letting them know that we're helping out, that if there's anything we can do, we will. For example, numerous people have offered to make food and drop it off, but we don't want a bunch of strangers calling the families. I figure they'd be more comfortable talking with one person, a friend."

"That makes sense."

"Would you be interested?"

"Yes."

"Excellent. I've actually got something for you to do right now."

"What's that?"

"We're circulating the pictures that were copied by the police, but I thought it would be good to put up more on the Facebook page. Not only so people have a better idea of what the children look like, but so they get a better sense of the children, as real people. You know, pictures of them with their families, or maybe out somewhere like a park or a pool. I think it will help rally support."

"Good idea."

Gordon pulls out his phone and asks Reagan for her number and email address. He then sends her the Facebook link, as well as the contact information for each family. "Could you give them a call and ask them for more pictures?"

"Sure."

"You'll then pick up the pictures, scan them, and then return them. Can you do that?"

"Go to their houses?"

"Is that a problem?"

"Um, no. I can do that. I can absolutely do that."

"Thank you, Reagan."

Gordon turns and walks back to the crowd of volunteers that has coalesced behind four group leaders in orange vests. There are roughly thirty people and Reagan is glad she is not one of them. She heads back to her car, away from the volunteers, so she can make her calls in private.

Regan first talks to a woman named Natalya who is kind and receptive, asking questions about the search party and thanking her profusely, glad to get some pictures together and actually be doing something. She then talks to a man named Steve, who responds brusquely, but agrees to her request. So far, quick and easy

Reagan then looks at the number next to the names Jim and Carrie Hughes. It's their house phone, the one she almost dialed last night, her cell in one hand and wine glass in the other, ready to tell Jim that she loves him, ready to tell Carrie about their affair. She dials the number, pausing once again before the last digit and feels a chill beneath her winter parka as the first ring signals a connection.

A woman's voice answers. "Hello?"

"Hello, is Jim there?"

"No, he's not available. Can I ask who's calling?"

Reagan says nothing.

"Hello?" the woman asks again.

"Carrie Hughes?"

"Yes. Who is this?"

"My name is Reagan. I work with Jim." Reagan can hear the other woman stop breathing, and wonders what she knows, what she suspects. "I'm calling from Tate Park. I'm here with the search party, with about thirty volunteers or so."

"Oh." The woman exhales. "Yes, thank you."

"I'm calling because there's a Facebook page being put together to help round up support. It's supposed to keep everyone informed with the latest updates and help coordinate volunteers."

"All right."

"We also want to put up some more pictures of the children, more than the ones being circulated, just so people have a better idea what they look like. I'm sorry to bother you, but I was wondering if you would mind gathering some pictures for us? Someone will stop by and pick them up. They'll just scan them and bring them back later today."

"I'm sure I can get some," Carrie replies.

"Okay. Thank you. Goodbye."

Reagan begins to hang up the phone when she hears, "Hello? Reagan?"

"Yes?"

"So you're at the search site right now?"

"Yes. At Tate Park."

"Could I call you? Just to see how it's going?"

"If anything happens, we'll contact you right away."

"Oh. Okay."

"No, that's not what… I mean yes, of course you can call me."

"Thank you," Carrie says, "Really, thank you."

"No problem," Reagan says. She finishes the conversation, puts the phone in her pocket, and heads back toward the park and finds Gordon breaking down tables and chairs. "I've made the calls," Reagan says. They'll all have the pictures ready by 1:00, so you can send someone over.

Gordon smiles. "Grab the other side of this table," he says. "We're just breaking everything down and putting it by my truck over there. The silver one."

Reagan grabs the other end, and as they lift and turn it onto its side, Gordon walks over and kicks the legs down. "You'll have to go over there. I don't want them dealing with different people all the time. You're the person they trust; you're now our liaison." Gordon flips the table back over, so that he and Reagan can carry it sideways. "I'll forward you my grandson's address. Like I said, he's in Tippington. Once you've scanned the photos, they'll probably be too big to email, so you'll need to bring them on a USB stick. You can do that, right?"

Reagan is still thinking about his previous words, "You're the person they trust." Her thoughts move from this general statement to the specific case; Carrie Hughes trusts you.

"You know how to do all that, right Reagan? Scan the photos? Put them on a USB stick?"

"Yes," Reagan replies. "You can trust me."

13

Carrie enters the family room and pulls a photo album off the shelf. She assumes recent pictures are what they want. Emily's birthday party last spring, at the roller rink. Pictures from her class trip to the zoo. Fifth-grade graduation. Carrie keeps turning the pages to see her precious child beaming into the camera, her head tilted, her straight chestnut hair falling over her shoulder, the sparkle in her eyes, the tiny gap between her front teeth, only visible when she was really beaming. Emily had asked about braces, as kids seemed to be getting them over the tiniest of imperfections, but Carrie always told Emily that her smile was perfect.

She flips back to last Halloween. Emily's best friend Arielle dressed as a fairy princess while Emily was a frog, burrowing her chin into her chest and elongating her face as she made "ribbit" sounds. Carrie still wonders why she wanted to go as a frog, but that was the way Emily worked, getting strange ideas out of nowhere and following through with unwavering enthusiasm.

There are almost no pictures of Jim or Carrie, with a simple explanation. Jim was always behind the camera, taking the picture, and Carrie always stood in the periphery, watching quietly, concentrating on holding herself together. Jim never said anything, never encouraged her to step into the pictures, and Emily let it go too, afraid she might tilt the fragile stability her mother used for balance. Carrie thinks of the first time Emily came home and caught her crying. She tried to explain there was no reason for her tears, but it was a concept no child could understand. After more and more questions, Carrie finally raised her voice, "There is no goddamn reason! Just let me be!" And Emily did, retreating to her room and crying herself. But Emily now knows the rules. Mother is not well. Do not ask her why. Do not say anything. Pretend everything is all right, because acknowledging mother's issues only made things worse.

From the most recent photo album, Carrie pulls out five photos, two of Emily and Arielle together and three of Emily alone. The pictures are from different angles and lighting, which is what she was asked to gather.

With pictures in hand, she continues flipping through albums, wondering where she has been these past years. In many cases, the photos seem staged, the girls making faces and laughing, as if they are having fun in this very house. Carrie doesn't remember any joyous times in her house. Not for years. Yet she holds proof in her hands, with glimpses of her turning away in the background, or maybe off to the side with crossed arms, proving that she had stood right there, right next to two giggling girls, and yet can't remember their joy. After going through all of the albums on their bookshelf, she wants to see more.

Carrie walks downstairs to the basement and into the laundry room. The cement floor is cold and only a narrow slit of morning light shines through the window well, drawing shadows across the walls. She pulls the dangling string and a bare light bulb illuminates the room in a grim yellow tint. She studies the stack of boxes against the back wall. Many are new, but some of the boxes still have room names written on them, Kitchen, Master Bedroom, Garage, and even Baby's Room. These are the boxes that were never completely unpacked, waiting in the basement beneath the constant weekend resolution of, "We better unpack those boxes." After six months, they stopped talking about them altogether, and about two years later, they came up under the question, "Should we take any of those boxes to Goodwill?" But it turned out newer boxes of junk stacked nicely against the old ones, adding to the pile until this part of the basement became an eyesore their eyes never saw.

Carrie pulls open boxes and looks in. Old jackets and gloves fall out of one. Another box contains ticket stubs and various knick-knacks, like an extension cord, cuff links, and an old wallet. These must be from Jim's junk drawer. Stepping further into the boxes, Carrie notices an orange furry arm sticking out of one box and opens it to find Mr. Orange-O-Tang, along with many more of Emily's stuffed animals. She pulls them out and holds them up like collector's items, priceless souvenirs. These are from good times she can remember, when Emily was only a few years old and would lie in bed, surrounded by her extended, stuffed family: Orange-O-Tang, of course, Raggedy Anne, Minnie Mouse, Zippy, Curious George, and Ee-yore. She pulls each from the box and watches it stretch and straighten.

Carrie remembers and, to her surprise, does not cry. With something that probably should bring up real tears, she instead looks at these creatures with a surreal questioning, wondering how they became part of her life. She stuffs them back into the box and closes it, looking around and trying to remember the contents of other boxes, grasping at forgotten memories. She reads the room names near the back and finds two at the bottom of a stack labeled "Books." She unstacks the boxes and opens one, thumbing through books they once had on display in their first apartment, many of them warped and yellowing. She rearranges more boxes to get to the bottom one, and upon opening, immediately finds the black binding of the book she is looking for. She pulls it out and reads the cover.

The Spying Toes

by Art Morrell

The doorbell rings and Carrie looks around to find herself tucked away in the furthest depths of her house and her memories. She takes long steps around the mess and climbs upstairs, grabs the pictures of Emily she placed on the counter, and opens the door to find a young, attractive woman standing awkwardly before her. "Hello."

"Mrs. Hughes?"

"Yes."

"Hi, I'm Reagan. We spoke on the phone. I'm here to pick up the pictures for the website."

"Right."

"I'll bring them back later today." The woman reaches out and Carrie remembers the pictures in her hand, carefully handing them over.

"Thank you," the woman says.

"Thank you."

The woman turns and heads down the front walk and gets into her Jetta. Carrie goes back into the house and realizes she is still holding the black book from downstairs. She turns it in her hands while experiencing a moment of guilt. That was the woman who called, the one who asked for Jim, and out of nowhere, she had suspected that she was the woman Jim had been spending so much time with. The truth is, she doesn't know what Jim is doing, and that girl was probably just young and idealistic, simply trying to help out. She is probably trying to make the world a better place, a cause Carrie once believed in too.

Outside, Reagan sits in her car. Only a moment ago she sat here, in the Hughes' driveway, looking at the house's brick façade with green shutters, the white pillars on the front porch, and peered through the many windows thinking she belonged in a house like that. She belonged in that house. And though she found many things wrong with Carrie, from not treating her husband right to answering the door in a shoddy robe without make-up, she finds herself looking at the same house, trying to dismiss this strange new feeling of guilt.

14

Terry pretends he has phone calls to make, preferring to wait alone than with an anxious father, so Steve Cardell leads him to the back room past the garage. Once alone, Terry studies the family pictures on the wall. Most of them are of the whole family smiling for the camera. The mother is now dead. A car accident four years ago. He remembers that one, out on County Road 18. She swerved off the road and into the side girder of a small bridge. Skid marks showed she swerved once, hit the brakes, and turned sideways so that the driver's side door lined up perfectly with the girder, the car wrapping around it. Nobody knows what really happened, whether she fell asleep, swerved to avoid something, or the car malfunctioned. There were no witnesses, and when help arrived, she was already dead. There were no drugs or alcohol involved, and there was no reason to believe she was tired or texting. It was an accident, if one can accept that the same word used to describe a stubbed toe can also capture a young mother's death.

Terry wasn't the investigator on that case, because the accident occurred in Meigs County, about forty-five minutes away. He gave some advice since the family lived in his precinct, but let the investigating officer deal with telling the family. Terry pretty much forgot about the whole accident until a few months later when, coming back from a weekend fishing at Lake Caldwell, he drove across the same bridge. The dirt was new, as was the guardrail, and he saw the small wooden cross, laden with flowers, with the name "April" painted across it. There was a teddy bear at the base, and he remembered she had a little girl.

Now here he is, hiding out in April's craft room, looking at pictures of her family, about to discuss her missing daughter. Terry wonders how much a man can take, and forgives the distant behavior Steve has displayed so far.

He hears a clamor out front as someone enters the house. Terry assumes everyone has arrived. A few more minutes and he will go in. With little to do but think, Terry picks up the phone, listens to the dial tone, and puts it back down. He looks at the red receiver and sees that his fingers have left an imprint against the layer of dust. A white sewing machine sits idly in the corner, with spools of thread and fabrics still gathered around. This room has been sealed off, mentally if not physically, ever since the mother who labored here stopped coming. Terry wipes the receiver clean with his shirtsleeve, sending a burst of dust flakes into the air, spinning chaotically in a ray of light. Enough waiting. He takes a deep breath and starts towards the front of the house, like an actor walking on stage for opening night.

In the front living room, Jim Hughes sits on one end of the couch, leaning back, with arms crossed. Antonio is on the other end, perched on the edge with his elbows on his knees. Steve sits on a wooden chair, while officer Baumgardner rests in the adjacent one. All three fathers look gaunt and tired, sitting in silence, refusing to discuss their shared torture. As Terry shakes hands with each man and gives a nod of acknowledgement, he feels like he has just entered a funeral parlor.

"Thank you for coming," Terry starts, and then pauses, forgetting his next line. These people are looking for something, anything, to comfort them, and he can't do it.

Steve is the first to speak. "Yes?"

"Yes, before we get started… I want you to know that there haven't been any major breaks. Not yet."

Jim straightens up. "We are all well aware that there haven't been any breaks. There hasn't been any progress at all."

"I can assure you, Mr. Hughes, that we're doing everything we can…"

"I'm sure you are. I don't doubt that." Jim wants to remain rational, in control, but finds that beyond the situation. "But to be completely truthful, I don't really care. You can say how everything possible is being done, how you're doing your best, but this isn't about doing your best. This is about finding our children. That's all that matters. A half hour ago, I was out with a search party, helping look for Emily. We've already been interrogated, answered everything we could, and now I want to know why I was pulled away from looking for my daughter!"

Terry nods, opening his notebook and starts from the top. "There is a search party of almost forty people combing through Busey Woods from the Tate Park entrance. Another party of forty started at the Mansing Trails entrance. Thirty more from Cooper Road, thirty from Woodfield Road, and from what I've gathered, small parties of five or six from all around the county are taking hiking expeditions into the woods. That's nearly one hundred and fifty volunteers looking for your children. We have trained assistants coordinating most of these searches, as well as three canine units from across the state, covering every inch of those woods. The state police also have a helicopter operating low-level fly-bys for support."

"Locally, every officer in Edgebrook is working overtime on this case: collecting data, interviewing residents, and trying to piece together every minute of what happened that night. Every officer in Ohio, Pennsylvania, and West Virginia has a picture of your children, and is looking for anything suspicious that could help us find them. Missing posters are going up across the state, ensuring millions of eyes will be looking for your children. If they make even the slightest appearance at a gas station or fast food restaurant, somebody will recognize them."

"In addition to that, the FBI is helping in every way they can. We shipped the computers in the girls' rooms to a hard drive recovery team in Virginia, and every connection they've ever made on the internet, every note they ever wrote, every website they visited, will be dissected and analyzed along with its digital trail. They've delivered a mobile lab with two forensic specialists to help analyze any evidence. They're polling through all national databases, including registered sex offenders in Ohio and all surrounding states."

"Locally, we've instructed the search parties to quickly and efficiently cover the largest area of the forest and to gather anything and everything they come across that looks as if it were put there within the last few weeks. Whether it be a Coke can, a piece of fabric, or a fallen barrette, it will be sent to the forensic team to run every test imaginable, including fingerprinting and DNA testing."

"I understand you are upset that you can't be out there looking right now, and I know I'm being vague when I say that every stone is being turned, but I wanted you to know exactly what that means."

Antonio can't help but feel a sense of pride. When Katya was sick, born with a defective liver, it was all he could do to get anyone to help. The doctors cared, as did the donor program, but everything came down to money, a resource they don't have. So they filled out form after form, called the insurance company every day, called the hospital every day, and tried to get anyone to give the authorization to run more tests and procedures. Invasive tests were finally run on little Katya, less than a year old, only to result in a half-hearted diagnosis. More forms were filled out, more explanations to the insurance company. Antonio used all his vacation days, sick days, personal time and future time off taking her to the hospital. Natalya lost her job at the department store, and he was close to losing his, knowing he would never find another job that would cover a family of seven, let alone provide insurance for Katya's pre-existing condition.

When everything finally came together, the day Natalya had a third of her liver removed and given to Katya, Antonio had to work. His mother called him from the hospital to report on the procedure, which was as successful as could be hoped. Katya would be on anti-rejection medication for the rest of her life, and at any time, her system could break down. But they finally had hope.

Now, with Alex in trouble, complete strangers, hundreds of them, were volunteering to help search for him. The police. The FBI. The entire country is on alert. He knows there are two other children missing, two children with nicer homes who are more upper-crust American, but he is still grateful for all that is being done. "Thank you detective," he says, "Thank you so much."

"And what have you found?" Jim asks.

"It's early in the search," Terry qualifies, "very early. I'm expecting a lot more through the course of the day, but here's a brief overview of what we know."

"On Friday night, at Tate Park, which is directly between the Hughes and Cardell houses and the most likely entrance for the girls, six cars were seen in the parking lot over the course of the night. A black Ford Thunderbird with two high school kids, a red Corsica from a family of four that was camping out, and four cars from a group of kids that were drinking in one of the nearby clearings. We've interviewed everyone extensively, but no one else was seen that night."

"On the other side of the park, the entrance off State Road 32, there is a house that resides along the trail leading into the woods. They had two friends over who parked alongside that trail, and neither of them saw anything all night."

Antonio guesses at the house. "The Matejas?"

"Correct. They were entertaining by their back bay window, which gave them a clear view of the forest entrance. Mrs. Mateja remembers seeing Alex go by, around 6:00 PM, but no one saw anyone else the rest of the night. We're still gathering more information, going door to door throughout the neighborhoods, but to be completely honest, we don't have any promising leads yet."

"So Mrs. Mateja was the last to see Alex? She never saw him come out?" Antonio asks.

"She probably assumed he did," Jim says. "I doubt she kept watch all night. I see kids walk by my house all the time, and they always make it home."

"That's correct," Terry says. "No one specifically watched for him, and they assumed he came back out. The Matejas are quite broken up over this."

"I must talk to them," Antonio says, "This is not their fault."

Sunlight seeps through the front shades, silhouetting Steve Cardell and Officer Baumgardner. Steve keeps unusually quiet for a father with a missing child, watching over the proceedings with a distant interest. Baumgardner watches whoever speaks, uncomfortably stroking a tassel on his chair between finger and thumb.

Terry continues, "Criminal psychologists are creating potential profiles while crime scene specialists are piecing together theories of how such a crime could actually be carried out. An encouraging point is how difficult it is for anyone to abduct three children at once, against their will. To not leave any evidence would be extremely difficult. If the perpetrator, and I'm going to discuss worst-case situations here, but if he wanted to seriously harm any of the children, that would have been easy and we would have found some sort of clue by now. Instead he went through a lot of effort to kidnap the children without leaving any evidence, which means he probably did not intend to harm them that night. That is a good thing."

"Maybe you're looking in the wrong places," Steve finally says.

"That is a possibility. But we have to assume the children were in close proximity at the time of abduction. We don't think he abducted the girls, then drove around town to find Alex and take him too. We are assuming it was one act, and the only place where all three children could be nearby and unnoticed, is the woods. We know Alex was there…"

"But why?" Antonio asks, "Why all three?"

"That is puzzling. Besides family cases, where a mother or father takes their own children, it is almost unheard of for someone to kidnap three children, let alone of different genders. Of course, the children aren't related, so we're not sure what we're dealing with. And going back to worst-case scenarios, let's say this is the work of a pedophile. They would generally want either the girls or the boy, but not both. This is truly atypical."

Steve finally speaks coldly, almost casually, saying, "Maybe he wants their toes."

"What?" Antonio asks.

"Maybe it's true. Maybe there was an accomplice," Steve continues.

Jim leans forward and asks, "An accomplice?"

"*The Spying Toes,*" Steve answers. He spent most of the previous night looking at missing children websites, and at one point cross-referenced a search with Edgebrook. Links to *The Spying Toes* came up, and he spent the rest of the night studying that case. Steve recites the facts as if he is recapping the major points of what he had for breakfast. "A little over thirty years ago this same thing happened in this same town. A man kidnapped three children, two girls and a boy, and imprisoned them in cages buried in the woods. He had a foot fetish, and for three days tormented them while worshipping the girls' toes. On the third day, the boy escaped from his cage. He made his way to safety and alerted the authorities, who found the man and shot and killed him because he had just cut off one of the girl's toes and was about to murder her."

Steve stares straight ahead, allowing Jim and Antonio to grasp the story before continuing. "*The Spying Toes* was a book written shortly after by a local college professor. According to the author, Art Morrell, there had been no cases combining a strong foot fetish with strong pedophiliac behavior. Morrell argued they were not characteristics of the same personality. After the case was closed and everyone assumed things were safe again, the doctor theorized that there were probably two abductors, a foot fetishist and a pedophile. The foot fetishist was killed, and the pedophile was still out there."

"So what happened to the pedophile?" Jim asks.

"Nobody knows," Steve answers.

"There wasn't any real evidence of a second abductor," Terry adds. "The police didn't suspect an accomplice. The kids never thought there was someone else. For two months after the case there was not one mention of this second accomplice until that book came out with its made-up theory to get attention. Nobody really believed it."

Antonio, Jim and Steve all watch Terry, waiting to see if he'll finish their thought, but when he says nothing, Steve finally adds, "Nobody believed it until now."

15

Antonio feels distant, almost delirious, from not sleeping the previous three nights. He is unaccustomed to this, normally able to sleep through anything. When Natalya's contractions started with Gemma, their first child, they were far enough apart that the doctor told them to wait a few hours before coming in. Antonio crawled back into bed and went right to sleep. Late bills, kids fighting, even the lightning strike that blackened the elm in the back yard, nothing woke Antonio when he wanted to sleep. The night before Katya's surgery is the only night he remembers being unable to sleep. He now has three more restless nights, and no idea what the final tally will be.

Last night Natalya and he lay in bed pretending to sleep, wondering if the other was awake, but unable to say anything when it became evident they both were. They would turn away from each other, turn back, hold hands, let go, and then repeat the routine, again and again. At 2:00 in the morning Antonio got up for a bowl of cereal. Gemma came in and he made one for her too, never speaking to her as they finished and he tucked her back into bed. He shuffled back to bed, squeezed in a few more hours of restlessness, and finally rose for the day at 5:30. After a shower, Antonio called his boss, with eyes closed, his head dangling forward with exhaustion.

"Hello Mr. Alvarez. This is Antonio, and I can't come in today."

"What's happened?" asks a slightly concerned, slightly annoyed voice from the other end.

"It's Alex. He's missing."

"Missing? Where?"

"I don't know."

"So you're taking the day off?"

"I may have to be gone all week. I don't know."

"Antonio, you know you don't have any time off…"

They had been through this before, with Katya's illness and surgery. Antonio used all of his time off, sick days, and managed to exchange all of his future holidays that year for more time off. He tried to go in, but more often than not, when he looked at his daughter in the morning, a baby that should be learning to crawl but barely had the energy to cry from all her tests and medications, when he held this baby girl with yellow skin and sunken eyes, he could not bring himself to leave her. "Tomorrow," he kept telling Mr. Alvarez. "I'll be in tomorrow." It was Natalya that finally convinced him to go. She understood what was at stake: not only his job but their insurance. Natalya even forced him to go in on the day of the transplant surgery. Mr. Alvarez had been as flexible as he could be, but Antonio stretched this generosity to the limit. And now it was happening again.

"He's been missing since Friday," Antonio continues, "with two other girls. It's in the papers."

A spark of recognition occurs. "Wait a second." Antonio hears the ruffling of papers followed by Mr. Alvarez's low whisper as he reads, mouthing the words. "Okay Antonio. I mean… this can't go on for… well, whatever. I hope everything turns out all right."

"Thank you." Antonio knows the position he is putting Mr. Alvarez in. The company is already paying exorbitant rates for Antonio's insurance, and everyone in the shop has his own specific skill, his being the lathe, so without him, nothing ships on time and the projects back up. This will show up directly on the bottom line. And even if Mr. Alvarez wants to keep him, Antonio knows the company will eventually force his hand, threatening to terminate their entire crew. It almost happened last time. They couldn't continue running at a loss. As Antonio hangs up the phone, he knows in his heart though that he has no choice. He must look for Alex.

Steve logs into his home phone account and has all calls forwarded to his cell phone. He packs his charger and starts off to work, an hour-long commute. His eyes are baggy and bloodshot, and he rubs them vigorously. Driving down Main Street, he sees all the MISSING posters taped in storefront windows. The Country Cafe on 57 has "God Bless our Children" written on their signpost. The local radio station talks about the three missing children, giving quick descriptions, who to contact if anyone sees anything, and how to help with the search.

To Steve, it almost seems excessive, or at least curious. When his wife April died, there was not much more than a three-paragraph article in the paper. Although many people attended the funeral, there was no public outcry. That following weekend, the Fourth of July, Edgebrook still had its parade down Main Street. Fireworks went off at The Community Center. Neighbors still had friends over, gathered in their backyards with a cooler of beer, various plates of meat, and a flimsy volleyball net. He could remember hearing the talk and laughter sifting in through the back windows. Meanwhile his daughter was upstairs crying, while he and April's parents drifted through the house, buffered from each other by a soft haze of numbness.

Where had Edgebrook been then?

He suspects they want another miracle. Another chance to find three children on the verge of disaster and have them delivered to freedom with hardly a scratch. They want to evangelize his plight now, declare it a national story, and ignore the hypocrisy that April's death warranted little more than those three paragraphs in the local paper. He is keenly aware of his sad resentment at this contradiction, but has no way to express it.

And then there are the ideas that roll through his head at night. It seems so apparent that some pervert has taken Arielle. He can't fathom any other possibility, no scenario where they miraculously come home unharmed. No person would take three children, not allow them to call home, and have good intentions. He fears he already knows the outcome, whether he receives the phone call today or a year from now. He is already bracing for that sympathetic, muted voice on the other line, starting off similarly to that previous call, "I'm so sorry to have to say this, but your wife... April... she was in an accident."

Steve's knuckles whiten against the steering wheel. A man in an SUV to his right sips his coffee. Somebody in the passenger seat is reading the paper. The woman in the Lexus in front of him talks on her cell phone. Life goes on.

Damn them all.

At work, Laura comes out from behind her desk and gives him a hug. Marc Trill, the Area Sales Director and Steve's boss, knocks on his door and asks how he's doing. Marc says he can take the day off, take as much time as he needs, but Steve declines. He needs something to do. A few people walk by outside with their morning coffee, their heads down or turned away. But there is a voicemail from the marketing department, somebody on the west coast who doesn't know, and there are emails that need responses. Steve knows he has to make a trip report from last week, fill out the QBR report, and draw a block diagram of the system board for the ABG team. He writes "To Do" on a scrap of paper, writes down five items, and starts at the top. The list makes no mention of his daughter.

Carrie lies in bed while listening to Jim move about the darkened bedroom. He shuffles between the bathroom and closet more times than usual. Not hearing anything for a while, Carrie opens one eye to see his silhouette standing with arms folded, staring inside the closet without moving. He turns away, paces across the room and then returns. He is looking for the right outfit to join the search parties and look for his daughter. Carrie knows he is not being vain, just delirious with exhaustion. His repetitive yawns confirm this.

She listens to him rummage around downstairs, make a few phone calls, place a plate or bowl into the sink, and finally grab a jacket from the hall and leave.

Carrie lies there for another hour, then reaches under her bed and pulls out *The Spying Toes*, whose folded page marks that she has just started the book. Yesterday, she could not convince herself to begin. She talked to her father, repeatedly telling him not to come out. She talked to the detective again. More neighbors called. She talked to that girl Reagan, who brought her pictures back and updated her on what was happening at one of the search sites. A forensic scientist had come by, collecting Emily's fingerprints, as well as DNA from Carrie. They went through the house again, especially Emily's room, looking for any clues on what her plans were the night she disappeared. As they searched around the house, Carrie sat at the kitchen table and waited.

Carrie turns on her bedside light and flips to the marked page. Three kids had just left their families to camp out for the night. They are figuring out where to set-up while covering gossip from school that day. The children are distracted, and Carrie knows evil lurks in the next few pages.

Terry Kruthers has slept little the past two nights too, but after talking to the parents, realizes how much rest he is getting. He needs to be on top of his game and make certain that no stone goes unturned, no lead unexamined. But instead he sits at his desk, goes over what others have planned, and grows more frustrated that on his most important case, he is best utilized as a desk jockey rather than being out in the field.

He will meet with the forensics team at nine o'clock. Afterwards he will call Agent Samperson again, just to see if there are any updates. The FBI is targeting all registered sex offenders within a hundred mile radius, just to question their alibis and verify their validity. That tactic seemed the most promising, but so far, nothing.

The press conference will be at one o'clock. Terry will skip lunch and go over his prepared statement one last time. He dislikes public speaking, knows he is not good at improvising, and worries about how little he has to say. There will be a round of questions and answers, but most likely, it will just be devious reporters trying to get something to slip out. He underlines the two statements that are the most crucial: There are no leads at this time, and we are looking into every possibility. These are statements he has heard before, unsure if they are from a movie or a real press conference, but not really caring. He may look silly, repeating the same mantra over and over, but he is fine with that. Imprecise answers leave the door open to implications the press can run with. No matter how he words his answers, the press will pick them apart and reconstruct them for quotes.

Repeat, there are no leads at this time, and we are looking into every possibility.

After the press conference, he will visit some of the search party centers. They are expecting almost three hundred volunteers, and Terry wants to make sure competent people are running each site.

Throughout the day, he will contact his officers and the families to keep everyone up-to-date. The schedule looks exhausting, and he knows this schedule is dependent on how the day proceeds. If there are any new leads, he will have to quickly provide new instructions to everyone. He has to remain sharp.

Terry sighs, closes his eyes, and rests sitting up.

16

Megan was just getting used to being a full-time teacher, and this was the first weekend she spent away from Edgebrook. She went on a road-trip back to Columbus with her college friends and watched Ohio State romp Northwestern. She seldom went to the games while at school, but loved cheering for her alma mater without a care in the world.

She had no idea what happened until she got near Edgebrook and began seeing the missing posters. She finally pulled into a gas station to fill up and walked up to one of the signs to get a better look. Her heart raced as she saw the pictures and read the names, instinctively pulling her phone out and calling the one person she could count on. "Mom," she says, "Emily and Arielle, they're students in my class. They disappeared over the weekend. I'm looking at their missing poster right now."

Unable to sleep, Megan rises almost three hours before she has to be at school. She dresses in her conservative tweed jacket and black pants, her most professional looking outfit, as she needs every reminder that she is now an adult.

She arrives almost an hour early, hopeful she can talk to some of the other teachers. At the very least, Principal Gorman will be there. He will have something to say.

As she works her way up Kingston Street, which turns through the school's front parking lot, she sees a maze of cars up and down the street. Cars are everywhere. Some park along the side of the road with their hazards on, while others maneuver around them, slowly creeping past one another with quiet understanding. Megan drives through the mess, watching minivans and SUVs with worried parents at the wheel, trying to remain patient. She pulls into the lot and parks in one of the last faculty spots.

Normally, the lot would be empty at this time. The band kids would be inside practicing, but the school buses, walkers, and children who are driven would not arrive for at least another half hour. Megan has never seen it this busy. She grabs her shoulder bag and heads toward the front entrance behind a blonde girl with a ponytail, her hand held tight within her mother's grasp.

The girl turns her head and says, "Hello, Miss Dermot."

Megan politely waves as she readjusts her bag's shoulder strap. "Good morning, Anne." Anne's mother turns too, and Megan acknowledges her, realizing she does not remember her name. "Good morning."

"Good morning, Miss Dermot," Anne's mother says with a determined seriousness Megan seldom sees in parents. She slows down so they can walk together. "I assume the school is keeping a watchful eye on our children today."

Megan instinctively responds, "We always do."

"I understand, but today, with what's going on...."

"Yes, of course." And it occurs to Megan exactly what is going on, why the lot is so busy. No parents will let their children walk to school. No parents will let them wait at a bus stop, unprotected, while there is a child abductor on the loose in Edgebrook. Today, a majority of the seven-hundred children will be driven to school and escorted to the school's front door. At the end of the day, nearly seven hundred cars will return to pick up their children, afraid that any time their child is out of sight, they might never be seen again. Megan senses the heightened responsibility of having them in her care. "We're going to care for them as you would."

"I know. I don't mean to be so over-protective myself, it's just that..." Anne's mother looks at her daughter and whispers, "...this scares me to death."

"I understand. I'll do everything I can to ensure Anne's safety, all of the children's safety."

"Thank you."

Upon entering the school, Megan watches the eerie promenade of parents leading their children to the gymnasium, followed by their slow, nervous hand-off to a teacher. She watches the big hugs and kisses, the anxiety on the parents' faces as they leave. *Please let me see my child again.*

The children sit on the gym floor, clustered by homeroom. The silence is amazing. No talking above a whisper, no snickering or giggling, just hundreds of middle school children sitting patiently. She has never seen the students so reserved. A commotion breaks out on the other side of the gym, and Megan watches a girl who begins to sob, and is then led out of the auditorium, probably to the nurse's office. They don't want the emotion to spread.

"I would like to start with what everyone knows," Principal Gorman begins, reading from a note he holds out so he can focus. "Arielle Cardell and Emily Hughes, along with a fourth grade boy from Carver Elementary, have been missing since last Friday. We don't know where they are or what happened, but there is a massive search taking place to find them. And just as important, we are all praying in our own way for their safe return. But until then, we want to make sure every one of you is kept as safe as possible. "

Principal Gorman looks up at the students, making sure they are following him, and then goes back to his notes. Megan catches a glance from Tracy, the teacher closest to her, who shakes her head, silently agreeing in their assessment of Principal Gorman. What an insincere ass. He is probably more concerned with potential lawsuits than any child's safety.

"This means no student should move around the school unsupervised. We have volunteer parents who will be assisting with each classroom, so whenever you need to go to the washroom, the principal's office, or anywhere else in the building, we have a parent who will accompany you."

"Also, a guard will be positioned at every exit, to keep track of all comings and goings. We will be taking attendance during lunch, and recess will now be held inside the gymnasium. This way, there will be no reason to go outside, and we can be sure to keep anyone unknown from entering our school. This is all being done to protect you."

"The one thing that I do ask is that you do not spend the eight minutes between classes socializing. Instead, please proceed quickly but calmly to your next class, so that your teacher can take attendance and we can be sure everyone is accounted for. Again, this will help guarantee everyone's safety."

"I hope everyone can abide by these rules, and as soon as Arielle and Emily are found and safely returned to us, we can go back to our normal routine. Thank you all for your cooperation."

The teachers do one last attendance count, and then lead their students out, homeroom by homeroom. As Megan waits her turn, Tracy meanders towards her and whispers, "Nice little Nazi state he's running here."

"Tracy…"

"I know, I know. It's for the children's safety. But I bet Gorman would run the school this way every day, if he could get away with it. Uh-oh, one of the guards has spotted me," Tracy says, heading back to where her homeroom sits after getting a stern glimpse from the assistant principal.

When it's her turn, Megan leads her class to their lockers, where they hang their coats and backpacks, get their books and line up again, still under the belief that if they misbehave, they're putting themselves at risk. Their fear is tangible, and Megan can't help feeling heartbroken for them.

Children this age should not have to experience this. She never experienced anything like this until now, and at twenty-two, Megan feels she is too young.

Within minutes, they are all at their desks and Megan can begin her lesson plan, discussing the short story, "The Secret Life of Walter Mitty." Hopefully it will distract them. Hopefully it will distract Megan, who can see the profile of someone's dad, standing outside her door like a prison guard.

She introduces the story by asking her students if they ever play make-believe? The children are not responding, and as she asks more questions, Megan notices Sheila's eyes watering up. Sheila is friends with Arielle and Emily, and is slowly getting worse as the class progresses. Trying to draw as little attention to the girl, Megan kneels by her desk and asks, "Sheila, would you like to come outside with me?"

The little girl with curly brown hair doesn't say anything, wipes her eyes with her fingers, and walks out with her head down. Megan leaves the room with her and asks the father standing guard to watch her class. Megan kneels down in front of Sheila and asks, "Are you all right?"

The girl can't look her in the face, and when Megan finally moves so they are eye-to-eye, the girl sobs uncontrollably. Megan hugs her. "It's all right, Sheila. It's perfectly all right to miss your friends." Megan holds the scrawny girl tight and feels her sobs, which echo up and down the hallway. Two parents, sitting outside classrooms down the hall, nervously look away.

"I'm sorry, Miss Dermot."

"Sorry? You don't have to be sorry, Sheila. None of this is your fault."

"But it is my fault. It is."

Megan's arms tense up, clutching the girl within them. She doesn't want to frighten Sheila, but can tell by the conviction on her face that this is not an idle statement. "What do you mean?"

"It's my fault. I'm sorry."

Megan takes Sheila's shoulders, looking directly into her eyes. "Sheila, do you know anything about what happened to Emily and Arielle?"

"I don't want to get them in trouble."

"Nobody is going to get in trouble, I promise you that. We only want to know where they are, so they can return home safely. Now, do you know what happened?"

"No, but it's my fault they're missing."

"How is it your fault?"

"I'm so sorry, Miss Dermot."

"Sheila, it's very important you tell me everything you know. Like I promised, you are not going to get in trouble and neither are they. Okay?"

"Okay."

"So what happened?"

"They were going to stay at my house. My parents were gone all night."

"And what happened?"

"We were supposed to meet in the woods."

"Why would you meet in the woods?"

"To meet him."

"To meet whom?"

"Him."

"Sheila, who were you going to meet?"

"I don't know his name. A kid from another school. Somebody who could... who could..."

"Who could what, Sheila?"

"We've never done it before. I swear."

"Done what?" Megan asks, terrified of what the answer will be.

"He was going to buy us beer. My parents were gone and we were going to try a beer at my house."

"Who was going to get the alcohol?"

"Somebody from another school. I don't know him. He said he made money buying for kids at our school. He knew the names of all these older kids. He said they did the same thing."

"How did you meet this person?"

"We talked to him on FnP."

"What?"

"It's on the internet."

"F-N-P?"

"It's just called FnP, but it means Facebook, No Parents."

"Okay, Sheila. We need to talk to some other people. Tell them what happened. Okay? We need to go to the principal's office."

"I'm sorry, Miss Dermot."

"This is not your fault."

Megan takes Sheila's hand and leads her down the hallway. There are no other noises besides Sheila's sniffles, and Megan finally asks, "Did this person have a name? Like a screen name?"

"Yes."

"What was it?"

"Toehead."

17

Jim Hughes makes his way through the crowd and into the police office without speaking to anyone. Workers lay cable to the podium microphones atop the front steps, while reporters and their videographers search for the best shot. Up and down Main Street, cameramen try to get sweeping shots of the idyllic downtown while trying to avoid having each other in the picture. They try to capture the wallpaper of missing signs that cover the store fronts, the hand-painted sign over Doc's Drugs that reads, "Closed. Out Searching for Our Children." Anyone who happened to be going down Main Street for other reasons, to pick up a newspaper at the Book Nook, get a haircut at Ruthanne's Hairstyling, or deposit a check at Edgebrook National, would be met by a barrage of reporters asking questions.

"It just doesn't feel safe around here anymore," says one man, walking a Great Dane, clutching his tattered robe while holding a hand spade and a full doggie bag.

"I'm just so worried for those poor children," an elderly woman says as she runs errands. "Who would do such a thing?" she asks the second interviewer. "I just want them to come home safe. We all do," she says, taking a moment to look away from the camera. When the camera light goes off, she looks to the reporter and asks, "Was that good? Should we do another take?"

Once the press conference finishes, the reporters plan to head out to the search sites. The best footage will be there, interviewing volunteers who took the day off to join the search. They should have the most riveting statements.

"Can I get you anything? Did you have lunch?" Terry asks Jim, debriefing him inside the station a few minutes before the press conference. He studies Jim, tries to determine if he looks thinner, more angular. His mouth hangs slightly ajar; he is wide-eyed, tired and lost.

"I'm fine."

"It's important you eat, even if you don't feel like it."

"I know."

"Let me have Barb get you a sandwich or something from the deli."

"Fine. Thank you. Something simple."

Terry gives a sandwich order to Barb, throwing in fries and an apple. He is glad to be able to do something for Jim, no matter how small, considering he has not done the one thing that he's supposed to do.

"How are you holding up?"

"Fine."

"And Carrie?"

Jim gives his head a slight nod and looks away, not wanting to discuss it.

Terry wonders how much they talk. Over the few interviews he had with them, he could tell they were having troubles. Especially when compared to the Collinis, who sat next to each other and held hands, talking to each other as much as to him, confirming each other's statements and working together to try and answer all of Terry's questions. Jim and Carrie Hughes, on the other hand, acted like total strangers.

"Are you sure she doesn't want to come down, say a few things too? It's alright for her to leave the house for a little while."

"No," Jim insists, "She's fine."

"Alright. Do you have a prepared statement?"

"I have a good idea what I'm going to say."

"There's not going to be much to this. I'm going to go out and quickly describe the facts of the case. At that point I would like you to make your statement. As soon as you're done, I'll go back to answer questions. It's as simple as that."

"Good. I'm ready."

"Do you want to go over your statement with me?"

"I speak in public all the time. I'll be fine."

"Alright," Terry says, thinking again about the break they just received, wondering if he should tell Jim. There is not much, yet. A classmate of Emily's had just come forward, claiming that the girls had been planning on going to her house that Friday night. They had met someone on the internet, someone claiming to be a student from another school, who was going to sell them alcohol. The girl's computer was already at an FBI lab, and Terry had questioned the girl for every bit of information she could remember.

But they don't know who this internet person is, and Terry does not want the perpetrator to know that they have a break. He wants him to remain confident that he has gotten away with the abductions. Terry will answer questions the same way he has every day. *There are no new leads at this time, and we are pursuing every possibility.*

Terry goes outside with Jim and, when given his cue, walks up to the bouquet of microphones and begins his prepared statement. He describes again how the children were discovered missing, gives a description of that night, and some of the steps being taken to find them. He asks anyone who knows or saw anything suspicious, anything at all, to immediately call the police department.

Terry steps back and nods to Jim, who proceeds to the microphones. "I only have a few things to say," he starts, clearing his throat. "First, I want to thank everyone who has helped out so far. From the many people who are searching in the nearby woods and fields, to all the people who have put up posters and called in with tips. I would also like to thank the Edgebrook police, as well as the FBI, who have been assisting in this search."

He's not getting an award, Terry thinks, why is he thanking people? He analyzes how much Jim has pulled himself together, looking much more poised and self-assured than he had just a few minutes ago. He watches Jim stop to look into the cameras and nod, as if he were announcing his candidacy for political office.

"I want to say that, although I don't know Alex Collini, both Emily and Arielle are extremely strong children, and I have the utmost faith that we will see them safely returned. I am looking forward to it, and again want to thank everyone helping to make it possible."

A reporter's hand rises timidly from the front row. They're not supposed to ask Jim questions, but before Terry can interrupt, Jim calls on him. "Are you concerned for your daughter's safety?"

"Of course I am. I don't know where she is, and I'm sure she misses her family just as much as we miss her, but I am confident that she will make it home safely, unharmed, and we will take it from there."

Terry realizes his mistake. Jim is trying to be a good public speaker, trying to put a pretty picture on the situation, an air of confidence. Terry wanted the exact opposite. He wanted Jim to break down, to sound lost and afraid, desperate to find his missing daughter. He wanted more emotion, inspiring the current volunteers to keep searching, encouraging more people to join in, and most importantly, stirring anyone who might have any information to come forward. Instead, Jim sounds cocky, like he's about ready to call off the search parties and tell the police they can go back to writing parking tickets.

Another reporter asks, "Do you have any information we don't know about, something that would lead you to believe in your daughter's safe return?"

"Yes, I do. I know my daughter. I know how strong and courageous she is. I know what a wonderful life she has, and I know what a wonderful life she will continue to have once this is over. It's these things that confirm to me that she'll come home safely."

Terry quickly walks up to Jim's side and whispers into his ear, sidling his way between him and the microphones. "I'll handle the questions from here. Thank you, Jim."

Most of the reporters' hands shoot up as Terry point to one. "Are you as confident the children will be found unharmed?"

"I'm confident we are doing everything within our means, everything possible."

"Are you as sure as Mr. Hughes that the children will make it back safely?"

Terry pauses. He needs to recover the situation. There was a message he hoped Jim would convey, and now Terry has to do it. "I do not know what the outcome is going to be, and I do not want to speculate. But I do know that we need as much help as we can get. We don't know where the children are. We are following every lead we have, but there's nothing that leads me to believe we're going to find them in the next hour, or for that matter, the next day. So if anyone has any information, anything at all, I ask that you please contact us."

"So the children have vanished without a trace?"

"I wish we had more. We don't know where the abduction took place. We don't know how the abduction took place. As far as what happened, we hardly know anything. And the basic fact is, when children go missing, with every day that passes, the odds diminish of them ever returning safely. It's been three days now. Three days for the kidnapper to get farther away. Three days where anything could have happened. Time is critical. I cannot emphasize that enough. Time is critical." Terry looks at the reporters and realizes he has just spoken his mind and shown that he's afraid. He hadn't planned on doing that, but it may not matter, as he told the truth.

18

The following day, when the various newspapers land on driveways and line the newsstand racks, one quote is used over and over. All three families read it, as well as the townspeople of Edgebrook and much of the nation.

"We hardly know anything."

Tuesday passes under this evaluation. Tuesday night courses endlessly, eventually ebbing into a Wednesday, promising to be a repeat of the previous day. The searching and questioning continue, but there are no significant breaks. The strongest lead, the only lead, has been provided by the girl who was supposed to meet with Arielle and Emily. Since Sheila was providing a place to stay, the three girls agreed Arielle and Emily would meet the stranger, buy the alcohol from him, and bring it to Sheila's house. The police found the clearing where Sheila thought the meeting was supposed to take place, about a mile into Busey Woods, but could not uncover any useful evidence, leading Terry to believe the kidnapper ambushed them somewhere else, along the way. But they didn't know where. The FBI labs had dissected Sheila's computer, recreating the conversations she had with this on-line stranger, this Toehead. He was skilled at making vague statements and purposely discreet comments, so the only hopeful lead was to get Toehead's information from the FnP chat board, as it was a paid account and they must have a credit card on file. For now, the west coast company, as well as a judge, were stonewalling their efforts, claiming their privacy rights from an illegal search. An FBI legal team was driving that lead, but to no avail. The issue could be pressed by going around the law, perhaps by threatening to portray the company as a guise for pedophiles, but it was taking way too much time, a commodity they could not squander.

"With every day that passes, the odds diminish of them ever returning safely." This quote permeates the investigation, a deep pressure on every thought and every action.

And so the Hughes, Collinis, and Steve Cardell spend another sleepless night. Edgebrook holds its breath as people pray, some ceremoniously kneeling and clasping their hands, others thinking informally, "Dear God…"

19

"Try this," Gioia Collini says, holding out a wooden spoon with a meaty mush gathered on the end.

"What is it?" Natalya asks, once again annoyed that her mother-in-law insists on having everyone sample a bite of everything she cooks.

"Just try it."

Natalya obediently opens her mouth and uses her upper lip to dredge the mush from the spoon. She smells, tastes and inhales raw garlic, but replies, "Mmm. Good."

Gioia nods. Of course it is.

Natalya has been through this before. When Katya was sick, the week before the liver transplant, Antonio's mother and two sisters moved in. They wanted to help, which meant they cooked, cleaned, and fussed about every little thing in their little house. When they finally left, the house was spotless. The linoleum floors were freshly waxed, the carpets were vacuumed, the windows were taken out and washed; it was as if every inch of the house had been dismantled, meticulously cleansed with every chemical possible, and then reassembled. Plus the fridge was stock full of Tupperware dishes, each one sealed with another night's meal. Once they left, Natalya was exceptionally grateful.

But while they were in her home, she wasn't sure how much she could take. Sitting at home, waiting patiently for a surgery that would completely remove Katya's liver and replace it with a section of her own, Natalya needed things to do to keep her mind busy. Instead, they instructed her to lie down, not to bother with anything, and catered to everything she wanted and everything they thought she should want. They took over her home.

The shelves were stocked with food Natalya never bought. The kids' lunches looked different, as Nonna couldn't help but give in to their requests for sweets. Clothes were folded into new shapes and put into different drawers. Cleaning supplies were restocked under cabinets throughout the house, not in the garage, where the little ones couldn't reach them. But how could she tell them what to do? The one time she tried, explaining that all the cleaning supplies had to be kept in the garage or else they were endangering the children, Gioia sulked away, feigning a hurt deeper than Natalya ever thought possible, retiring to the family room's rocking chair to brood. In the end, Natalya apologized, explaining that she was just nervous about Katya's operation. Gioia accepted this explanation, and in return started putting the cleaning supplies in the garage. So Natalya won, in a way, but she did not have the strength to battle Gioa's every whim.

So she sits, half lies, on the living room couch, listening to a local radio station she never knew existed playing upbeat Christian songs she has never heard before. Antonio's mother and sisters know them, but they are too busy gabbing in the kitchen to really listen.

Where's Alex, momma?

Katya has long tired of this line of questioning, but her voice echoes in Natalya's mind, repeating the question over and over. *I wish I knew, baby. I wish I knew.* What kind of sicko abducts three children? If he's a pedophile interested in boys, what horrible things has he done to Alex? And possibly worse, what if he's not interested in boys? Why keep Alex alive?

Natalya bats these questions around, finding the only way to drive them from her mind is to concentrate on her own self-pity. Why does this keep happening to her family? Hadn't Katya's surgery been enough? Even after a successful operation, wasn't it punishment enough to live with the prospect that any day her liver could fail? The doctor said two years was a good sign; that would mean they were out of the woods and her body had accepted the liver, but it hasn't even been a year yet. So they are still in the woods.

What a terrible expression, "out of the woods." Natalya now has one child in the proverbial woods and the other quite possibly in the physical woods? *Please Alex, please break free like that other boy. Please break free and come home.*

And under it all, there is always the debt. Antonio could lose his job if he doesn't go back, but he won't even discuss it with her. As long as Alex could be in those woods, as long as Antonio's help increases the odds of finding Alex, even just a little, he will continue searching. That is that. As kind and genial as her husband and his family come across, Natalya continues to be amazed at how foolishly stubborn they can be, how oblivious they are to their situation when their hearts point the other way.

And what does that make her, lying on the couch, doing nothing to bring her son home? Lazy? Heartless? A horrible mother? She knows none of these are really true, but can't help thinking them. Gioia enters the room carrying a large bowl wrapped in a towel, steam rising from the top. She sets it on the table in front of Natalya, and stirs it a few times, releasing the pungent aroma of slightly cooked garlic. "Whenever you're up for it," she instructs her daughter-in-law. Natalya tightens her upper lip and nods.

"They should be coming later today," Gioia informs her.

"Who?"

"*Time.*"

Natalya remembers. The magazine is running a story on each family. Pictures, interviews, the whole works. *People* magazine comes tomorrow morning, and then a few others. Detective Kruthers said, as long as they were up for it, the exposure would be good. Keeping it in the headlines might help bring someone forward with a clue, keep the volunteers working, keep everyone working. So she agreed. Let the media carousel whirl up. At least she'll have something to do.

20

The urgency inside the Edgebrook police station surges and wanes all morning. Terry feels the search approaching a sense of routine, analyzing the same evidence over and over, again and again. He watches Baumgardner at his desk, pretending to look at sign-in sheets from the search parties but mainly reading the newspaper underneath. Baumgardner is not slacking; Terry knows one can only go over the same sheets of paper so many times before it becomes completely meaningless. A momentary distraction allows one to come back with renewed intensity. Terry looks at the folders and papers around him and struggles with the same problem. At times he thinks he could study the case files for a hundred years and never find anything. There is just nothing there.

But then, at other times, Terry seems to flip a switch and inspire himself to the task at hand, renewed into a flourish of industry. Terry knows what the stimulus is. Whenever he looks at the photos of the children, or thinks about the families involved, not as facts in a case but as real people in a dire situation, he gets keyed up, internally cheering himself on, just like he does before stepping into the batter's box. Except this isn't recreational softball, striking out is unacceptable, and he feels himself slipping from one of these frenzied moments into quiet distraction, taking a moment to look around the precinct.

Barb comes out of the office where they're sorting mail, approaches Terry's desk with a pleasant smile, and places a brown package in his In Box. Other officers are going through the general mail now, opening every letter addressed to the station and deciding if it is worth passing on or just filing away. Most are letters of encouragement, praise or thanks. Although appreciated, the officers quickly throw them in a box labeled "Non-Evidence." Some people send donations, usually five or ten dollars, which they file in a manila envelope to be dealt with later.

Then there are the tips and condemnations. These are passed along so the FBI can study them, as they have received all sorts of tips. Psychics claimed they were getting feelings, messages from the beyond, whether they be from the children, kindred spirits, or evil spirits, all claiming to know some generic clue, like the children are near water or a large tree. One claimed the spirit of Fred Rogers, yes Mr. Rogers of *Mr. Roger's Neighborhood*, was guiding her to the children, which the officers passed around for a chuckle. Other letters were more wrenching. Parents of other missing children, children who weren't getting the same exposure, suggesting that the cases might somehow be related, that by going through the facts of their children's cases, the police might uncover some clue to find them all. Parents from all over the country were connecting the dots. One mother from Hawaii was sure the person who took her daughter was responsible for this case too, even though her daughter had been abducted on the island of Kauai more than twenty years ago. She is still searching, she still holds out hope, and Terry hopes from the bottom of his heart this investigation will not still be open twenty years from now.

Some people claimed to know why the children were abducted. Sin topped the list, whether it was the parent's sin, the town's, America's, or society in general, people wrote page upon page on how we must pay for our sins. Satanists and anarchists took the other side and claimed that this was their work. Cranks and crazies, that was how everyone felt about the people who wrote these letters, but each one had to be investigated.

Terry even received a marriage proposal, a side effect of appearing on TV. Terry couldn't help being a little curious, wondering who could be taken by a plain-faced fellow like himself. His best traits are height and weight, which can only be described as above average and below average. Otherwise his thick brow, his bowed out ears, and his bluish-gray eyes which sit just a tad too close have never done much for attracting the opposite sex. The only compliment he can remember, usually from little old ladies, is that he has an honest face. "Must be a practical joke," Baumgardner concluded, "but to come up with a joke like that, she also must be a little crazy." Terry agreed.

And that was only the mail. Every article written on the internet, along with every blog, seemed to have an overflowing "Comment" section. There were hundreds, maybe thousands of them. It wasn't Terry's responsibility to look through them, but he found late at night, when he couldn't sleep but couldn't concentrate, they provided at least a glimpse of something else to study, somewhere else to take his thoughts and still be on the case. More often than not the comments and blogs quickly degenerated to someone going on a rant, finding some sort of causation between three abducted children and whatever injustice they saw in the world. Socialism, capitalism, or tiger-mom parenting, there was always a connection. Whether it be gun control, charter schools, or the trade deficit, people seemed to find a connection by the thinnest of threads. Things only made sense if some global issue, like climate change, child vaccinations, or legalized abortion, was responsible for the children's disappearance.

Terry didn't think that way. Going back to the original case, a dysfunctional man had a severe foot fetish, and ended up kidnapping three children. That is not common. There are no universal truths that could have predicted that. In the end, the children escaped because the abductor carelessly left a knife by one of the children, and that resilient boy used it to escape. Nine times out of ten, the outcome would have been completely different. For Terry, the truth is knowing what happened, what is happening, and nothing more. There are no grandiose connections, no all-encompassing theories or covert forces, that dictate outcomes. Things happen, all sorts of nearly random things, and that is the only truth. His job is to uncover what happens, and he'll let others worry about why.

Though he does wonder why Barb pulled this small brown-paper package and placed it on his desk. It might be the way it is tightly wrapped with perfect folds of brown paper. It might be the deep red ribbon, made of cloth with black trim, that wraps around the box and loops into a small bow. It might be the small letters so neatly typed on the front. Or it might be the postmark, which reads Lovely, Texas. Whatever the reason, Terry reaches across his papers, picks it up, and turns it carefully in his hands. Lovely, Texas, he thinks, is that really a place? He pulls the ribbon's loose end and the taut knot on top dissolves into curled twine. He folds open one end of the wrapping, then a flap of the cardboard box inside, and removes a velvet jewelry box, the same kind men clasp in their pockets before proposing. A small square of paper falls out, which he unfolds and, seeing the magazine-cut letters, begins to read:

I am offering a lovely,
An angel I yearn,
To make you aware,
Of my return

Terry rereads the curious note and sets it down next to the ring box. With one hand, he holds the base down against his desk, and with the other, he flips the top open. The inside has a soft black liner, cushioned for holding an engagement ring. But instead of a ring, Terry sees a small, perfectly polished, cleanly severed, pinky toe.

21

"Hello," Terry says into his cell phone, wishing he had not answered it.

"Detective?"

"Yes, Natalya."

"Hi. I'm just calling to… well, there's not a particular reason. I just wanted to see if there were any updates?"

"I'm sorry, Natalya, but I really can't talk right now." Knowing he should not say it, Terry slips out, "We do have a potential lead, and we're tracking it right now."

"Oh my God," she shrieks.

"No, no, no," he says, realizing the magnitude of his blunder. He needs to remember the situation she is in, how completely on edge she must be. Just the thought that there might be a lead, that resolution may be coming, that she may find out shortly if her son is coming home, or if she may never hold him again, is the raw emotion he has tapped into. "No Natalya, we really have no idea right now at all. We're just checking something out."

"You just do what you have to," she says, her voice shaking, "and let me know." There's nothing he can say now. She's at the cliff's edge looking down, waiting for his phone call. He listens to the breaths rushing in and out, the anticipation swelling.

"Like I said, we don't know anything right now, but I will call you back shortly. All right?"

"I will be here."

"Goodbye, Natalya." Terry hangs up the phone, upset with himself for stirring her fragile emotions. "I do think this is it," Terry predicts aloud in the car.

"This is what?" Baumgardner asks, turning to look in the side mirror, eyeing the line of police cars behind them.

"This is the big break. I can feel it."

84

"How so?"

"Everything's been too clean. Too polished. I've spent every day of the past week wondering how three kids could disappear without a trace. There would have to be some sort of screw up. Some clue. But nothing. I think this is finally what we've been looking for."

ToeHead was the clue. It was the username of the person Sheila talked to in the chat room. After reading Sheila's cached transcripts with ToeHead on the FnP site, they clearly paint the picture of someone trying to lure young girls into talking to him, trying to pretend he's someone he's not. But once they had the alias, FnP would not provide the user's details due to privacy concerns. With some arm-twisting from the FBI, they finally gave up ToeHead's information, a credit card number, a name and an address.

Max Janikowski. 1443 Orchard. Three blocks east of the Hughes house. Judge Reinhardt signed the search order and they were on their way.

"What do you think we're going to find," Baumgardner asks, "when we get there and all? Do you think the kids will be there?"

"I don't know."

"What about the toe?"

"I don't know." The forensic results would be coming back soon enough, but Terry hopes this will break the case open. Why tell a family that their child's toe has been cut off when you can tell them the perpetrator has been caught, when you can hopefully bring their child home. If they are alive, Terry assumes that news will outweigh the fact that someone's toe was severed. And if they're dead, the same logic applies. As disturbing as it sounds, the toe is secondary.

Three of the patrol cars in the back of the procession take a right at the stop sign, surrounding the suburban block. Terry pulls their unmarked car into the driveway of a modest ranch house while the other cars park up and down the street or behind the block, trying to remain out of sight. The house's siding is a faded gray with large scrapes of paint peeling off, but Terry keeps his eyes on the windows as he approaches, searching for movement. The front lawn has yellowed beneath the cover of fallen leaves, and beneath an imposing elm tree, a row of bushes line the front walk. Terry reads "Janikowski" on the mailbox next to the door, knocks three times and waits.

Nothing happens and Terry knocks again. This time he hears movement inside, slow and patient, followed by a hoarse voice. "Who is it?"

"Mr. Janikowski?"

"One minute," the voice responds. The sounds inside don't indicate scampering, no last minute hustle before being caught, but instead make a slow swoosh, like slippers on linoleum.

The locks tumble, one, then the next, then a pause as the door handle turns, revealing an old man with a slight hunch. He holds his glasses in his hand, and puts them on to survey his guests.

"Max Janikowski?" Terry asks, knowing this man does not have the strength or speed to catch one kid, let alone three.

He looks from Baumgardner to Terry to Baumgardner and finally settles on Terry. "The name's Arthur, Arthur Janikowski."

"Is there a Max Janikowski at this residence?"

"What's this about?"

"I'm Detective Kruthers and this is Officer Baumgardner. We would like to talk to Max Janikowski, if he's here."

"You sure about that?" the old man asks.

"Positive. We have a search warrant," Terry says, unfolding the form from his jacket pocket and showing it.

"A search warrant? For Max? Hmph. You can come in, but you're not going to get him to talk."

"Where is he?" Terry commands, aware that they are wasting time.

The old man laughs. "You can talk to him detective, detective, what was it?"

"Kruthers."

"Detective Kruthers, but like I said, don't be upset if he doesn't answer your questions." Arthur Janikowski's liver-spotted hand opens the door wide as he shouts out, "Max! Come here, Max!"

Terry hears the crisp scrape of nails on linoleum and knows what's about to happen before Max appears. His heart sinks as a Boxer turns the corner at full speed, then tries to stop on the sliding hallway rug, crumpling it into the door frame.

"Good boy, Maxie. Good boy." Arthur is laughing now, watching the expression on the detective's face. "Say hello, Max. Say hello, boy." Max barks at Terry. "Awww, be nice, Maxie."

The boxer rises onto its hind legs, holds the pose, then leans forward and puts his paws onto Terry's chest, sniffing the search warrant.

Arthur Janikowski, a man in his late seventies who has lived on Orchard Street for most of his life, wipes a tear of laughter from his eye and says, "Now if that search warrant says you have to look around, you better come on in and look around, but maybe you can tell me what's this all about."

"We have a credit card in Max's name."

"A credit card? That's all? He's been getting those things for years."

"He has?"

"Yes indeed."

"Your dog gets credit card applications?"

"Yes sir," Arthur laughs.

Terry thinks. There must be something here. Arthur isn't the person they're after, but he must somehow be connected. "Who knows that?"

"Damn near anyone who wants to. It was in the paper a while back, more than five, maybe ten years ago. An article about how people get a million of those damn applications every day, how they'll give 'em to anyone, although I think Max's probably more responsible than most people. Since then it's only gotten worse. I read about a boy's goldfish that got an application. Although you probably already have that goldfish in custody."

"What paper was it in?"

"*New York Times*," Arthur says proudly. "I've still got it, if you want to see it."

Terry plays this out in his mind and asks, "How did your dog get mentioned in an article in *The New York Times*?"

Arthur smiles. "Let's just say, if something ain't right, I do know how to raise a stink about it." He grins, proud of his standing as a cantankerous old man.

Terry instructs Baumgardner to go back to the car and let the other officers know this is a bad lead. Shit, he thinks. Terry steps into the house, Max jumping up on him in defiance of Arthur's commands. Not only is this a bad lead, Terry realizes he has to call Natalya back and let her know they don't have anything. Now the toe is front and center, their only clue, and once they determine whose toe it is, he'll have to break that news to the family. Shit, shit, shit.

22

Carrie Hughes closes *The Spying Toes* and clutches the book tight, having re-read the ending a third time. The author, Art Morell, was a professor of literature at Trinidad Community College, a small school nestled in southern Ohio. Due to the book's success, he quit about a year after its publication and dedicated himself to writing, although none of his subsequent books came close to the success of *The Spying Toes*.

The book follows the typical true crime formula, starting with the back-story of the three children, Andy Frempt, Susan Waldorff, and Elizabeth Pierce, leading up to the day all three were abducted. These introductions would be quite mundane except Art enjoyed the flair of foreshadowing the coming tragedy. He peppered their daily routines with lines like, "Susie played fetch with her golden Labrador Buster, but just as she expected him to return the ball every time she threw it, he also expected her to return when she left on her bike to play in the nearby woods."

He portrayed the abduction from the children's point of view, a chaotic ambush as a man wearing a tattered black ski mask tackled Andy and Susan, while Elizabeth froze in fear. He corralled the children at knifepoint and forced them to endure a nine-mile hike into the woods. They fell down, they cried, but eventually they reached a valley not far from the beaten-down shack he called home. He then made them lay down in pre-built wire cages on the forest floor, and covered them with leaves. Art finished their point of view as a handful of leaves were dropped over Elizabeth's face, and the three children were trapped in darkness.

At this point Art Morell introduces Calvin Landess, piecing together bits of his history and weaving a story. Born in southern Indiana, Calvin was an only child, homeschooled until the age of fifteen, when he ran away. There is little information over the next eight years of his existence, besides a few odd jobs and an indistinct police record. Public drunkenness, petty theft, but nothing out of the ordinary until his trespassing arrest at a department store in Tuscaloosa. He was arrested for hiding in a rack of clothes next to the women's shoe department, and though only charged with trespassing, the police report indicates a witness thought he was masturbating. A year later he was admitted to a hospital in Birmingham with various cuts and bruises and a broken jaw. The accompanying police report is vague, but it appears he jumped a woman in her mid-thirties as she entered her apartment building, only to find her boyfriend following shortly behind. No charges were filed due to the extent of Calvin's injuries, but once discharged from the hospital, Calvin was pretty much asked to leave Alabama.

The third incident was the most brazen. He snuck into a suburban backyard that abutted a nearby forest, where a young mother was out sunbathing and had fallen asleep. Calvin carefully straddled her chest, facing away from her, and pinned her down with his weight. According to her testimony, she awoke not to his weight, which he didn't apply until she struggled, but to the sensation that her toes were being licked. One efficient kick to his previously broken jaw allowed her escape, and running to the front yard, there were plenty of people out on a Saturday afternoon to hear her cries for help. This time, Calvin was arrested, prosecuted, and sentenced to six months in jail.

Two more years passed without anything more than a few rumors of Calvin's whereabouts. Some homeless people claimed to have seen him in Richmond, Virginia. A volunteer remembered talking with him at a soup kitchen outside Pittsburgh. Each sighting pieced together a trail that wrapped around Ohio, but there was nothing concrete until the three children were abducted.

Up to this point in the novel, Art portrays Calvin not only as an unsympathetic, foot-fetish pervert, but as a buffoon. He was caught three times, and each time was more out of simple carelessness then the time before. A crowded department store, a woman who lived with her boyfriend, and another woman sunbathing in a busy neighborhood on a Saturday afternoon. Calvin was not a criminal mastermind, merely a slave to his compulsions.

As for compulsions, not once was there any record to indicate an affinity for children. The youngest woman he attacked was thirty-two. So breaking from his tale, Art directly asks how this bumbling fool could plan the abduction of three children, having clearly built the traps in advance, and why a man with a foot fetish for older women would want to abduct children?

With these questions laid out, Art returns to the abduction, to the shack Calvin was living in, where the reader finds him talking to another man. He has no name, but he is the intelligent one, telling Calvin how he made sure no one was watching when they abducted the children, how he built the traps, and how he was going to have his way with the children when Calvin was done. Art admits he doesn't know where Calvin met his accomplice, speculating it could have been from his time in jail, one of the odd jobs he worked, his time on the streets, or just some twisted stroke of fate that brought the two together. Regardless, this second abductor is the intelligent one. He is the pedophile. And when Calvin was shot and killed on the forest floor, he is the one who got away.

There was never any proof of an accomplice, and while most of the book was well researched and stuck to the facts, the police dismissed Art's theory as pure fiction. Though it may not have had traction with the police, it was this theory that propelled his book to fame thirty years ago, and it is this theory which now goes through Carrie's head as she puts the book down on her nightstand. If two men abducted those children thirty years ago, a bumbling fool with a foot-fetish and a genius pedophile who masterminded the abduction, and only the fool was killed, then the genius mastermind is still out there, and he has Emily.

23

Terry massages his temples and sighs. The FnP web account, which at one point was their best lead, turned out to be a dog. Not only that, Arthur Janikowski allowed a number of websites to reprint the credit card numbers, which meant anyone would have known them and anyone could have opened the FnP account with them. The whole investigation of Toehead proved to be a dead end, without any new suspects and without any useful leads.

Much, much worse, the other lead, the one packaged in a jewelry box and mailed directly to him, was not a dead end.

Terry sits in the driveway for another minute.

"Do you need me to go with?" Baumgardner asks.

Terry almost says no, reprieving Baumgardner from this grievous task, but decides this is part of the job and they will tackle it together. "Come on," he replies, opening his car door.

Walking up the front steps, Terry feels like the house is waiting for them, expecting. Confirming this, Jim opens the door before they knock.

"Hello, Jim."

Jim takes one look at Terry's solemn face, Baumgardner's averting eyes, and asks, "What's going on?"

"Is there someplace we can sit?"

Jim just stares at them, wondering if he can just close the door, and mutters, "No."

"Jim," Terry tries to assure him. "This isn't… it's not what you're thinking."

Jim squints, tries to confirm what Terry has said, before leading them into the family room, where Carrie already sits. She watches the men enter and says nothing. She expects the worst, and it occurs to her that maybe the emptiness she has been carrying for so long is not some inexplicable imbalance, but instead a preemptive safeguard, a defensive mechanism shutting down her emotions so that she can handle this very moment. Maybe that inexplicable hollowness is about to transform into a real experience, starting with the horrible words, 'We found your daughter's body …'"

Terry sits on one end of the couch, while Baumgardner sits on the opposite side, as far from the conversation as possible.

Jim does not sit, and when Terry glances at the open chair next to him, he says, "No, I'll stand."

"All right," Terry sighs, "I'm just going to come out and say it. Yesterday morning I received a package. A small package about so big," he says, cupping his hands together.

Carrie's brow contracts. This isn't the news she expected.

"We get a lot of mail concerning the case, and numerous packages, so I opened it without much thought. Inside the package was a velvet ring box, and inside of that… inside of the box…" He looks to Baumgardner but gets no support.

"Yes?"

"Inside the box was a pinky toe."

"A what?" Jim exclaims.

"A pinky toe. At the time, we had no idea if it was a real lead. We've received all kinds of strange mail, and it could have been a prank, from a cadaver or something, somebody long gone, so we didn't say anything. But the DNA tests came back this morning. I'm sorry to have to say this, but the tests confirmed it was the left pinky toe of your daughter. It was Emily's toe."

Jim looks around the room, at Baumgardner staring at the floor, at Carrie, who somehow maintains her stoic expression. Finally, he goes back to Terry, the only one willing to recognize him. "How?" he asks.

Terry understands the question. How could this happen to Emily? How could someone cut off a little girl's toe? How could they put it in the mail? How could this be happening? Terry can only reply with facts. "This is not like before, with *The Spying Toes*. It was a clean cut, probably from a scalpel. The lab is also quite sure, from the way the blood coagulated, she was alive when the toe was severed."

"You mean she felt it? Emily was awake when her toe was cut off?"

"I don't know if she was awake or not, but she was alive. And, if she were awake, from what I've been told, a scalpel cut is so precise that the pain would have been minimal."

"What?"

"It wasn't an old, serrated knife that was used, like the previous abduction. This time a professional cutting instrument was used. I don't want you to assume it was done like in the movie. It wasn't that painful."

"You're trying to tell me that having your fucking toe cut off is not painful?"

Terry hardly believes it himself. "Of course it is. I'm just saying, it's not as bad as the movie."

"What the...! It's not that bad? Bullshit it's not!"

"I'm sorry."

Jim slumps into the open chair, pounds his fist against the arm, and then slides further down, covering his eyes with his hand. "What the fuck is going on?"

Terry looks helpless, feels helpless, and can only repeat, "I'm sorry."

"Jim," Carrie says into the silence. Everyone stares at her as she waits, savoring the thought before committing to it. "Jim," Carrie repeats, "she's alive."

"Yes," Jim says, "I know that. Of course she's alive."

"You didn't know that, Jim. You hoped. You believed. You tried to convince yourself you knew, tried to convince others that you knew, but you never really did. But now, now we do know."

"She's right," Terry says. "Statistically speaking, based on other abductions, if a stranger did it and they were gone this many days, the odds were not good. But she was kept alive. We don't know what his plans are, but he's definitely keeping Emily alive."

"Bleeding from her foot? In pain?" Jim asks.

"We don't know."

"Being tortured some other way."

"We don't know."

"You have to find her!"

Terry opens his mouth but says nothing, knowing the phrase "We're doing everything we can" emanates from his breath, his body, like a noxious odor.

"What about the other children?" Carrie asks.

"There was no mention of them."

Jim exhales, puts his head in his hands and squeezes, then relaxes. Terry doesn't want to bring up the other children, doesn't want to make the statement aloud, but knows they all understand the strange math, that it's better to receive your daughter's severed pinky toe in the mail then to receive nothing at all.

"Where did the package come from?" Carrie asks.

"That part is strange. The package came from a town called Lovely, Texas."

"Lovely?"

"Yes. I was also confused, but it's actually a service the town provides. People send items like love letters, valentine's cards, or wedding invitations, and for a fee, they postmark them with "Lovely" and send them back out.

There are towns throughout the country that do the same thing: Peace, Oregon; Valentine, Oklahoma; even a Loveland, Ohio."

"Why would someone do that?"

"To make a point. There was a letter with the package. I have two copies here." Terry unfolds two sheets of paper and hands them over, waiting as Jim and Carrie read the simple statement and contemplate what they are dealing with.

I am offering a lovely
An angel I yearn,
To make you aware
Of my return

"Angel," Carrie finally speaks up "That's from the book. That's what he called them. They were his angels."

"Yes."

"So there was an accomplice," Carrie states.

Terry surveys Carrie as she looks right back at him, but he can't read her at all. If she were hysterical, worried that some toe-loving child molester from thirty years ago had returned and kidnapped her daughter, if she were crying or shouting or anything that showed emotion, he would understand. But instead, she seems to hardly care, stating facts from *The Spying Toes* as if they were answers to a game of Trivial Pursuit. "Not necessarily," Terry says, "this isn't any sort of proof. 'Angel' was the term the author used, but it was part of a make-believe story told to support a make-believe theory. The reality is that there wasn't a single bit of physical evidence or testimonial that suggested another person was involved. Not one."

"Until now."

"Using the word 'angel' doesn't mean there was a second abductor; it just means he read the book. Look, there's definitely a connection. Either it's the accomplice from the original case, acting again after thirty years, or it's a copycat. We're pursuing both leads."

"Leads?" Jim asks, "Don't you mean guesses?"

"We're contacting everyone involved with the original case, as well as experts who have studied copycat cases. That's in addition to three criminal psychologists already working on the case, the FBI, every officer in Edgebrook, and hundreds of volunteers." Terry wonders how many times he has repeated the number of people and the amount of expertise involved. It is the only reassuring statement he can claim.

"Are there any leads? Do we know anything that the kidnapper wouldn't want us to know? Are there any clues that weren't mailed directly to the police station?"

"I can assure you," Terry says before he can stop himself, "we are doing everything we can."

"Who's the lead FBI agent helping you? I'm wondering if he's more qualified to handle this."

Baumgardner finally looks up and glances at Terry.

"Look," Jim continues, "my daughter has been missing for almost a week. And the only thing we know is that her goddamn toe has been cut off! I am not going to be polite nor am I going to give a damn about hurting anyone's feelings. I want the best possible chance of getting my daughter back alive and that's all I care about."

"And that's all you should care about. I'll have agent Samperson call you as soon as we're done and you can talk to him. Right now, we've split up our responsibilities by what we are best suited to handle. I'm managing the local aspects of the investigation, the searches in and around Edgebrook, while the FBI is analyzing the data and providing exhaustive technical support. They are also heading up the questioning of all convicted pedophiles in the area."

Jim nods, knowing this makes sense, but hoping something is being overlooked, something that can be corrected.

"The FBI has also made another suggestion. They are providing a therapist to come by, to help you cope with what's going on."

"No," Jim interrupts, "that won't be necessary."

"Jim, I can't possibly imagine…, but I'm sure…"

"No. Period. I don't want to talk to any therapist right now. I want to find my daughter."

"I understand. Carrie?"

Carrie calmly glances at Jim and then back to Terry. She nods. "No thank you, Detective."

"All right. But at least let me give you his card…" Terry pulls out a business card and sets it on the end table. "Just keep it around, in case you change your mind." He gets up and starts to leave, realizing he just made it through telling two parents someone had cut off their daughter's toe. It hadn't gone as expected, but his expectations had been wrong all week. He remembers that as of last Friday morning, he expected to be fishing this weekend. The Hughes expected their daughter to come home. And nobody, except perhaps one person, expected the Edgebrook police department to have a girl's pinky toe delivered from Lovely, Texas.

24

It's 5:30 in the morning and Antonio sits outside his boss's office. Up since 4:00, he has little else to do. The search parties don't meet until eight, and he understands what he's been told, that it would be counter-productive to go out on his own. He would just cover the same ground. Although over the past two weeks, with the number of volunteers growing with the news coverage, many sites have already been covered twice, if not more.

At first, there was the hope of finding new evidence, a swath of fabric or a shoe, anything that would allow the authorities to pin down where the abduction took place. The police would bring the canine units, allowing them to search each area and hope a scent or other marker would bring them closer to finding the children. The volunteers then came through, collecting a surprising amount of garbage, all of which went through forensic analysis. So far, none of it proved useful. There were thousands of acres to check, tens of thousands including the Alleghany Mountains, and they had nothing, not a single clue. The forest had swallowed their children whole and was now keeping its mouth shut.

Then *The Spying Toes* connection leaked. People believed there wouldn't be just a scrap of clothing or a child's shoeprint. The children themselves might actually be out there, buried alive. If that was true, it was more important to cover as much area as quickly as possible. Call out their names. Spread the volunteers wide, search for three children lying flat, not some miniscule scrap of evidence. The nights were cold and getting colder, so if they were going to find them alive, it would have to happen quickly.

Still, nothing.

"We've already been there," Antonio interrupted the day before, when his search party was instructed to meet at Belthoff Park the next morning.

"We need to look again, more carefully," was the response, and everyone nodded. No one came out and said it, but when they thought they might find the children, they searched with speed and little else. Now it was time to backtrack, to be more thorough, each volunteer just an arm's length from the next, treading slowly while beating back the bushes, searching for miniscule clues within the vast reaches of the forest.

The number of volunteers was dwindling. At one point, there were almost four hundred people divided into multiple parties, but now they were lucky to break one hundred. Antonio's brothers and uncle were with him. Jim Hughes was also in his search party. They gave each other a sullen acknowledgement, accepting that their separate groups had merged into one. Most of the others had left, gone back to work and to their own lives, looking for updates in the paper and wishing they could have done more before turning the page. They left because of work and life's obligations, which Antonio understood, or at least accepted, but he also knew there was another reason. People thought it was too late. They wanted to look for children, not bodies.

A reporter asked him about the search, catching up with him one early morning as the volunteers gathered before heading out. "Is there anything you would like to say?" she asked, a moment after agreeing with her cameraman that they should shoot from the opposite angle, to catch a glimpse of the rising sun.

He could only respond as he'd seen Natalya, as he'd heard the other parents respond. "I want my son back. Whoever has him, please let him come home. Please let me see my son again. That is all I want."

"And how is the search going?"

"We're still searching. We will continue searching. I will keep searching, even if I'm the only one out here. I'm going to keep looking for Alex. I'm going to find my boy."

The reporter nodded, holding back a smile, knowing this would make the evening news. "You're in everyone's prayers," she replied, allowing the cameraman to focus on Antonio, making sure they captured his determination.

And he will keep looking. If all the other volunteers leave, if the police give up and the other parents try and move on with their lives, he will keep looking. He is sure of that. How could he not? So here he is, 5:35 in the morning, sitting in a plastic chair outside Mr. Alvarez's office, waiting. The work floor is empty and all the lights are out except for one lone bulb outside the front door. The place seems foreign, like a snapshot taken long ago. How could he go back to working the lathe, sculpting decorative patterns into the table legs of high-end furniture sets? How could he listen to the easy listening station from the radio hanging on the peg board? How could he join his coworkers banter as if nothing has changed? He can't and he won't.

A car pulls into the parking lot and Antonio watches the headlights cut through the upper windows, the shadows sweep across the factory wall. The car engine dies, a door shuts, and footsteps make their way across the pavement. Every sound is audible this early in the morning.

"Jesus!" Mr. Alvarez shouts, surprised to see the silhouette of his missing lathe operator sitting outside his office, "You startled me."

"Good morning, Mr. Alvarez."

"Shit. I didn't think you'd be here this early."

"You said in the morning."

"Yeah but… that usually means eight or so."

"That's when we start searching. Eight."

"Right," Mr. Alvarez says uncomfortably. He searches through his keys and unlocks his office door. It is the only separate room besides the bathroom, and most of his office is just a large glass partition, blocking out noise but little else. "Come in," he says, turning on his office light, illuminating Antonio's slumped profile.

Mr. Alvarez's hands are sweating. He looks through the papers on his desk, searching for the name of a project to talk about, anything that will make for easy conversation, anything to delay what he has to do. Mr. Alvarez, tired and balding, uses his thick hands to pull up the sleeves on his worn blue sweater, readjusts his belt and sits down. Antonio sits across from him, looking directly in his eyes, and says nothing.

"How are you?"

"Getting by."

"And Natalya?"

"The same."

"Are there any leads?"

"Some. One. I'm not supposed to talk about it," Antonio says, reciting what Detective Kruthers told him, but also just preferring not to talk about severed toes.

"I understand."

The office's dim yellow light provides refuge from the gloom of the still-dark manufacturing floor. Mr. Alvarez inhales the thick air, keenly aware of the underwater silence that accompanies pre-dawn.

"You've been out for almost two weeks."

"Yes. I don't expect to be paid."

"It's not that. I mean, it is, somewhat, but that's not the point. We need someone working the lathe, someone with your skill. We were just catching up, and have now delayed shipments by another two weeks, and the backlog of unfinished goods is getting in the way of shipping. Normally everyone would be working overtime right now. The Christmas orders aren't that far off. But now…"

"Yes."

"You know we can't get by without moving product. You know how it works. Corporate gives us the business, makes sure we've got a steady supply going through the doors, and that's the way we stay in the black."

"I know."

Mr. Alvarez clasps his meaty hands together and squeezes them in frustration. He's not sure what he wants Antonio to say. Not an apology, just some sort of acknowledgement of the situation. He understands Antonio has much larger problems, but that does not mean he can ignore everything else. "I'm going to put this bluntly. I've talked to corporate, I've explained the situation, and they have explicitly told me, to keep my job, I have to make sure there's a skilled lather here next week. There's no way around it."

Antonio nods.

"And I've found someone. He can be here next week, and can do the job. Fifteen years' experience with good references. But here's the problem. It's not part-time work. He'd be coming from Georgia. He'd be moving here to work full-time." Antonio's expression does not falter the slightest. "Antonio," Mr. Alvarez says with raised eyebrows, "he'd be taking your job."

Antonio blinks, but nothing more.

"Shit," Mr. Alvarez mumbles, leaning back in his chair, "I know what position you're in. I know how much we're paying for your insurance. If it weren't for the union, we'd have let you go already, for that alone. But you're locked in, locked in with a good job, and I'm glad of that. But if you give corporate a reason to let you go, there's nothing I can do. And if that happens, you won't get a job with these benefits anywhere else. Not one that could cover your insurance. So then what? You'll get Cobra for a little while, unemployment. That'll end and you won't have a job, won't have a way to pay for Katya's medications. What are you going to do then? What's going to happen to your family? Antonio, are you listening to me?"

"Yes."

"Do you understand?"

"Yes."

"There's nothing I can do. If you're not here by the end of the week, if you don't come in Friday, then I have to call that other guy and offer him a job. He's ready to show up Monday morning. He's ready to sign a contract. This is not bullshit. I am not bullshitting you. I have no control. Either I let you go and hire your replacement, or they'll let me go and do the same. It's out of my hands."

"I understand."

"Are you going to come in?"

"I don't know."

"Antonio! You're jeopardizing your whole family, how you live, whether you'll get by. You're jeopardizing Katya's health. You're gambling with your children's lives."

"Mr. Alvarez, I want to find my son. It's that simple."

"No! No it's not! There are many people looking for Alex, people more qualified than you. The police, the FBI, the search parties. I've read about them all. Adding you to the mix hardly helps, and risks so much more."

"But it does help."

Mr. Alvarez sighs, unable to see a way around Antonio's obstinacy. "Look," he says, calming down, "continue going out with the search parties until Friday, but most importantly, talk to Natalya. Tell her the whole situation. Tell your kids, your family, and then decide, as a family. But I don't want you doing any pig-headed thing by yourself."

"No matter what you say, I don't see how looking for my son is wrong."

"It's not wrong! It's just... dammit! It's more complicated than that. Just promise me you'll talk to your family, explain the whole situation to them."

Antonio says nothing.

"Antonio, promise me you'll discuss this with Natalya."

"I will."

"Promise."

Antonio looks at his hands, clasps and unclasps them, and says, "I promise."

"Thank you."

Mr. Alvarez thinks of what to say next while Antonio watches. They sit in silence, until Mr. Alvarez finally says, "You can go now."

Antonio nods and rises, and Mr. Alvarez wonders if he'll see him again.

25

Terry's phone beeps as Baumgardner drives to the Collini house. Terry knows it's a text message from Steve, in response to the voicemail Terry just left him. This has become their usual mode of communication. Terry calls, Steve doesn't answer. Terry leaves a voicemail and Steve texts back a few minutes later. Text messages, Terry knows, are for communicating without having to talk. He looks at his phone and reads the message.

"Is it urgent?"

Terry wonders aloud in the cruiser, "What is wrong with this guy?"

"Who?" Baumgardner asks.

"No one," Terry replies, before continuing, "If the lead investigator in your daughter's disappearance leaves you a message, do you really have to ask if it's urgent?"

The other parents hang on his every word. Their lives are on hold and nothing matters except the return of their child, while this guy hasn't missed a day of work and seems to be inconvenienced by having to answer his phone now and then. Terry doesn't have the patience to play phone tag, but what is he supposed to do? Should he leave a message claiming the perpetrator has begun cutting off the childrens' toes? Should he follow up with a "Take care," or "Have a nice day?" He dials Steve's cell phone again, and after listening to the polite greeting, irritably says, "Hello Steve, this is Detective Kruthers again. I understand you are very busy at work, but I would appreciate it if you would answer my calls. I am admittedly unfamiliar with this text messaging thing, and I really can't fit important information into a quick message. We have received a small but disturbing package that directly relates to the case and I would like to discuss the contents with you. Please call me as soon as possible."

Terry watches the leafless trees go by as they drive toward the Collini house. He likes the Collinis. They are good people. He knows Natalya will thank them for coming, even though it was Terry's request. She'll offer them something to drink. She'll ask how the other parents are doing. Antonio will thank them for everything they've done so far. They will act as parents should act. Terribly worried, terribly concerned about their child. Antonio will pace. Natalya might cry. Antonio will sit back down and comfort her. The Collinis are good people, plain and simple.

As they head up the country road to the Collini house, Terry watches the sparse passing of houses, most of them in poor condition, some abandoned, overgrown, and wasting away. Terry has handled too many domestic disturbances in these houses, brought too many mischievous kids home to these houses, to not look disparagingly on them, especially when compared to the perfect suburban homes of the Hughes and Cardells. He regrets his prejudices, putting the Collinis into this mold the first time he pulled into their front drive.

His phone rings and Terry sees "FBI OFC" flash on the caller ID. "Kruthers here."

"Terry, Agent Samperson."

"Glad you called. I just left the Hughes' house."

"How'd it go?"

"It's done. But they're starting to doubt me. I don't blame them. I said you would give them a call."

Samperson pauses. "We've got something else I'd like to discuss."

"What?"

"We've been contacting everyone concerned with *The Spying Toes* case. The author Art Morrell is driving in as we speak and should be here this afternoon. The lead detective passed away a few years ago, although we're talking to one of his deputies. We're even calling the kids in the old case. Susan Waldorf, whose last name is Shoemaker now, lives in Oregon. She's the one who lost her toe. Elizabeth Pierce also lives on the west coast, in Santa Barbara. And the boy, Andy Frempt...," Samperson pauses.

"Yes?"

"He still lives in Edgebrook."

"Okay."

"He's a mailman."

"Yes."

"And the Cardells and Hughes are on his route."

26

"Can you stay here while I go for a walk?" Carrie asks, realizing she has not set foot outside once since Emily went missing.

"Sure." Jim answers, not looking up from his desk.

She asks him so little nowadays, she already feels uncomfortable with this little exchange.

Carrie places her cell phone into her parka and pulls on a knit hat and mittens. It isn't cold enough to warrant this, but she likes being covered. It's not quite the comfort of her bed, but it helps her feel more secure as she heads into the open expanse of daylight.

At the end of the block, the man who lives in the tan brick house with black shutters, Bob or Rob she thinks, is home early for a Friday, raking the leaves in his front yard. He takes a peek in Carrie's direction from behind his hooded sweatshirt, and seeing her, rakes faster, pretending he does not see her. As she walks by, he takes another peek and inadvertently makes eye contact. He freezes in discomfort, purses his lips and nods before turning away. Carrie wonders if he looks so awkward because he doesn't know what to say to a woman in her situation, or if he feels guilty that he is raking his front yard rather than aiding in the search for her daughter.

Don't worry, she thinks, we just got her toe back, so that's a start.

This is how it's going to end. There won't be a single call or knock on the door with someone saying they found Emily, unwilling to look Carrie in the eye. The news will come piecemeal, as slow and torturous as possible. Carrie shudders.

They will have a funeral. Or a memorial service, depending on the situation, and the simple quiet of each day will wail inside their house, echoing inside their walls without abatement. Jim will leave. He won't put up with having a ghost of a wife, and she won't blame him. He'll just send money every month, enough for her to rent a small apartment and buy groceries. She won't ask for more and won't need more, just enough to hold on for a while, enough to make it look like she tried.

She never thought about suicide, never thought of it as an option since she didn't have real problems, but now people will understand. They will say, that poor thing, having her daughter sent to her in pieces, her split with Jim, it was just too tough, too much for her to handle. People won't ask why she threw her life away. Her life was already disappearing, seeping out her pores and evaporating, leaving nothing more than a walking body, a placeholder. And whatever still exists of her will be ripped out by Emily's abduction. That poor thing, they will all say, and she will at least have sympathy.

She crosses the street and finds it peculiar that she still looks both ways, still waits for a car to pass, surviving out of habit rather than will. Carrie walks down Black Partridge Street to Tate Park, past the tennis courts and the playground equipment to the line of trees that steal foul-tipped balls from the baseball diamond. A small opening exposes a path, and Carrie enters. The undergrowth separates enough for her to pass, but an occasional bush or sapling reaches out and brushes against her ankles. The tree limbs stretch overhead into a web of branches, while the forest floor is thick with red and brown leaves. Carrie usually does not walk this far, but finds moving forward simpler than finding a reason to turn around.

She occasionally stops and listens to the silence, hearing only the sound of a squirrel in the distance, scampering across crusty leaves. An overhead bird might flap its wings, gliding to another branch, keeping watch on the sad figure below.

Carrie cannot get *The Spying Toes* out of her mind. It seems so fitting as a story from the past, the way things used to be. Children were kidnapped then, just as they are now, but those children escaped. They found their way home. The police killed the evil kidnapper. The town celebrated and they lived happily ever after.

Life is so different now. Stories don't have happy endings. They drag on, lurching toward the dismal end, everyone shaking their heads and wondering what kind of a world they live in.

Emily, her poor Emily, is in the eye of the tornado. Everything whirls around her, and Carrie wonders how much she knows. She wonders if the winds are quiet in the center, if there is just a flutter, a lack of pressure, a stilling fear. She knows Emily is not all right, but prays her experience is not too horrific.

The path opens into a large clearing, an open field surrounded by trees, and Carrie starts across it, assuming the path will pick up again on the other side. The fallen leaves cover the field in a thick blanket, blown in from the surrounding woods, and Carrie's feet swoosh and crunch as she walks. She looks up at the sky, framed within the surrounding treetops, and her heart beats faster as she approaches the halfway point. The air hangs with a piercing stillness as a thought creeps into her mind.

Whether her daughter's kidnapper is a copycat criminal or an accomplice from thirty years ago, he is recreating the original crime. Abduct two girls and a boy. Worship the girls' toes. Cut one off. And if that is the case, in order to truly recreate the crime, the perpetrator would trap the children in cages beneath a layer of leaves. *In these very woods.* Hundreds of volunteers have searched these woods, but the forest is enormous. The searchers could have missed them, especially if the cages were well hidden. That means, right now, Emily could be buried beneath these leaves, bleeding to death or already dead. Emily's body might only be a few feet away, and Carrie's next footfall might uncover her lost daughter.

Carrie halts, her leg frozen in midair, and wonders where she can put it down. Where can she go without stumbling across the dull gray of children's corpses? How could she have wandered into this? Her daughter is trapped in the grime and dirt, perhaps with an opening just large enough to see a glimmer of sky, bleeding from a severed toe, crying for her mother. Or perhaps she has already made her last cry. Perhaps this open clearing is not a prison but a cemetery. Carrie puts her foot behind her, turns back towards the way she came and finds that blowing leaves have covered her path. It is impossible to retrace her footsteps, to cover the safe ground she has just walked. She bends over, her lips quivering as her hands shake, and feels the ground with her fingertips. Anchored by its touch, she crumples to the forest floor, lies down within the same leaves that conceal her daughter, and looks up to the sky.

God, please let Emily be alive. Please let her be all right. Please don't let her be trapped here. Please don't let her be tortured. I'm sorry. I'm so sorry for letting go of my family. I'm sorry for doing nothing, for falling into the shadows, for letting my family slip away. Please, please, bring my daughter back. Please God, please.

Time crumbles beneath Carrie's thoughts as she lies in wait, pleading to the heavens. She wonders if her daughter sees the same sky, if the faded gray of autumn is their only connection?

Finally, she pulls herself upright. She studies the line of trees surrounding her in the distance, the leaves piled all around. She looks toward the break in the trees she came from and knows she can't make it. The thought of running across Emily, a trapped Emily who can't speak or move, an Emily who was abandoned by her mother and left to die in the woods, is too much for her to handle. She removes her cell phone from her jacket pocket and stares at it. This is her connection to the outside world, but she has no one to call.

She does not speak to Jim, at least not if she really needs anything. There are no friends she confides in anymore. She scrolls through the recent calls and finds the number that last called her, someone who called to help. Carrie dials. When the call is answered, Carrie listens to the voice and hangs up. What is she supposed to say? She looks around, weighing the fear of calling a stranger against the fear of her predicament, and dials again. "Reagan?"

"Yes."

"I need help."

"What's going on?"

"They found her toe. They found Emily's toe."

Reagan gasps. "They what? How? Where?"

"It was sent to the police department. Emily's kidnapper cut it off and sent it to the police station."

"Oh no. You poor thing. I'm so sorry."

"He's trying to taunt us or something."

"Taunt you? Why?"

"I don't know." The wind blows, rippling through Carrie's phone.

"Where are you?"

Carrie wonders if she should tell her. Lying in a field of leaves, too petrified to stand, petrified with the fear of uncovering her daughter. "Out, on a walk."

"Oh."

"I... I needed to talk to someone."

"That's okay. You can talk to me."

"Did I ever tell you," Carrie asks, aware that she has told Reagan nothing, "that we had grown apart? Emily and I?"

"That's normal. I used to fight with my mom all the time."

"No, we don't fight. Fighting means you care about something. We don't fight, we don't talk. We don't do anything."

"Does she avoid you? That's pretty common too."

"No, it's my fault. I don't talk to her, I don't talk to Jim, I don't talk to anyone. I mean, I met you less than a week ago and you're the first person I'm calling right now, the only one I can turn to."

"I thought that was a little strange."

Carrie pauses.

"I'm just kidding, Carrie. I'm glad you called, that you felt I could help."

For a moment, Carrie does not feel so alone, and stands up, careful to avoid touching any new ground. "Emily is just the sweetest girl. She'd probably open up to me in a second, like she does with Jim, but I never ask her to. I never even try."

"Why?"

"There's something wrong with me. I mean I don't talk to my own daughter. Not even small stuff, like how her day was, what she wants for dinner. I let her lead her own life and I stay out of it."

"That's not normal."

"It's so not normal. Something's wrong with me. I feel so embarrassed by what I've become. I'm so afraid that they'll notice me and notice what's wrong, so I just sit there and watch, like we're not even in the same room."

"What are you embarrassed about?"

"I'm embarrassed by what a wreck I am. I'm scared half the time, alone all the time. I lay in bed all day and I never sleep. Some days it takes all my effort to not break down and cry; other days I can't manage that."

"How long has this been going on?"

"Too long. Years. I don't know what's wrong."

"Do you cry without reason?"

"Yes."

"Are you always tired?"

"Yes."

"Do you feel afraid and alone?"

"Constantly."

"Girlfriend, you're depressed."

"About the way I've been acting."

Reagan gives a matter-of-fact sigh, almost a laugh. "Not emotionally depressed. You're chemically depressed. It's no big deal. I mean, it's a big deal you've been suffering through it and all, but it's not a big deal. You just need to see a psychiatrist. Try some medications or something. You'll be fine."

"I'm not crazy."

"Where did you grow up?" Reagan asks. "Pick up a *Cosmo*. Depression doesn't mean you're crazy. Nowadays, it means you're pretty much normal. But you have to do something about it and get some help."

"I don't want to be drugged up."

"Honey, you've probably got a chemical imbalance, which means you're already off. You just need a little help to get you feeling closer to normal. So it's like you're already drugged up, and this will help fix you."

Chemical imbalance. Off balance. That is a good way to describe it. Like over time, not a specific day or moment, she'd been slowly losing her balance. And once it was gone, there was nothing to hold onto, nothing to pull herself upright.

"I mean," Reagan continues, "I take a little something myself, although my psychologist doesn't think there's a strong chemical imbalance or anything, just that, well, I care about things too much. That's my problem. I care too much."

Carrie says nothing, lost in her own realization.

"But what the fuck do I care, as long as I feel better."

Carrie takes a step, a small step, towards the break in the forest, concentrating on the voice casually talking on the other end. "How does this happen?"

"I have no clue, but it's common. At least according to the magazines. And it's in the movies a lot too. Either way, no big deal. You've just got an old-fashioned way of thinking about this, like you're going to end up in a padded room giving yourself a permanent hug. But it's not like that at all."

"I know, I just thought…"

"You were better than that? It's all right. I have girlfriends that feel the same way. But I'll help you out. I'll help you get through this."

Carrie keeps her thoughts on the conversation, taking step after step, wondering if Reagan is right, if things are that simple and she somehow missed it. She approaches the end of the clearing, at the break in the tree line where the path begins. She bounds onto it, scurrying the last few steps as if the leaves might reach up and pull her back. Inside the forest, the leaves scatter loosely to the sides and expose a well-trodden trail that she can walk with confidence. "Thank you," Carrie says, "You've already helped."

"That's what I do. I help because I care so much."

Carrie holds the phone and listens, letting Reagan talk about herself while Carrie follows the trail back to Tate Park. She finds Reagan's voice distracting, taking her away to a different place, a different view of the world where everything lies out in the open, where problems don't hide and solutions are simple. She listens the whole way back and emerges onto the park's expanse, where she can see the passing road, the town homes across the street, and a man playing catch with his dog. She feels safe, or at least safer. She has a direction, something to latch onto.

Reagan has somehow steered the conversation elsewhere, talking about one of her girlfriends and her "asshole" boyfriend. Carrie barely listens to the details and just clings to the friendly voice. "You know," she interrupts, wanting to say something, letting a pause change the subject. "I often fall asleep in the family room. I won't make it to bed until it's almost morning. But when I'm lying there in that dream state, and when it's time for Emily to go to bed, she'll always come in and give me a kiss. I'll open my eyes just enough to catch a glimpse of her in her pajamas, and she always says good night. Sometimes she'll rub my hand, or move the hair from my face, but she always kisses me good night. Always."

Reagan does not respond. She can talk for hours about medications, about how one should feel and what pill they need to get that way, but she cannot talk about a child's caress. She doesn't know anything about a daughter's kiss good night.

A resolution comes quick and strong to Carrie, and she utters it with force. "I want my daughter back."

"I know you do, sweetie. I know you do."

Carrie walks the last block home with her cell phone in her pocket and her head held higher than when she left. Once inside, she takes off her shoes, hangs up her jacket, and goes to the family room, where the therapist's business card is still on the end table. She pulls out her cell phone and dials.

27

The two-story house is painted a dark chocolate with white planks surrounding the frame. It is old and run down, but a large number of planters and flower boxes with autumn flowers cover up the aging structure. Terry first interviewed Andy Frempt at the station, but this time he wants to do it on Andy's turf. He wants to keep the interview as casual as possible and has come alone, not wanting anyone dressed in full uniform. This visit is just for talking.

There is also the concern that Terry won't say out loud. As of right now, too many things revolve around Andy. There are the initial similarities between the new abductions and Andy's. Same number of children, same genders, roughly the same ages. Same town. Of the original three children, Andy is the only one to remain in Edgebrook. He's the only one still around who knows key details from the previous case. As a postman, he'd have a better understanding of the mail's inner workings, how credit cards could be sent to Max Janikowski's dog, how packages could be postmarked through towns like Lovely, Texas. Most suspicious of all, he's the postman for both Emily and Arielle. He knows them and their families.

The flip-side is that when Terry first interviewed Andy, he seemed about the least likely person to abduct three children. He was kind and open, easy going. He wanted to help as much as he could, although at the time it didn't seem like he could be of much help. In Terry's experience, guilty people don't offer to help, at least not genuine offers, and everything about Andy seemed genuine.

And why in the hell would Andy abduct three children? Terry can't understand why anyone would but it's now happened twice. The first time was, Terry honestly felt, a toe-obsessed freak that he would never understand. What's the motive this time?

Terry rings the doorbell once, does not hear anything, and rings again, putting his ear next to the window beside the door. Footsteps emerge from inside and a man opens the door, wearing a black apron onto which he is busy wiping his hands. "Detective Kruthers, sorry about that. Just putting dinner together. Come on in."

At least this time Terry is prepared. Of course he read the book, *The Spying Toes*. He studied the flip of black-and-white photos in the middle. A picture of young Andy before the abduction posing with a baseball bat over his shoulder. The missing posters were copied. Finally there were pictures afterward, Andy in the front car of the Edgebrook parade, with bright eyes and a crooked smile, waving to the cheering crowds.

Terry also received from the FBI a DVD of the made-for-TV movie. Andy Frempt was played by a young actor with tousled blonde hair. He had freckles, a cowlick, and a small-town naivety that made Terry think of Opie Taylor. Knowing it was coming, Terry still jumped at the scene when young Andy romped happily through the woods and was suddenly tackled and violently abducted. Later, Terry's heart wrenched as the kidnapper threatened Andy, sticking his knife into the chest of the dirty, emaciated boy. But all of his struggles were forgotten by the end, when the child-actor Andy rode down Main Street in a celebratory parade, his smiling face framed in a halo of sunlight.

These are Terry's visions of Andy Frempt, the child actor and the snippet of book photos. But once again, here stands a man recently turned forty. His blonde hair has darkened and thinned out, receding at the top. He is stocky; his potbelly pushes against the black apron. Thick arms protrude from an old blue polo. As he turns up the stairs, Terry follows and looks at his shirt, partially tucked into wrinkled khakis which hang over old, worn-out sneakers. The boy-hero of Edgebrook has grown up, become a man, and suffers all the marks of aging. There is nothing wrong with this. Andy doesn't look much different than the average forty-year-old, but the average forty-year-old doesn't look like the child hero of Edgebrook.

"I guess I shouldn't be happy to see you."

"How so?" Terry asks.

"Well, it's just that I assumed I'd be a dead end by now. That you'd have other leads."

"I can't really go into the leads we have."

"I know. Of course. I'm just saying that I doubt I have anything useful that hasn't been said before. I'm probably not much help."

"You never know."

"That's true. Here, have a seat."

Terry sits in a chair beside the coffee table, thinking about the questions he wants to ask, but Andy jumps in first. "Originally, when the papers tried to connect the abduction to what happened to me, I thought it was a stretch. I thought they were trying to sell papers. I refused all interviews because I didn't want to take any attention from those missing children. But it seems to keep coming back."

"How so?"

"Well, if you're here to interview me, you think there's some sort of connection. Or…"

"Or what?"

"Or you don't know anything and are still…" Andy says, putting finger quotes in the air, "… investigating all possibilities?"

Terry's signature phrase has become a cliché. "Well, we either know something or we don't," Terry answers, "I can't say much more than that."

Andy smiles. "Of course."

Similar to the previous interview, Andy is an open book, willing to talk before any questions are asked.

"You know," Andy says, "I'm just not happy that this is similar in any way to what happened to me."

"Why is that?"

"I was called a hero for escaping and finding help, but let's be honest, it wasn't any great feat. The guy left a knife with me. He left a knife where I could reach it and then disappeared for the night. Not exactly an evil genius, and I wasn't exactly James Bond. Our escape had more to do with his incompetence than any miraculous feats on my part."

"You're selling yourself short."

"Doesn't matter. He left a knife with us, and that had as much to do with my escape as anything. That was a one-in-a-million type thing, and if he hadn't done that, who knows?"

"You still might have been found."

"Yes, but in what condition? I don't like to dwell on it; it's in the past. But the point is, what are the odds of something like that happening again? These children have already been gone longer than we were. If they're going through something similar, what are the odds of a one-in-a-million thing happening again? That's the part I don't like to think about."

"This isn't a casino. You don't play the odds."

"Of course, Detective, you don't play them, not by choice. But it's still hard not to ask yourself, at least subconsciously, what are the odds?"

Terry doesn't acknowledge it, but finds himself asking that question all the time. The odds of the children returning unharmed is zero, since they already know one of the girl's toes has been severed. Who knows what else has happened?

"Plus…" Andy says.

"Plus what?"

Andy looks around the room, as if he hasn't looked at it in a long time, debating if he should finish what he was about to say. "Plus… I need to check on my dinner."

Andy disappears into the kitchen while Terry looks around. The carpet is mahogany-colored shag, old and stained. A chess set with oversized marble pieces sits on a glass coffee table, curved legs of gold propping up the corners. The couches are a worn cloth, a brown stitch with an underlying orange. Terry looks at the wall and notes family pictures, a much younger Andy, closer to the boy Terry pictures in his head, standing next to a proud mother and father in various settings. Most are black and white.

"Yeah," Andy exclaims, walking back in from the kitchen, "I've been meaning to change those pictures, ever since the house became mine. But after four years I guess I don't have much of an excuse. I haven't really turned this place into the bachelor pad it should be."

"How long have you been living here?"

"My whole life. I still say it's my parent's house although it's officially mine. Mom passed away seven years ago; dad four."

"I'm sorry."

"Thank you. But I doubt that's what you're here to discuss."

"No, I guess not. You were about to say something, before going into the kitchen?"

Andy half-smiles and nods. "Yes. It's kind of strange, and I don't like admitting it, but there's another reason why I don't like this current situation being connected with what happened to me."

"Why's that?"

"To be perfectly honest, I don't look on my abduction as a bad thing. Yes, we were imprisoned and tortured, scared and alone, but I've forgotten most of it. It's a distant memory at least, and sometimes feels more like a story told to me than something that actually happened. More importantly, it had a happy ending. We survived. We thrived. And so it's not a bad memory. But if something happens to these kids, and it's in anyway related to what happened to me, that's going to taint our ordeal."

"I see."

"That sounds horrible," Andy quickly adds. "Those missing children are all that matters, I don't have to say that. It's just…. It's just something I feel. Never mind."

"No, I get it."

"Thanks. Now about your questions?"

"Let me start with a question I have to ask. Where were you last Friday night?"

Andy freezes for a moment, slouching on the opposite couch. "Whoa," he utters, realizing the implication and then pulling himself together. "Sorry." He grabs a chess piece, the rook, and studies it in his hands. "I understand. I just hadn't thought of that. You know."

"Mmm-hmm."

"Let's see. I mean, I know where I was. At home. Watching TV. Read a little. That's about it. Like I said, my life in bachelorhood hasn't been too exciting."

"Is there anyone you talked to, anyone that can verify your whereabouts?"

"That's what I'm trying to remember. I don't think so. Nothing I can recall. Is there a reason that, I mean, I know the reason, but do you really think I could be involved?"

Terry watches Andy and feels bad for doing this. He sees the strained concern of a man without an alibi. "I have to ask everyone. Standard procedure."

"You didn't ask last time."

"Last time we didn't realize how connected you were to the case. Besides your history, you're the mailman for two of the missing children's families."

"True. Not that I know either of them. They're seldom around when I make my rounds."

"It's still something, and like I said, I have to ask. I have to ask everyone involved with the original case."

"Why?"

"I can't go into detail, but we do believe this new case is associated with your case. Whether it's a real connection or some sort of copycat, I don't know, but we're re-interviewing everyone, and we're re-checking all alibis."

"I see."

"Let's talk more about the original case, specifically Art Morrell's theory of another abductor."

"Yes."

"What's your impression on that?"

Andy looks at him earnestly. He scratches his arms and sits back. "You have all the transcripts, from the interviews after it happened. Right?"

"Yes, and we're going over them."

"Okay. I'll answer any questions you have. I'll tell you everything I remember, but you have to keep in mind that whatever I say now has been tainted by thirty years. After those original interviews with the police, after the first round of hoopla, there was the book and then the movie. I sometimes think that I've told and retold that experience so many times, dwelling on the same points, that I remember the book and movie more than what actually happened. My quotes in the book, which were a good while after it happened, feel more real than my original interview."

"Really?"

"I was a kid. I was impressionable. I'm sure my interview was a frightened ramble. But in the movie..." Andy says, "..remember when I escaped, er, when the actor escaped? He said something along the lines of, 'Follow me and I'll take you to him. We have to hurry. There's no telling what that monster will do!'"

Terry listens and remembers this line in the movie, a thin boy with dirt smeared on his face, summoning the courage to save his friends, ordering the two police officers into the forest before they could call for back-up.

"I never said anything like that," Andy continues. "I never showed the police where I escaped. I didn't even know. Alice, the woman who picked me up, told the police where she found me and they worked their way back from there. And I believe they did wait for back-up, but that wasn't dramatic enough."

"Well do your best. I'm just trying to understand if there might have been a second abductor, even a slight possibility."

"The first thing," Andy starts, "was how we were kidnapped. It was fast. Sue, Beth, and I were out in the woods, just exploring paths. I was tackled out of nowhere, by someone much larger than me, naturally. It was rough and quick. I remember a hood being pulled over my head, my hands were tied, and then I was left alone, bound up and blind for a while. I remember hearing screams, from Sue I think. But the same thing happened to both girls. Tackled, blinded and bound, each one of us. Whether it was one at a time, or two people working together, I have no idea."

"But you didn't see anyone else?"

"I was the first one tackled, so I didn't see anything. I'm not sure if the girls ran or what, but they were blindsided too. At least that's what they've said."

"So you couldn't say one way or the other?"

"No. I mean, I only saw and heard one person, so my inclination is that he worked alone. I never thought about a second abductor until that book came out. But that other big thing was definitely true, even if that doesn't offer any real proof."

"What big thing?"

"He wasn't a pedophile. I mean, he didn't do anything to me, at least sexually. The girls say the same thing. Their feet were fondled, and I'm sure their feet were, um…"

"What."

"I'm sure their feet were… sexualized…, but he didn't do anything to the rest of our bodies. He never touched us in a sexual way."

"You're positive?"

"I'm positive he didn't do anything to me. I could only hear what happened to the girls, so I can't say I know for certain. But we've talked many times about it and I've never had the feeling that they've held back."

"Okay."

"And also," Andy starts, then stops.

"Also what?"

"It's just that he talked to me, about their feet. I think he wanted someone to talk to, and so he got down and talked to me. He told me how perfect they were. He told me he loved them. He opened up to me, and I just think if he were doing other things, he would have told me that, too."

"And no one else ever came by when you were trapped?"

"Not that I was aware of, but I couldn't see much of anything."

Terry is certain this is a copycat case, that the only links to the past would be what could be found in the book and the movie. Whoever is doing this might not have even been alive when the original case took place. Andy Frempt is a dead end. Terry asks more questions about the kidnapping, while Andy often scratches his head or fumbles with the chess pieces as he tries to remember details from so long ago. But as Andy predicted, there is no new information to share.

"What about the two girls, Sue and Beth?" Terry asks. "Do you keep in touch?"

"Actually yes, quite a bit. And they'll have better alibis than me," Andy says with a smile. "Elizabeth lives in Long Beach, California. Owns a clothing boutique there. And Sue is married to a programmer in Oregon. She has two daughters and coaches their volleyball teams."

"Do you talk often?"

"Probably once a month with Sue. A few times a year with Elizabeth. Might I say they're both doing wonderful."

"Good."

"I mean, they're both about the nicest people you'll ever meet. Wonderful families. Loving, kind."

"I'm glad. I imagine sharing such a traumatic experience has created quite a bond."

"Yes, it has. And they don't shy away from it, pretend it never happened. We try to get together once a year. 'The Survivor's Club' is what we sometimes call it, jokingly. But yes, there's definitely a bond. I'm the godfather to both of Sue's girls."

"Have you talked since this recent abduction?"

"Many times. It's mainly just me filling them in on what's going on in town, what people are saying. They're both deeply concerned. Both of them considered flying back, but we thought it would be more of a distraction than anything."

"That's probably true."

"Detective?"

"Yes."

"I was wondering. How are the families doing? The families of the children?"

"It's difficult for them. Very difficult."

"I'm sure."

"They're probably doing the best they can though, under the

circumstances."

"I see. Well, I was kind of wondering, actually I think it was Sue's idea, but I was wondering if I could do anything to, you know, help out. I mean, maybe just talk to them about it, since my family went through a similar... experience."

"Mmmm. Thank you for the offer. We've got professional counselors, so it's probably not necessary, but... let me bring it up. Thank you."

"It would mean a lot though, to me, to try and help in some way."

"I'll see, but again, that probably won't be necessary."

"I understand, but the offer's always there."

"Thank you. That's very kind."

"Just a minute," Andy says, jumping up and running back to the kitchen. He bangs about for a bit and yells back, "It's all right. Nothing's burned. You want to stay for dinner? Pork chops and green beans, I have plenty."

"No thank you," Terry says, finding this to be going nowhere. "I really should get going. Thank you for your time."

"Whatever I can do," Andy says, returning from the kitchen. "Good luck catching that guy. Good luck finding them. Good luck with everything. My thoughts and prayers are with them."

"All right. Keep thinking positive." Terry stands and shakes Andy's hand.

They say goodbye and Terry gets into his car, validated that Andy doesn't have any useful information. If anything, he just helped reconfirm Terry's suspicions that there was only one abductor and this is a copycat case. He checks his cell and there are two messages from Agent Samperson. Terry dials the number and pulls out of Andy's driveway.

"We've got something," Samperson tells him.

"What?"

"We're still confirming, but it's a detail we glossed over. A detail from the toe you received."

"A print?" Terry asks, doubting if the velvet jewelry box would even hold a viable print.

"No. The actual toe, the way it was painted. Remember the black line?"

Terry could picture the toe any time he wanted. More often, he saw it when he didn't want to, imagining what it must feel like to have it... removed. No larger than a button, the nail was polished in a sultry red, a provocative siren for whomever desired such a thing. "A black line?"

"Yes, surrounding the nail."

As Samperson describes it, Terry recalls the black band around the nail, a thin dark outline carefully drawn to separate the nail from the dried, pink skin. "I remember."

"Eyeliner was used to make that line," Samperson continues, "to outline the nail."

"Okay."

"At first we glanced over it. Running DNA tests, fingerprinting the attached note, all the usual stuff was our first priority. But we compared it to the first case."

"Compared it to what?"

"There's a picture in the original file, of Sue. A picture was taken after they sewed up her wound, just for documentation. In that picture, the other toes are still painted, in a similar red. And they all have that same black line, carefully drawn, separating the nail from the skin."

"Is it identical?"

"Yes."

"Who knew?"

"That's what we're confirming. So far it's not in the book. It's not in the movie. We've been going over the testimony, pulling up every article written about that case, and nowhere is there anything documented about a black outline."

"There's got to be something."

"It was such a small detail, nobody mentioned it. I'd be surprised if the two girls even knew. They never saw their feet until after they were rescued. And after such a traumatic experience, it was probably irrelevant, like what color socks they were wearing. Nobody cared."

"So you're saying nobody knew about the black line?"

"We have to tread carefully, Terry. I'm saying it doesn't appear to have ever been recorded. Besides this one picture of Susan's foot, a picture sealed away thirty years ago and stored in the archives, it doesn't appear to have ever been mentioned. So if this is a copycat crime, if the perpetrator just read the book, watched the movie, maybe researched some of the old newspaper articles, he would not know that detail. There would never have been a black line on the toe you received."

"Shit." Terry pulls over, grasping at the many thoughts running through his mind. "So whoever did this had to be there during the original abduction?"

"That's what it looks like."

"So Art Morrell was right?"

"Probably."

Terry slams his hand against the steering wheel. Once again, every suspicion and every instinct Terry has about this case has been wrong. Shit.

28

Antonio bends over and kisses Natalya's forehead. Her eyes open as she mumbles something, then sees his jeans and tan work shirt and asks, "You're going to work?"

"I have to," he answers. "They're so far behind. Mr. Alvarez said I have to…."

"But …" Natalya starts, sitting up with widening eyes as she studies his face. She says nothing and eventually falls back to her pillow and closes her eyes, "…yes."

Antonio knows what that look means. It does not accuse; it simply acknowledges the inevitable. He will go back to work. His brothers will check out of their hotel and drive back to New Jersey later this week, going back to their jobs. The kids will spend fewer nights at friends' homes, eventually quitting altogether. Mama will leave. They both knew this would happen. Even if he did not go back to work, other things would force his hand. A leaky transmission on the station wagon, a child's flu, or even a run to the grocery store. Things would come up that had to be dealt with, and they would handle them. This is the beginning of the gentle nudge into new daily routines, the day after day that constitutes life, a life that will progress without Alex. Antonio guesses Natalya has expected it, deep down at some level that can't put up a fight, and as long as the steps toward this new life are small, an unperceivable upward grade, they will never be able to look back and say how it happened.

Antonio kisses Katya in her bed, baby Vincenzo in his crib. Gemma and Gregor are staying with friends, a temporary relief. They still come home, still eat dinner together, but family friends pick them up afterward, have them spend the night, make sure they do their homework and get to school. When they eventually do come home, for good, Gregor will have the hardest time. He roomed with Alex, sleeping on the top bunk. Antonio

119

passes their room and is unable to look in.

Mama, who sleeps on the couch, is already up brewing coffee. It is only 5:30, and Antonio acknowledges her nod that, if things were right in the world, neither would be up at this hour.

She looks at his buttoned work shirt, his name patch improperly displaying Anthony. "Where are you looking today?" she asks, pouring a cup from the still brewing coffee and handing it to him.

"I'm not."

"You're not?" she asks, forcing surprise into her words.

"I have to work today."

"Hmmm." She turns her back to him, picks up a sponge and makes circular swipes at the spotless counter.

"I have to, Mama," Antonio says, and then whispers, "I'll lose my job."

"Mmmm-hmmm," she mutters, not listening, "I can't imagine who would fire someone for looking for his son."

"Mama…" Antonio starts, knowing it is useless.

Then, as if changing the subject toward inconsequential pleasantries, she says, "It might freeze tonight."

But Antonio understands exactly what that means. If Alex is imprisoned outside like those other children were, then he won't last the night. *Alex will freeze to death and you're going to work.*

He checks the fridge for his lunch, but Natalya isn't up, hasn't made it yet. He pours some coffee into a thermos and grabs his wool jacket from the front closet. On impulse, he bends over, pulls out a large cardboard box from the back of the closet and rummages through it for his thick gloves and winter hat. Antonio also finds Alex's GI Joe gloves and red hat and pulls them out, stuffing them into his jacket pockets. He kisses his mama goodbye, who barely acknowledges him as she scrubs the counter.

The morning is dark and cold, and he stops at the gas station. Antonio doesn't bother putting on his gloves, rubbing his hands together while he waits for the tank to fill. He looks at the front page displayed in a newspaper kiosk and sees the headline announcing "BRRRRRRRR!!!!!"

Antonio drives to work, pulls into the empty parking lot, and sits, staring at the brick complex. A small fluorescent light shines dimly above the entranceway. Antonio gets out of the car and feels the low-pressure winds against his cheeks. He pulls Alex's hat out of his jacket pocket and puts his hand in it, curling his fingers into a fist, forming the safety of a miniature fetal position. It provides immediate relief as his hand warms and the joints ease into fluid motion. Antonio curses himself, curses God, pulls out his Italian horn and kisses it, and then gets back into the car. The engine turns as he pulls onto County Road 47, which leads to 33, where his search party will meet at sunrise.

29

Jim steps out of his car and senses, once again, that something is wrong. When his daughter disappeared, Reagan called him repeatedly each day. Dealing with her ramblings became the last thing he wanted to do, and so he ignored her calls completely until they eventually dried up.

After a while, he actually found himself missing her. He missed her cut-and-dry way of looking at things. He missed the way she said everything would turn out all right, even when she did not really believe it, even when she herself would be the one to sabotage the situation. He missed having someone envious of him, having someone whose entire dream was to be with him. He hates to acknowledge it, but he misses Reagan because he misses being needed.

That was why, when his phone rang with Reagan's name on the ID, he answered. She talked quickly, inviting him over with little reason, insisting he come, persisting until he relented. But it was not the usual flighty, chatty Reagan. She seemed to have a purpose, driven by something she would not say, and this is why he feels something is wrong.

Jim walks to her apartment complex with head down and presses the button for her unit. A buzzer goes off, unlocking the front door, and Jim takes a deep breath as he opens it. He passes through sconces of light, spread too far apart for the dim yellow glow they emit. The final door is open a crack and Jim enters.

Standing in the hallway, Reagan turns toward him and grins. Her eyes tighten and she looks sadly triumphant. She does not speak, just steps into the living room, out of view. Jim follows, and as he enters, he sees Carrie sitting on the armchair, her arms folded and chin against her chest. Reagan meekly utters, "Surprise."

Jim does not flinch, hardly slows down as he removes his coat and hands it to Reagan. She takes it and says, "I think the two of you need to talk."

Jim nods toward Reagan. You are correct, you conniving bitch.

He sits on the couch across from Carrie and studies her.

"You're probably wondering why you're here," Carrie says.

Jim waits carefully. His fingers tingle as he tries to focus, tries to stay calm and in control. Emily is missing, and he's going to have to defend his actions in their failing marriage. Failed marriage? This setup is so Reagan. Jim wonders if Carrie weren't in the room, if everything weren't so strangely calm, what he would do to Reagan. He has never raised his hand against a woman, and doubts he ever would, but he has never had so much reason. Telling Carrie about their affair while Emily is still missing, it's all so Reagan.

"I thought," Carrie begins, "it would be better to meet on neutral ground."

Neutral ground? Jim thinks. I've fucked on this couch.

"Reagan offered her place. She's been so helpful."

"Helpful?" is all he manages, unsure of what question to ask first.

"Thank you," Reagan says.

"How?" Jim asks, looking from Reagan to Carrie and back.

"How do we know each other?" Reagan asks.

"Yes, how do you know each other?"

"Reagan called me," Carrie says, "when Emily first disappeared, that Sunday afternoon. She was helping with one of the search parties."

"Called you about what?"

"She was collecting information to help with the search, from Steve, the Collinis, and us. We just got to talking and..."

Jim turns toward Reagan in time to catch her eyes squint, accusing him of thinking exactly what he had been thinking, that she had told his wife about their affair. Instead, she transforms into a gracious host and states in a pleasing manner, "Well, this isn't about me. I think I should leave you two alone."

"Thank you," Carrie says as Reagan pads down the hallway and closes her bedroom door.

The two of them are alone, and Jim is still unsure of what Carrie knows. He doesn't trust Reagan at all, and he's sitting here in the lion's den. He waits for the meltdown, for Carrie to explode into rage and disgust. He has no idea what he will say, sitting at the end of the couch, head down. Carrie's voice starts, a weak, shaky voice, and she says words that are the furthest from what he ever expected.

"I've been a terrible wife and I'm sorry."

He looks up at her, staring in disbelief.

"I'm sorry for disappearing like I have."

"What are you talking about?"

"You know what I'm talking about, Jim. When was the last time I asked you about your day? Or told you about mine? When was the last time I looked you in the eye, acknowledged you, or made my presence known? I have problems, and I just closed myself off, walled out everyone around me."

"Carrie…"

"No, it's true. You know it. I've been nothing like the woman you married, and I'm sorry."

"Carrie!" he pleads again.

"I wish I could say why. I wish I knew why."

"Carrie, stop. Please stop." Jim wants to vomit. He wants to wretch like an animal. He wants to beat his fists against the glass table top. Anything but listen to his wife apologize in the very same room where he has been cheating on her.

"I went to that therapist. And then a psychiatrist. Dr. Henry. I told him how I've been feeling, what's been wrong with me the past few years. He basically diagnosed me with depression. Not just emotional, but chemical. I have a chemical imbalance."

"When did you determine this?"

"Two days ago."

"Two days ago? How could you know in two days?"

"I don't know anything, yet. But it's the first explanation that makes sense. If you look at the symptoms, if you read about how depression feels, it could be my diary. I've been talking a lot to Reagan, too. She's been helping me with it. She knows a lot about this kind of thing."

Jim knows Reagan's travails. A chronic complainer, he listened to her tales of woe-is-me and wished her doctor, who listened to the same stories, would stop prescribing different levels of different medications and just tell her to deal with it. Carrie is not like Reagan at all. But there is no denying it, Carrie is no longer anything like the woman he married. Could it really stem from that catch-all diagnosis, a chemical imbalance? Why didn't she say anything? Why would she keep this to herself? "But how long… how long has this been going on?"

"I don't know exactly, but years, many years. There was no definitive starting point. I never went to sleep one night and then woke like this. I think I've had symptoms since college."

"College? But you were never like this in college."

"Not in front of you. I could control it then. I could put on a smile whether I felt it or not. But there were shadows. I remember times…"

"But…," Jim huffs.

"I don't know everything about this, Jim. Not in the slightest. But it makes sense. For the first time in years I haven't felt so helpless, so completely hopeless. It's nice to have something to point to, something else to blame rather than that empty feeling that this could only be my fault. Dr. Henry said it's going to take a lot of work, years, possibly a lifetime. But at some point I might get out of this. It's been so long, Jim. Like I've been lying in bed for years, in a room with the shades pulled down, but now, just to stand and look outside, to know the outside still exists… I feel almost hopeful. The thing is, I need you to forgive me for what I've been. I need you to help me move forward."

"Wait, wait, wait! Wait a minute." He is supposed to forgive her? They're sitting here in Reagan's condo, with Reagan just down the hall, the woman he's been sneaking off to and fucking, and Carrie is asking for forgiveness? "I can't. I can't forgive you because you haven't done anything wrong."

"Jim."

"No! If you've been sick, then this is out of your control. And yet, for me, the supposed healthy one… I mean, I never said anything. I never…"

"It's all right Jim."

"No!" he exclaims again, unable to find the words, hardly comprehending what Carrie is talking about, hardly understanding why he is apologizing for what he did not do, when he should be apologizing for all that he did do.

"What is it, Jim?"

"I… this isn't right. I don't know. I'm sorry, I just don't know what to say."

"I know. I'm not asking for anything more than that you listen to me, and then perhaps at some point, you can forgive me."

"No! It's not that. I forgive you completely. It's not you. It's just… I don't know. I just don't know. I'm so confused right now."

Carrie rises from her seat and sits next to Jim on the couch. She places her hand on his knee and takes his hand. "I know this is not a good time, that this is really so unimportant when compared to Emily. I think that's another reason I wanted to do it here, to make it a small escape, a step aside so we could talk about it briefly. We need to talk about Emily, need to concentrate on finding her. I just wanted you to know where I am, what I'm going through."

Jim hates himself for every word that Carrie speaks, every kindness, every thoughtful concession. His heart aches, and he wants to unveil all his secrets to the woman holding his hand. He looks at her with watering eyes, and though he cannot tell her everything, they can connect in their sorrow. They both love Emily, and they can share that. Carrie leans into him, hugs him tight, and whispers, "Let's go home."

They leave without saying anything, and as they walk to the parking lot, Jim sees that he parked two cars down from Carrie's Lexus and never noticed. He stands by as Carrie gets into her car, watches her with a protective eye, and shivers.

"Where's your jacket?" she asks.

Jim looks down at himself, his hands buried in his pockets for warmth, his breath visible. "I must have left it inside."

"Go get it."

"I can get it later, at work."

"You haven't been going to work. You need your jacket. Go get it and I'll meet you at home."

Carrie gets into her car, pulls out, and waves as she drives away. Jim can't remember the last time she waved to him.

Walking back to the apartment, Jim is surprised by his calmness, how little regard he has toward Reagan right now. The relationship is over, but he needs to find out if she considers it over, what she will do next. He presses her buzzer and the door unlocks without a word. He walks in to find her sitting on the couch, arms folded. He sits across from her and returns her stare.

"What?" she asks.

"I want to know what you're thinking."

"About what?"

"I want to know why you called my wife. I want to know what you thought was going to happen by inviting me here, having us meet here like this."

"I was helping."

"Helping? What if I saw Carrie and confessed right away? What then?"

"If that was meant to be…"

"Are you shitting me? Meant to be?"

"Yes, if it was meant to be, then I would still be helping."

"You're a regular saint. What if I walked in here with flowers and a bottle of wine?"

"We both know you weren't going to do that. We both know we're over. I've been down this road before, Jim. I've had enough people tell me this was never going to work and I should have realized it a long time ago. But it doesn't matter, it doesn't matter to me and I know it doesn't matter to you. I just saw that I could help."

"Of course. It's always about you, what a good person you are. I'm glad you can end this thinking you helped me."

"You? You're an asshole." Reagan says. "I'm helping Carrie. I did this for her."

Jim turns, and unexpectedly feels his eyes water up. He stands and wipes them. He grabs his jacket from the kitchen chair and puts it on as he heads to the door. "I'm supposed to help her. That's my job."

125

30

Steve Cardell dials his voicemail and punches in the pass code. He taps his pen against an empty sheet of paper, prepared to take down messages. His cell has been rattling all day, and each time it goes off, he checks the caller ID. If it's not business, he puts the phone back down and lets the call go to voicemail. He is not up for talking about personal matters. He prefers the large mocha phone, his office phone, which is always business. He always answers it, willingly discussing CDOCIs, allocation schedules, and pricing strategies. This phone provides an outlet, something he understands, something he can control. But whenever that cell phone crackles to life, Steve's stomach drops and he holds his breath, waiting for it to end.

The first message is from Detective Kruthers. He wants to talk.

Another message from the detective. He listens but only writes a squiggly line across the empty sheet and then circles the doodle.

The third message is unexpected, and his pen drops. "Hello Steve, I think this is still your cell phone. We tried the house but can't seem to get hold of you. Anyway, this is Ruth. Could you give me a call when it's convenient? We're just trying to find out what's going on. We've been following the situation in the papers, but that's all we know. Please call." There is a long pause, something that wants to be said but isn't spoken, until the voice finishes with a terse, "That's all. Bye."

April's mother. Arielle's grandmother. Steve has not talked to her in months, and most of their conversations haven't involved more than handing the phone over to Arielle. It's not that he doesn't like them, but it's just not the same since April's accident. Arielle still flies out for two weeks each summer to visit them in Scottsdale, but since the funeral, he has never invited them back to Ohio. When they call, he says things are good, politely asks how they are doing, and quickly gets Arielle.

But they deserve a phone call now, deserved one that Saturday Arielle

126

went missing. But Steve was just unable to make the call. The last time he called was when he told them that April, their only daughter, had died in a car accident. He's never dialed their number since. The last message plays, Detective Kruthers again. Something about new evidence related to the case. This is the call to make first. He deletes all the messages and looks outside at the trees swaying in the wind, then dials Terrence Kruther's number.

"Hello detective, this is Steve Cardell."

"Thank you for calling me back."

Steve cannot tell if there is sarcasm or not. If there is, it is deserved.

"There's something new?"

"I didn't want to go over this on the phone..."

"Please do."

Terry coughs twice, short little bursts that he forces out. "Yesterday I received a package..." Terry starts, explaining everything except for the eyeliner, the black outline, keeping that piece of evidence confidential. The important facts are whether a copycat or not, our kidnapper is recreating the previous case, and so there's a decent enough chance that the children are still alive. That's what Steve needs to know.

"I see," Steve responds, as if he has just been told it might rain. "Thank you."

"Do you have any questions?"

"You've told me everything, right?"

"Yes."

"Then thank you."

"Steve, I really can't fathom what you're going through, but I want you to know we have a therapist ready who specializes in things like this."

"Thank you, but no thank you."

"It's just someone to talk to, someone who has a better understanding."

Steve laughs to himself, wondering if someone could really understand this. What do you look for in the psychiatrist's book of mental disorders, the DSM? Dead wife? Kidnapped daughter? Foot fetishist cutting off her best-friend's toe? How much information is there in cross-referencing those little facts? "No thank you," he repeats.

"It's your choice. Could I at least give you the counselor's name and number? It would make me feel better."

"Sure. Go ahead."

"Do you have something to write it down with?"

It's almost five on Friday afternoon, which means people have been sneaking out for the past hour, getting a jump on the traffic, starting the weekend early. "Uh-huh." As Terry recites a name and number, Steve wonders if anyone is going to The Shamrock, the nearby pub they sometimes visit at the end of the week. Doubtful. No one would have invited him even if they were, not because he doesn't occasionally make an appearance, but because no one has talked to him all day. Most of his phone calls have come from customers, or from the home office, from people who don't yet know.

The Shamrock is more for talking about how to seal a crack in the driveway or whether to paint the kitchen or hire someone. A few stories about your kids always kept things moving. Someone will make a comment about Shannon, the saucy waitress with an authentic Irish brogue, and people will start making comments about it getting late before their escape. Mentally, everyone knew the code. Don't get too personal with coworkers.

"Got it," Steve responds as Terry finishes reciting the therapist's name and number. Steve looks at his paper, which only contains angular doodles, and tells Terry he has to go.

He hangs up the phone and calls the answering machine at home, more out of curiosity, and discovers 23 messages were left before the mailbox became full and stopped taking messages. The media has his home number, so he does not listen to or erase any of the messages.

Instead he works on until 7:00, when, after skipping lunch, the gnawing in his stomach feels good and real. To keep working on the new account, he needs information from people on the west coast, but they are going home now too, calling it a week and not thinking about work until Monday morning. They'll enjoy the weekend, spend time with their families, maybe watch some football, and complain Sunday night about having to work the next day. It doesn't seem fair that Steve's productivity depends on them.

The cleaning crew finally comes in, politely taking out the garbage in each office, lightly cleaning while the sound of a vacuum whirs down the hallway. A young girl knocks politely on Steve's door and points toward his garbage can. He nods and begins putting papers into his briefcase while powering down his laptop. He goes to his car and sits, wondering where he's going, while two people on the radio debate the trade deficit. Steve turns the radio off, then back on, finding their banter pleasantly distracting, as he eventually pulls out of his parking space and heads to The Shamrock.

The turnover begins around this time, as the happy-hour people in business attire head home and the Friday night regulars arrive. Steve looks around, doesn't recognize anyone, and sits at the bar. The bartender, who couldn't be much over twenty-one, is talking to a waitress, glancing at Steve every few seconds to see if he's ready.

Steve studies the bottles of hard alcohol behind the bar, remembering drinks he used to order when he was young, but none of them sound good now. His coworkers usually order Black and Tans, which is Guinness and something, but that isn't what he wants either. He doesn't feel much like alcohol and wonders why he's in a bar.

"What'll you have?" the bartender asks.

"Umm," Steve starts, taking one last sweep of the spirits and finding none of them appealing, asks, "What do you have that's non-alcoholic?"

"Like pop or coffee? Perhaps a Shirley?" the bartender kids.

"No, no. Like one of those beers, I guess. One of those non-alcoholic beers."

"We've got O'Doul's, that's it," he says, reaching into a cooler and holding up the bottle. Steve reads the label and nods. The bartender turns his back as he opens it and pours it into a glass, throwing the bottle into the garbage. He places the drink on a coaster in front of Steve and walks back to the waitress, who has been waiting patiently. Steve watches the kid lean onto his forearms as the waitress reaches over and squeezes his tricep. The kid looks once more around the bar before acknowledging her.

What Steve should get is food, but he doesn't want his dinner to be bar food. He is also unsure if he wants his hunger pangs to go away, glad to have a physical reason for pain. With what he's been going through, hunger pangs, direct and understandable, are a welcome relief.

A few people sit at the tables and booths while the stereo switches between Van Morrison and U2 songs. Everyone is busy enough, consumed in themselves and their alcohol. This is better than going to a coffee shop, where everyone sits wide-eyed, pretending to read or work but always looking around, always taking stock. Here he can disappear.

The non-alcoholic beer starts with a crisp bite on the tongue which fizzles into a bland swill. A man walks behind him, returning from the bathroom, and sits on the stool next to Steve, announcing, "Hey, the Silver Fox."

"Hello, Randy," Steve acknowledges. Randy Hinton, the office IT guy. When something goes wrong with a computer, printer, or network connection, the office relies on him. He has total job security with little incentive to work too hard, and he is fully aware of the situation. He wears jeans and Hawaiian shirts most of the year. He's quick with a joke without questioning its appropriateness, and he has a simple belief that he is responsible for keeping the office running, that he's the man behind the curtain.

Since it's Friday, today's Hawaiian shirt is silk. Large toucans perch amongst wildflowers across his chest and expanding belly. "When'd you get here?" Randy asks.

"A few minutes ago."

"Hmm. Some of the other guys were here earlier, but they all left." Randy's breath is thick with alcohol, and his eyes seem incapable of focusing. "I'm just talking to some senoritas in the back."

"Good for you."

Then Randy, who jokes about everything, asks a question in a tone Steve hasn't heard in the six years he's known him. Even when April died, and the whole office came to the wake, Randy just shook his hand, frowned, and looked up at the lights. The only way he knows how to not be inappropriate is to not say anything at all. But placing his hand on Steve's back, he sincerely asks, "How are you doing?"

"Fine," comes without hesitation, too quickly, to which Steve qualifies, "considering."

"Yeah, it must be tough." Randy looks up, tries to think of what else to say, both of them just sitting there, when the bartender heads over. Randy points to their glasses on the bar, makes a circle with his finger and makes the peace sign, sending the bartender for two more drinks.

"You know, I think I'm going to try and help and all, you know, with the searches and all."

"Thank you. I appreciate it."

"It's the least I can do. I'd be there right now, but I know they stop when it gets dark."

Steve nods as the bartender puts another glass of non-alcoholic beer in front of him, his first one still almost full. Randy gets a glass three-quarters full of some golden liquid, no ice.

"Can I ask you, and I know it's none of my business, but do they know anything? Do the coppers have any leads?"

A toe, Steve thinks. A goddamn toe. But he can't really relate the toe to Emily, Arielle's best friend, who he pictures singing and giggling from Arielle's room during their sleepovers. The correlation is too grotesque to register, and he finds himself thinking of it more like a lost button or hair braid. Insubstantial miscellany. "They've got some leads they're pursuing."

"Good. They better find the son-of-a-bitch. It's just so fucked up."

"Yes it is."

"You know, they say life's not fair. And it's not. But sometimes it's just fucking ridiculous."

Nail on the head, Steve thinks. You just hit the nail on the mother-fucking head, ole Randy. "Where are your lady friends?"

"Oh yeah, they're in back. I think they're just using me for drinks. Wouldn't hurt for them to buy a round themselves."

Steve nods.

"You know, I'm surprised you've been coming into work."

"Have to do something."

"I understand," Randy says, then corrects himself. "I mean, I can't imagine what you're going through at all, but I get it, having to do something."

"Uh huh."

"Are you getting any sleep?"

"Some," Steve answers.

"I imagine nights are the worst."

"Yep."

"I mean, days can't be good either, but nights are usually the worst."

"Yep."

"Sometimes they seem to drag on forever."

"Couldn't agree more."

"Do you ever take anything?"

"No."

"Nothing to help you sleep? You should. Sometimes it can be a godsend."

"Uh-huh."

"I mean, godsend isn't the right word. It's just getting you through the night, but sometimes that's a big help."

"I'm sure it is."

Randy takes a gulp from his drink, and lets the liquid sit in his mouth.

"I imagine your lady friends are missing you," Steve states.

Randy smiles. "I take it you don't want to talk about it."

"No, not particularly."

"Well," Randy starts, holding up his glass to assert his pontificating, "if it's any consolation, at least be glad you've had it."

"Had what?"

"The wife and kid. The whole family. The American dream and all. Some of us probably won't ever have a chance."

Steve looks at him incredulously. He doesn't know where to begin, is not even sure why this statement bothers him so much. Randy is more drunk than Steve first thought, oblivious to the cold stare he's receiving. Instead, his plump face curves downward, saddened by the thought that he won't ever have a family. On most days, this is a condition Randy would proudly declare, rolling his eyes and making wisecracks whenever someone said they had to leave early to get home to their family. But right now, Randy Hinton looks truly sorry for himself.

Steve thinks of a quote, "'Tis better to have loved and lost than never to have loved at all." But that's not the point. Steve could live with his loss, if that were all there was. But what about April's loss? She's already missed three Christmases. Three of Arielle's birthdays. She was never going to see her daughter grow up. And now Arielle's loss. Arielle may never kiss a boy. Never graduate. Never get a job or get married. Never know the joy of being a mother. They're the ones who lost everything. Steve holds back, answering from a distance, "That's one way to look at it."

"Yeah, I'm sorry Steve. Don't know where that came from. Here, do a shot with me."

"No."

"Aw, just one. Two shots of Jaeger," he shouts to the bartender.

"No Randy. Not tonight." But the bartender sets out two glasses and pours them.

"Ready?"

"No," Steve says with raised voice, "I am not doing a shot."

Randy finally realizes Steve is mad and wonders where this anger came from. "No problem," he says, grabbing both shots, "I've got you covered." Randy downs both shots and then lets out a moan, sticking out his tongue and shaking his head. "Whoa-humditty, fuck yeah."

Steve watches in disgust.

"Well, I best get back to the ladies. Take care." He pats Steve on the back and heads to the depths of the bar.

Steve shudders that, with everything happening to him, the world keeps spinning. What a sick world it is. The bartender, looking around to see if anyone needs him, arches his eyebrows and shrugs his shoulders, as if to say, 'What did you expect?'

Steve finishes his first non-alcoholic beer, asks for the tab, and goes to the bathroom. He comes back to find Randy's drink and two-shots have been added, and he throws down his credit card with contempt. His second beer sits on the bar untouched. Twenty-five dollars for one non-alcoholic beer. Steve shakes his head and signs.

A hand slaps Steve on the back and he realizes he would be more than happy if he could leave down twenty-five and not deal with Randy again.

"You know Steve-O, sorry about what I said a minute ago."

Dammit. "Don't worry about it."

"No, no. I wasn't even thinking. Just drinking a bit too much. But I mentioned it to the girl I was talking to. Julie. Her name's Julie, and she said I was an asshole. I think that's why she left."

"Don't worry about it, Randy. Happens to the best of us."

"No, no, it happens to me all the time. I just open my mouth and out it comes, something stupid every time. What I meant before, I didn't mean to say anything mean or anything, it's just that as shitty as everything is, you can be glad that you've had a family."

"Randy."

"I've seen the pictures in your office, of you and your wife and kid. A real nice family, that's what I see. I think you should be real happy for having had that."

"That's enough."

"I want you to know, I want you to appreciate it. I'd kill for something like that, just for a while. To have a wife who loves me, a family. The whole kit and caboodle. That's never going to happen, and you know why? Because no woman will love me. I'm unlovable. I don't know why or what it is, but I'm just an unlovable sack of shit."

Steve looks around the bar, not sure what to do, but trying not to listen to this babbling idiot. There has to be a way out, a way to change the subject.

"I've tried to have a girlfriend, to be serious," Randy continues. "Remember that girl I brought to the Christmas party? I should have been more than good enough for her, cause you know, it's not like she was any prize herself. But she dumped me. Can you believe that? I don't think that's what I told everyone and all, but honest to God, she dumped me. But you, you found the right woman. A looker, too..."

"Randy."

"Be proud, my man. Loud and proud. I'll never hook up with something that fine."

"Randy!" Steve's fists clench in his pockets. He looks around, but everyone is oblivious to the hell he is going through. He has to change the subject, and asks the one question he wishes he hadn't. "Did you drive here?"

Randy looks at him, puzzled. "Sure."

"You're drunk."

"No way."

"Yes, you are."

"I only live a few miles away."

"Are you walking it?"

"Fuck no. It's cold."

"C'mon, I'm taking you home."

"I'm fine."

Steve only feels angrier. This may be the right thing to do, but it is also the last thing he wants to do. "Say the alphabet backwards."

"What?"

"Recite the alphabet backwards. If you can do that, I'll let you drive home."

"No problem. Z!" Randy declares, confident in his start. "Y." He murmurs the alphabet forward, starting with A, trying to find the next letter, q-r-s-t-u-v-w-x-y-z, "X, the next letter's X."

"What's the next letter."

"Q-r-s-t-u-v-w-x-y-z. Wait. Hold on," Randy mumbles through it again, "q-r-s-t-u-v-w-x-y-z. X!"

"You just said that."

"No I didn't."

"Randy! You're drunk."

The bartender comes up and says, "If he's offering a ride, you'd be wise to take it."

Randy looks at the two of them, the bartender smiling, happy to get the Hawaiian-shirt drunk out of his bar, and Steve, who is acting like the good guy, but can barely contain his anger. He finally smiles, and asks, "One more before we go?"

"We're going now!" Steve insists.

Randy nods in acknowledgement. "All right, hoss. I think I'm out with the senoritas anyway."

Steve fumes, furious at Randy for forcing this situation upon him, but even more furious at himself for coming here. He does not want this lush getting into his car. He does not want to hear him or see him a minute more. He puts on his coat and heads toward the door. Randy sits and watches until Steve turns and gives him the evil eye. Randy hops up, grabs Steve's second glass, still full of non-alcoholic beer, and chugs half of it before following Steve through the door.

Outside, beneath the parking lot lights, Steve spots his car and steps down from the curb, his fists still clenched, telling himself to just take Randy home and not say a word. He hears a gasp behind him as Randy misses the step, starting a slow-motion fall. Steve reaches out, grabbing his elbow for support, only to have the fat bastard grab onto him tight and pull him down too. Randy lands on his back and pulls Steve onto him. Steve immediately starts to get up, to distance himself from this drunkard, when he looks at the eye of a toucan staring at him from Randy's shirt, and Steve raises his hand and punches it as hard as he can. He lifts his arm again and punches Randy again, deep into his fat gut, producing a sharp exhale.

Steve jumps up, distancing himself from his coworker and his anger.

Randy curls up and tries to breathe, "Oh, Jesus!"

"Are you all right?" he asks, suddenly concerned with Randy's welfare. But the mass only rolls back and forth, whimpering. "What's wrong? Talk to me!"

Randy sucks in a few large gasps, just enough oxygen to look up at Steve with eyes watering and yells, "Why did you do that?"

"What's wrong? I'm sorry! You fell! You pulled me down! It was an accident!"

"That was no accident!"

"You pulled me down! It was an accident!"

"No, you did that on purpose! Aww, Jesus it hurts!" Randy's eyes are venomous, accusing Steve of the unthinkable. When Steve leans toward him, tries to get him to calm down, Randy curls up, protecting himself from another attack.

"Randy!" Steve calls out, his anger rising again, "Stop being ridiculous." He does not hit people for no reason. It is all just ludicrous paranoia from an annoying drunk. "It was an accident and I'm sorry. Now get in the car. I'm driving you home."

Randy eyes him frightfully.

"Now!"

Randy works his way up to his knees, pausing on all fours like an animal, sucking in deep breaths as he works up the strength and balance to stand.

Finding momentary sobriety, he follows Steve to his car and obediently gets in the passenger seat. He keeps his body pressed against the door, and with the whimpering of a freshly scolded child, squeaks out left and right commands until they pull into his driveway. Without a word, he opens the door and hobbles up to his front door, fumbles with his keys, unlocks it, looks back into the headlights like a frightened rabbit at the forest's edge, and disappears into the house.

Steve stares at his headlight's double halos on the garage door and wonders what's happening to him. Now that the accusations are gone, he admits to himself that he did punch Randy. Twice. And he enjoyed it. He really wanted to pick up Randy's fat head and drive it into the street, do anything to stop that despicable, whiny son-of-a-bitch from telling him he should be happy for having had a family, that he should appreciate what he's lost.

31

As far as Terry knows, very few people actually saw the original polish on the children's toenails, and nobody knew about the outline of eyeliner. The girls who were abducted, Beth and Sue, vaguely remembered it when reminded. Andy Frempt says he never actually saw the girls' toes. That left the police officers who found the captive children, the EMTs who brought them to the hospital, the doctors who stitched up the excised toe, and whoever washed the girls' feet in the hospital. Also, a photographer took the picture of their feet and put it in the case file. From there, a few people had signed in to look at the file: the detectives who did the follow-up investigation, a few researchers and journalists, and Art Morrell, doing research for his book. None of these people have been a suspect, but Terry must try to figure out if any of them even remember the black outline and in some way might have written it down or told others. Yet tracking down suspects from thirty years ago is not easy.

The girls that were abducted now live on the west coast. One of the officers who arrived on the scene and killed the kidnapper has retired to Florida while the other died of lung cancer. Of the EMTs who brought the children to the hospital, and the doctors who looked after them and sewed up the severed toe, only one still lives nearby, in Pennsylvania, but he was almost ninety years old. The investigating officer now works at a golf course in Tucson.

The FBI sent agents to interview all of these people or their surviving family members, and in the middle of a long interview process, asked them to carefully describe the condition of the toes. No one recalled the black outline.

Finally, there is Art Morrell, the author of *The Spying Toes*, who viewed the photographs of the children's toes in the case file. Terry doesn't think he has anything to do with the children's abduction, but does not entirely trust him either. Art studied the old case files with more scrutiny than anyone, but just because a description of the black outline did not make his book does not mean he wasn't aware of it.

According to the background report from Agent Samperson, Art's writing career never equaled the success of *The Spying Toes*. Although critics panned the book as bad writing on many levels, it sold well because readers were morbidly curious about the kind of monster that preys on children's toes and were frightened by the prospect that his accomplice might still be on the loose. When the television movie debuted, and was the most watched made-for-TV movie of the year, his book shot to the top of the best seller list again.

This first attempt at writing was more successful than Art Morrell could have ever hoped, so he tried to do it again, and again, and again. And based on his first book's secret to success, he continued making wild predictions and shocking accusations in order to drum up sales, only to ruin the little credibility he had.

Tag Team, his second book about a serial rapist in the nation's capital, followed a similar tack as *The Spying Toes*. Art Morrell claimed the man the police caught and convicted couldn't have been responsible for all of the connected rapes, and that an accomplice was still on the prowl. With little proof and shaky logic, he pulled together a thin argument while glancing over the concrete facts that opposed his theory. Although conspiracy buffs and fans of *The Spying Toes* purchased it, the book was mostly ignored.

His third book, *Uprising*, recounting two Chicago murders committed by a homeless man, went a step further. The book's premise ignored the simple, open and closed case of a homeless paranoid schizophrenic who killed two people in a drug-fueled delirium, and instead suggested he was part of an underground gang of the homeless, hell-bent on rising up against society. Mixing fact and shock were common tools throughout, with tag lines like "There are an estimated three million people in America who are homeless. Do you think they're content being kept down? Do you think they're going to allow themselves to be held on the bottom rung of society?" *Uprising* had one meager print run, most of which never sold. Only the most paranoid of conspiracy buffs could accept the monstrous leaps of reasoning he used to support his theories.

According to Agent Samperson, Art Morrell has been dropped by both his agent and publisher and is now self-publishing his latest works while supplementing his income with occasional freelance writing jobs.

Terry read *The Spying Toes* shortly after the children were abducted, and quickly thumbed through the other books, reading their jacket covers and skimming a few chapters. Terry finds the decline in the jacket cover art just as revealing as the stories. *The Spying Toes* looks professional, serious, almost a textbook with the title printed in simple letters and a line down the middle that divides the cover into black and white. The next book, <u>Tag Team,</u> about the serial rapist, has an outstretched hand whose shadow transforms into a woman. By *Uprising,* the illustrator must have given up on any attempts at credibility, drawing a pack of faceless vagabonds emerging from an alley onto a busy street.

Terry gets out of his car in the Holiday Inn parking lot and looks around. Television and newspaper reporters are staying here and they will recognize him immediately, having been through numerous press conferences already. Terry wants to keep a low profile, so agreeing to meet in the hotel bar late Friday evening was a bad idea. He has become something of a celebrity and isn't comfortable in the role.

Terry thinks of the time a reporter cornered him after a press conference and saying they were 'off the record,' asked, "Are you planning on writing a book?"

"What?"

"A book," the reporter repeated, "a memoir, something for people to remember this case. You're the center of the action. You're the one who can do it."

"No," Terry hastily replied. "I haven't thought about it, but the answer is no."

"You should. It's easy money. And it's a good story, as long as something happens."

Terry ignored the comment, but the reporter placed his hand on Terry's shoulder and finished with, "You're too professional to be thinking about this now, and that's good. But once everything's over and the smoke's cleared, call me." He slid his card into the front pocket of Terry's overcoat, grinned and nodded as if they had agreed on something and then walked away.

The reporter's words still bother him. "It's a good story, *as long as something happens.*" Terry knows what that something is. Whether he finds the children alive and well at some roadside stop, or he finds their corpses half-buried on the forest floor, it does not matter. How excited would that reporter have been had he known about the toe. Terry despises looking at the case through that lens, as if it were all a show. But here he is, about to meet with the ultimate spin-doctor. Who knows what he is thinking this time?

Terry enters the hotel bar and quickly recognizes Art from his book covers, sitting in the corner. Those pictures were black-and-white, but spotting Art's frazzled head of white hair and writer's outfit of a black jacket over a black turtleneck, little color is necessary. The big difference, which Terry could not discern from the picture, is noticeable when Art rises and stands at almost the same height as when he was seated. Terry guesses he is barely over five feet, as he shakes the man's hand. Terry's first thought is that Art isn't large enough to abduct three children, and he reminds himself it's his job to think everyone is a suspect.

"About time," Art says, heaving himself back into his swivel chair.

"Sorry." Terry glances at his wristwatch. "I thought I was on time."

"No, no, not that. It's about time you contacted me. You let two weeks pass before consulting the expert."

"The expert?"

"Yes," he says indignantly. "Who else knows this case better?"

"Okay. You're right," Terry concedes, "The expert."

"Good. So what do you want to know?"

Terry smiles congenially. He looks around, sure people are watching. Gossip for the reporters. Blood in the water. A waitress heads their way, the only person who could care less. "Since you're the expert, why don't you tell me what I should know?" Terry opens his notebook and takes the cap off the plastic pen clipped to an empty page.

"Fair enough," Art says. "Of course, you know who's responsible, at least the main person. Whether he has accomplices or not, I'm not sure, although I do have some theories."

"Theories are what I'm here for." The waitress smiles as Terry orders a 7-Up. Art points to his glass of ice with a thin pool of copper liquid at the bottom. The waitress nods and heads toward the bar. "Let's start with the main perpetrator."

"Hobbes?"

"You know his name?"

"No, not exactly. But if I'm going to write about him, I have to give him a name. I can't put 'the kidnapper' or 'the villain' in every sentence. It sounds silly. Readers need a name to hang their hat on, so for now I'm calling him Hobbes."

"Hobbes? How did you come up with that name?"

"Calvin was the first one. The criminal with a foot fetish whom the police found and killed. Calvin Michael Landess. I decided to name his accomplice Hobbes, not only because I enjoy the comic strip, but also because I enjoy the metaphor. Calvin was the man with bold intentions, bold plans, over which he was killed. Hobbes is the tiger. The intellectual. The stealthy one. The one no one else sees."

"Calvin and Hobbes? Really? You're naming these criminals after a comic strip?"

"The metaphor is too good. Hobbes was his friend, his confidant, but whenever a grownup came into the picture, he was nothing more than a toy stuffed animal. Completely overlooked, he was in every scene, but to the real world he was never seen."

"Was Charlie Brown the getaway driver?"

"If you're going to go Peanuts, Schroeder is the one I would watch out for."

Schroeder? The piano player? Terry opens his mouth to ask, but Art answers the question before hearing it.

"He had a temper," Art says.

Terry nods.

"But this is just Calvin and Hobbes."

"And you're going to keep that name? Hobbes?"

"That all depends on you. If you manage to catch the tiger, prove who it is and give me a real name, then I'll change it. Until then, as far as I'm concerned, the second abductor's name is Hobbes."

Terry nods in acceptance and takes a sip from the frizzy pop placed before him. The past two weeks have made him understand the need for a name. Constantly talking about *the perpetrator, the abductor* or the overly generic *that guy*, Terry likes pinning a name onto him. Only it isn't a real name. He senses that, if he would blindly follow, Art Morrell is capable of taking him down the path of the make-believe and will justify every step along the way.

"So this Hobbes character, what do you know about him?"

"What's he after?"

"Sure."

"I don't have everything yet. He's a pedophile, I'll guarantee that much. But that's easy. The bigger question is, why do it again? Why go back to the same town and reenact the same crime? I found that quite perplexing at first. Say you're a normal pedophile, you've got a thing for children. You could care less about creating a reenactment. The less likely you are to get caught, the better. And that means moving on."

"So why has he come back?"

"Probably because he can. Thirty years is more than enough time to wait before striking twice. Don't tell me anyone was telling their children to watch out, to be careful because three kids were abducted here thirty years ago. Most people don't even remember."

"No, but wouldn't he recognize all the attention he'd get because of the previous case? Wouldn't he know how much more likely we'd be to catch him?"

"But you haven't caught him."

Terry nods and swallows the truth.

"And with all the focus this abduction is getting, the fact that he hasn't been caught means he is pretty smart. Just think, he could have gone thirty miles down the road, to Reedsville or Lee Creek, committed the same crime, and it'd be down to a footnote in the *Columbus Dispatch* by now. Yes, there'd be an Amber Alert, but do you think the FBI would have gotten involved? Do you think it would still be making the front pages of national newspapers? Not a chance. Hobbes knew the extra scrutiny he would get.

He planned on it, welcomed it, and was certain he could still get away with it."

Terry has already come to mostly the same conclusions as Art, but he's got more evidence. Repeating the same crime in the same town is bold. Severing a girl's pinkie toe and sending it to the police is brazen to the point Terry can't fathom. Terry jots down a few notes to make Art feel like he is helping out. He needs to keep Art going, to see what else is in his head. "So Hobbes wants the attention?"

"Oh yes. In fact, that's his strongest motive. Hobbes is a proud man. A vain man. Of the three motives, I'm sure that is the most overpowering."

"There are three motives?"

"Most definitely. This isn't your usual small town case, detective. You can't just chalk it up to too many brewskis on a Saturday night."

Terry doesn't like the "small town" description, but must admit that more cases than not are alcohol related. "What are these motives?"

"The third motive, the least important one, is to actually abduct children. I'm sure you have this at the top of your list, but you're wrong to have it so high. Or it may be your only motive, as it's the obvious one. He's a pedophile, there's no question in my mind about that, but he has other urges driving him. The second of these is revenge. You see, the first crime was foiled. Calvin Landess, his partner and friend, was killed. The children escaped relatively unharmed and went on to live normal lives, unscarred from what happened to them. He wants revenge."

"That makes sense."

"Of course it does."

"And the first motive?"

"The very first motive, the most powerful impetus for Hobbes, is his vanity. He can't let go. He thinks he is better than that; he knows he is. To use an overused analogy, he lost the battle, but he plans on winning the war. He wants to prove he can get away with it."

"Get away with what, kidnapping three children? What's he doing with them?"

"I haven't written that part yet. I was hoping you could tell me. Or eventually, he will."

"What do you mean, he will?"

"When his crime is complete, he'll make sure everyone knows. He'll broadcast his success as far and wide as he can, which won't be difficult with the media so highly invested."

Terry finds Art Morrell's thought process fascinating. Number the motives, define his weaknesses like a Shakespearean character, and then set it in motion. There are no subtleties, no vagaries in human depravity. This is good versus evil, and he is sure the villain is pure evil. It's easy to do. Terry heard other officers comment about what they would do to the perpetrator if they had the chance. After cutting a little girl's toe off, a toe for a toe didn't seem harsh enough. And no one disagreed. Like the original villain Calvin Landess, shot dead, gurgling his last breaths on the forest floor, no one felt sorry for him. Many felt he got off easy, and maybe he did. But no one wondered what he had gone through before then, what tortured inner-strife led to those final events.

Terry must remind himself that he doesn't care either. His job is straightforward. Find clues, piece them together, locate the children, and apprehend the kidnapper. If circumstances require it, if it will save the children again, Terry will shoot him dead too. He is interested in these theories of motive only as clues. Terry will let the doctors and philosophers debate what they mean about society, the reflection of the so-called human condition. Art will have his book to write. Terry does not care. Terry always liked that about law-enforcement, the lack of ambiguities, the directness of it all. If you do your job to the best of your ability, you contribute to the greater good. Find the criminal, bring him in, expose the facts, and let the judges and juries, the media and the public, make their own verdicts. Terry believes in this doctrine whole-heartedly, and he likes his cog in the machine, which only requires working hard and figuring out the who and the how, leaving the why to others.

On the other hand, Art Morrell likes implications, delights in ulterior motives and unexpected twists, tying a narrative together more by stretched motives than by actual facts. He enjoys all that, and he enjoys selling books. Terry knows this and wants to pass off these theories as nothing more than a desperate man trying to get his name back in the papers and make a buck. But there is a problem. Art Morrell's profile has a lot in common with the FBI's. They've emphasized how the kidnapper wants people to know what he's done, enjoys flaunting his acts, just as Art is claiming. And Art doesn't even know about the toe.

"I still find it troubling that you think the kidnapper isn't motivated by his perversion for children."

"I didn't say he isn't motivated, I said it isn't his only motivation, or his major motivation. If he were some pervert getting his kicks off, Edgebrook is the last place to kidnap three children. He knows that. That's why you should have met with me right away, so I could point you in the right direction."

Terry reckons Art Morrell's arrogance annoys everyone. "If Hobbes were an accomplice in the first abduction, his motive would have been the children, right? If I'm not mistaken, your original theory stated there had to be another accomplice because Calvin had a foot-fetish but not a thing for children. So this Hobbes, he's the pedophile."

"Correct."

"So why did his motive change? Why would the first kidnapping satisfy his sexual deviance and the second one be about revenge? Pedophiles usually repeat. They have these urges that never go away, and if they're never caught, they'll continue to act on them. Why is his motive now revenge and vanity?"

Art's fingertips trace the circular rim of his glass. "I'm not abandoning my original theory, detective. Quite the contrary. You think this pedophile, the one who didn't get caught, has been sitting around for thirty years, plotting? Not a chance. He is and always has been a sexual predator. When he wanted to satisfy that urge, he went elsewhere, made sure he didn't get caught, and has been doing his thing year in and year out, getting away with it, and growing more confident every time."

"So you're saying this guy's been molesting children for thirty years?"

"Children go missing every year, detective. They never turn up. Young kids. You know that. He's intelligent. He's crafty. And think, every time he gets away with molesting some child, he grows more upset about that first time, more outraged at getting caught. Now he's out to make amends."

"Amends?"

"In his mind, yes."

"And of course, proving you right all along."

"Of course," Art says, ignoring the sarcasm. "I haven't been right in everything I've done. But don't tell me it doesn't add up. I'm guessing he's not finished, either."

"What do you mean?"

"The media keeps pressing *The Spying Toes* connection, and you keep denying it, saying it might be, but it might be a copycat, or maybe unrelated altogether. If I may quote you," Art goes to a monotone impression of Terry, "*There are no leads in this case and we're pursuing every possibility. I repeat, there are no leads in this case and we're pursuing every possibility.* It gets boring. It stops people from listening. I think he's going to try and prove he's back."

"How?"

"I don't know."

Terry studies Art intensely, looking for any sign that he knows something else; his premise is too accurate. Terry studies Art, but Art studies him right back, and the little man with dark eyes and a crumpled brow stares right back into Terry's eyes. Terry blinks.

"I'm right!" Art shouts, jumping up from his seat.

"Right about what?" Terry asks, too late to deny. His straightforward manner, his inability to lie, has always been an asset, but it is betraying him now.

"He has done something else, something you're not telling me!"

"I don't know what you're talking about."

"I'm right!" Art shouts out to the delight of the reporters in the bar, watching the little man next to Detective Kruthers pumping his fist in excitement.

"Sit down!" Terry commands sternly, scolding him as if he were a gloating child.

But Art knows he has the upper hand, sitting down and shaking his head in affirmation. "You've got to tell me."

"There is nothing to tell."

"No way. I'll let them know," he says, nodding behind Terry to the people in their chairs and barstools.

"Keep quiet!" Terry whispers.

"I will and you know it!"

"Let them know what? You don't have anything."

"I'll let them know that confidentially, off the record, you confirmed that this abductor was an accomplice to the original case. You said I was right, and you've got a clue to prove it."

"I didn't say that!"

"You don't have to. The reporters are watching us together right now. They'll quote me. They'll put it in the papers."

"You'll be lying."

"I'll be right."

"But you'll be lying."

"Tell me what happened and I won't say a word. Just give me the inside scoop."

Shit. This wasn't the way it was supposed to go. Terry was here to get information, the most important being if Art knew about the eyeliner, which he had planned to ask about without getting specific. But now this arrogant little shit was getting information from him. "You have to answer something first."

"Anything."

"You studied the previous case more than anyone; you studied the case files. So I need to know something."

"I am all yours, detective."

Terry focuses on Art's pupils, measuring just how small they are, steady pinpoints of calm. He wants to be sure to catch the slightest recognition in the question he is about to ask. "How were the toes painted?"

"What?"

"Describe to me how the toes were painted."

"You mean red?"

"And?"

"And? They were polished. Red. They looked manicured. You know, cut and filed. I don't think there were any hangnails or anything."

"Keep thinking," Terry commands.

"About what? Red toenails. I don't know the color. A darker red, not quite a burgundy. Why would it matter how the toes were painted, unless,

144

unless you got something? What?"

The only thing Terry reads from Art is pure confusion. "Art, you were in the case file, you saw the photograph of the injured foot. I want you to close your eyes and try to remember everything you can about it. I want you to describe it to me and be very specific."

Art closes his eyes as instructed, clutching the sides of the table. "I remember a girl's foot, after surgery. There was a garish mark where the stitches began. I remember thinking something was not quite right, besides the stitches."

"What wasn't right?"

"I knew the toe was missing, at least logically. But you're not used to seeing a foot with four toes. It not only looks wrong, it feels wrong. Even if the scar weren't there, intrinsically, it looks wrong."

"What about those four toes? What do you remember about them?"

"Like I said, they were painted red. Crimson red, maybe, but a little flashier. Ruby red? It was a long time ago. What am I supposed to say?"

"Was there just nail polish," Terry asks, "or was there any other make-up used?"

"No. Just the polish."

"Do you remember a black mark, outlining the toenail?"

"A black mark? I... no... I don't remember anything like that."

Terry believes him. How a woman paints her toes has probably never been a concern for Art Morrell. If Terry had been hard pressed before this case to describe a painted toenail, what was normal and what wasn't, he would also have been at a loss. In his mind, they were just different, that was all. He knew lipstick, and vaguely understood things like eyeliner, eye shadow and blush. But how a woman actually applied it was a complete mystery. And just like him, Art probably couldn't recognize the difference between a painted toenail and a painted toenail outlined in black.

While Terry contemplates, deciding where to go from here, Art continues connecting the dots. "You've got an M.O., right? You've definitely got something, but... how would you use that today? There's no way you found one of the children and hid that from the media. Did he describe it in a letter? Send you a picture? I've said all I know. It's your turn, Detective." Art grips the arms of his chair and leans forward. "You promised you would tell."

"I promised I'd tell you everything I could. But I've already said more than I should on this topic."

"What?"

"I can't say anything more."

Art, always thinking, understands he's losing the upper hand, reanalyzes the situation, and says, "You can't tell me because I'm a suspect."

"A suspect? In a way everyone's a suspect."

"Don't be coy, Detective. Of course I am and probably pretty high on the list. What is the first step in solving any crime? Determine the motive. And how do you do that? Ascertain who has benefited from the crime and voila, there's your list of suspects. For example, I'm going to sell books because of this. *The Spying Toes* is going into reprint right now. My old publisher is asking about a sequel, although I'm going to stick it to those S.O.B.s if they want a piece. Regardless, I'm benefiting, and therefore I'm a suspect."

Terry nods.

"I can't tell if you're just playing dumb, detective. You did have me as a suspect, right?"

"Yes but, but it is sick, abducting children just to sell books."

"Sick? There isn't any motive for abducting children that isn't sick. Just being sick doesn't disqualify anyone."

"True."

"Look, detective. I'm pushing this because I know I didn't do it. I'm not worried. But if that is a motive, let's call it by its real name. It's not just to sell books, it's fame and fortune, and that's a powerful motive."

"Agreed."

"With that motive I assume you realize you have to put your name on the list of suspects, too."

Terry stares into his drink as he takes a long sip, trying not to put too much into what Art says.

"You're surprised? Don't tell me there haven't been any book offers yet?"

Terry grins, changing his demeanor as if he knew this was coming all along, but wishes Art weren't so quick. Not for the first time, Terry wonders just how good of a job he is doing.

"So you didn't think of that one, Detective. Maybe you shouldn't be privy to my clues either, since we're not exactly engaged in open communication."

"I guess I may be a suspect," Terry says, stuck on this idea, "but I've never profited from a case. I've never profited from a child's abduction." Terry looks around the bar as he states, "I don't have a prior."

"Good, detective. Witty. Yes, I made money on <u>Thy Spying Toes</u>. But no one has proven me wrong. And if you solve this case, you're going to profit from it. You don't have to write a book or anything like that, but you'll be a hero, whether you want it or not."

Terry doesn't want to be a hero and is more concerned about the other side of the coin, that he'll be the detective who couldn't save those children. He doesn't want to be the hero, but he especially doesn't want to be the goat. "Whatever. I can't worry about it We're pursuing all leads, that's all I can say."

"Christ. Let me see what I can put together. The previous toes were marked in some distinctive manner that nobody knew about. You now have a clue that matches. Correct? What was it, a photograph?"

"I would like to thank you for your time…"

"But because Hobbes is smarter than our keystone cops, he made sure there were no fingerprints on it. Nothing for you to go with."

"You have my number in case…"

"So how did he deliver the clue? Email? The FBI would have traced that. It'd be too risky to drop it off. Cameras are everywhere. If he left it somewhere to be found, whomever found it would have most likely talked by now. There also would have been a reallocation of the search parties, to concentrate on that area, and I don't think that's happened. Still a possibility, but…"

"Goodbye, Mr. Morrell."

"Did he send something? That would get postmarked, so at least you'd have a general location."

"Unless it was repackaged," Terry says, wanting to see where Art takes this lead.

"Repackaged? What do you mean? The post office doesn't repackage."

"Some places do. Towns with significant names . . . "

"Like what?"

"Like Loveland, Ohio. People send Valentine's cards there, have them re-marked with "Loveland" in the corner, and then sent back out."

Art turns the concept over in his mind. "Loveland, Ohio?"

"Yep."

"What about Lovely, Texas?"

32

'Short on facts, Art Morell creates a tall-tale.' – *The Sentinel*

That was the review that burned Art the most. It came out shortly after the release of *The Spying Toes* and pained him because it was from the student newspaper of the very school where he taught. Even though some reviewers poked holes in his theories, none cast him aside so casually, pegging him as a fraud and a huckster. At the time, the review truly incensed Art. After *The Spying Toes* became a bestseller, it was this very review that sent him over the edge, convinced him to quit teaching and dedicate himself to writing.

Art bought two copies of that review, setting one afire over the stove and laminating the other. He now thinks about that laminated copy, filed away in the bottom drawer of his writing desk, and wonders how the laminate will burn, how it will smell as the smoke curls off, when he proves that he was right all along.

"So who is collecting your mail?" Terry asks again, driving to Plainfield, the town Art now calls home, a little more than two hours west of Edgebrook.

"Bart Gorski."

"He's your neighbor?"

"That's right."

"And he's not answering his phone, but you say he's probably there?"

"I'm positive," Art answers.

Bart Gorski. Apartment 210. Right next door. The neighbor who is collecting his mail while Art is away, who reads each item of mail to him over the phone, the same neighbor who said there was a package with no name or return address, only a town. Lovely, Texas, he said, making Art wonder why he would get anything from such a town but assuming it could wait until he got back. Art got a hotel room in Edgebrook and did his investigating by day, his writing by night, and he didn't plan on returning home until the case was resolved, whatever that resolution might be.

This is the neighbor Art never wanted to depend on, but when he had to leave for Edgebrook he had no choice. The neighbor who first knocked on his door one day, shortly after Art moved in, stuffing the last half of a pastry into his mouth, scratching.

"I think I got your stuff," he said those many years ago, licking his fingers.

Confused, unsure where this long-haired man holding out three letters and a furniture catalog had come from, Art took the offering.

"Next door," the man clarified, peering behind Art into his apartment. "I'm 210. Bart Gorski."

"Oh. Thank you."

"You are?" Bart asked, extending his plump hand.

Art glanced at the numbers on his open door. "211," he read, then held up the mail just handed to him, label side out. "Art Morrell."

Bart lowered his unshaken hand, nodding his head, unoffended. "Cool."

Art watched his neighbor and wondered if he was going to say anything else, realizing the animal at his door was not going away.

"You know," Bart said, deep in thought, "I bet they mixed up our mail 'cause of our names. Bart. Art. They're pretty close."

"Yes, I imagine that is the root of the problem," Art agreed, wondering for the thousandth time why he gave up tenure at the University to write. On the one hand, he had dealt with more students like Bart than he ever cared for, but on the other hand, they were never neighbors, never equals.

"You got any of my stuff?" Bart asked, now blatantly looking behind Art with suspicion.

"What?"

"My stuff. Mail for me. If they can switch Art with Bart, I bet they can do Bart with Art?"

"No, I don't believe I have. But if I do receive your mail, I'll be sure to bring it over."

"Okay."

"Well, thank you for your neighborly commitment, Bart."

"Hey, where's your TV?"

"My TV?"

"Yeah. I don't see any TV. What do you watch?"

"I don't own a television," Art said, watching Bart's expression glaze over. He wondered if he closed the door right then and opened it the next day, would Bart still be standing there, pondering life without television?

"That sucks. Must be quite a pinch."

"A pinch?"

"Tight," Bart elaborated. "Money. Must be tight on money."

"Oh, yes," Art nodded, knowing he will be viewed in a more sympathetic light as one who can't afford a television rather than one who chose not to purchase one.

"Gotcha," Bart said, his head bobbing as he turned toward his apartment. "That's too bad. My TV broke once. It sucked. It really, really sucked."

"Yes, it does quite suck," Art said, appreciative of Bart's empathy for his fellow man.

And now here Art sits, getting a ride back to his apartment building, about to uncover a crucial piece of evidence mailed directly to him, about to prove he was right all along. There is a second abductor. There will be a sequel to his book, another bestseller. He will prove he was right, and the key evidence is sitting in Bart Gorski's apartment.

"Are you sure he said it was a package?" Terry asks again, puncturing the car's silence.

"Positive." Art answers again, "A package from Lovely, Texas."

"Do you want to call him again?"

"I already left a message. If I keep calling and leaving messages, I guarantee the dumb ape will start snooping. He'll put his prints all over it, hold it up to the light, all that. I think it's better if we just leave it as is."

"You're right."

"I know," Art murmurs.

Terry follows Art's directions and pulls into the parking lot of a small apartment building made of deteriorating shingles and filthy windows. "This is just a temporary arrangement," Art says.

The meeting goes as Art described. Although Bart Gorski never answered the phone, after a few loud knocks and yelling from Art, a red-eyed Bart Gorski, smelling of marijuana, answers the door. He lets them in at Art's request. Once inside, Terry states that he is with the police, causing Bart's eyes to widen as he glances back towards his living room.

Bart Gorski has strewn Art's mail across his kitchen table, each letter dropped as Bart finished reading the outer envelope. "Whoa, dude," Bart says, watching Terry put on rubber gloves and pull out an evidence bag.

Terry spots the package right away, just like the one he received, the same dimensions, the same brown-paper wrapping, and the same red ribbon with black trim, tightly wrapped around the package and curled into a neat bow. "Lovely, Texas" is printed in the corner, and Terry's heart sinks at the prospect of what's inside.

Art sees his name on the shipping label and reaches for it.

"Wait!"

"What's in it?" Art asks.

"Just wait. Do you have a garbage bag, Bart?"

While Bart goes to the front closet and searches, Terry carefully lifts the package with gloved hand and puts it into the evidence bag. With that done, he takes the Hefty bag from Bart and puts the rest of the mail in it, securing it with a knot when he is finished. "All right Bart. It's time we all went to Edgebrook."

"What? I didn't do anything," Bart declares, looking nervously back into his living room.

"I know that," Terry says, taking off his gloves and rolling them together. "But do you know those kids that were abducted? In Edgebrook?"

"Yeah."

"The same person who abducted those kids sent this package, so we're going to lift all the fingerprints on it. Now did you touch the package?"

"Yeah."

"Did you kidnap those children?"

"No way!"

"Then you're going to have to come with us so we don't have to put out an arrest warrant for you when we uncover your fingerprints. Okay?"

"Yeah, okay, shit. Hey Art, why's this psycho sending stuff to you?"

"I wrote a book about him," Art answers.

"Really? You know who did it?"

"No," Terry interrupts, "he does not know who did it."

"Then how'd you write a book about him?"

"Look," Terry says, "the point is, we don't want to confuse any of your prints with the real perpetrator's. So let's all get going to Edgebrook where we can sort this out and make sure there are no misunderstandings. Otherwise, there'll be a gang of officers knocking down your door tomorrow morning."

Bart takes one last look towards his living room and agrees to go, putting on his shoes and jacket in the front hall. "Shotgun," he shouts out.

Terry drives in silence. Art talks some when they begin, but when Bart is the only one who responds, he resorts to silence.

"It's hot back here." Bart declares. "How long's it going to be?"

No one answers.

"So if this dude's writing you letters, do you think he's telling you where the bodies are?"

"Nobody's dead," Terry reminds him.

"Oh. What's he doing to them?"

No response.

"He's a pervert, isn't he?"

Nothing.

Bart goes quiet for a while, watching darkness pass through the side windows, when he says distractedly, "I really hope you catch this fucker. And hurt him too."

"Hurt him?" Terry asks.

"Yeah. Fuck his shit up."

Terry does not respond. Art wrinkles his brow but lets the comment pass.

A good ten minutes of silence pass before Bart continues. "My little brother, he was molested by one of those perverts. Messed him up big time. The fucker lived in our building. He tried some of that shit on me, too, but I was older and told him to go fuck himself. But I never said anything. Never told nobody, and then he ends up doing that shit to my little brother."

"What happened?"

"The fucker went to jail. Hopefully got what he had coming to him. It's been like twenty years though, and my brother, he's just not right. Tried to kill himself once. Only with aspirin and all, but still. He's quiet all the time and never has a girlfriend or anything, as far as I know. Just keeps to himself."

"I'm sorry to hear that," Terry says, glancing in the rearview mirror to see Bart still gazing out the side window, transfixed by the darkness.

"I really hope you find those kids. I hope nobody fucks up their lives like my brother's."

"So do we," Terry says.

"Those things just fuck things up," Bart says, grasping for the words. "I don't know how else to say it. They just fuck everything up for the rest of your life."

Terry ponders Bart's assessment, and realizes it's probably the most accurate description he's heard, and that even if the best case scenario happens, if his ultimate hope comes true and the children are found alive, the rest of their lives are probably already "fucked up."

A forensic technician paces outside the metal trailer used as a lab, stomping out his cigarette as Terry's car pulls into the police parking lot. Terry hands him the evidence bag as they head toward the trailer, holding it out like radioactive material.

Art follows at his heels, and Terry nods to the technicians to let him in. Terry walks Bart into the station, where Baumgardner meets him to start the fingerprinting process, before heading back to the trailer.

Inside, the package lies on a thick metal table, as one technician sprays the surface and another flips it with tweezers. A violet light goes on overhead as the surrounding tungsten lights are extinguished. Fingerprints materialize on the brown paper, exposing a trail of many hands. One technician takes photos while the others whisper to each other in their professional jargon. Art squeezes in between them, careful not to touch the table or envelope, but peering as close as he can, while Terry stands in the background, trying to hold his composure in anticipation of what's inside.

A technician carefully slices open one side with a razor, and with gloved hands pulls out a cardboard box. He lifts the top flap and pulls out a black velvet jewelry box. With a pair of metal hooks, the box is pried open, and there resting, just like before, is a single pinky toe, cleanly severed, meticulously polished in a brilliant red, and outlined in black.

The technicians had expected it, having worked with the first package, and they try to carry on with their jobs, try to remain objective to the severed toe of a child. Terry closes his eyes, as Art looks at him, then looks all around for anyone to answer, asking, "Is that...?"

"Yes."

"He's cutting off their toes?"

"Yes."

"But the pedophile, the one who cared about the toes, was killed. We know that."

"Yes."

"But Hobbes... he doesn't care about the toes... he's just doing it because...?"

"Because he's sick."

"Jesus."

As they talk, the technicians remove a single sheet of paper from the cardboard box. Terry sees inverted words through the page and waits as the back of the sheet is dusted, but there are no fingerprints.

Using tweezers, a technician unfolds the page, exposing the magazine-cut letters.

Time is not a singularity.

I have moments of want.
little precious needs.
To grow closer.
To unite.
To thrash.
Break upon.
Break open.
Dissect.

Then dispose.

So, so simple. And no one to stop me.

Except for other moments.
Moments of lucid normality.
Moments when i walk amongst you,
        creatures of singularity.
i understand your contempt.
Your disgust and your anger.
All for Me.
These moments restrain.
Moments of introspection.
Moments to reach out and ask for help.
Moments to write Lovely letters.
these moments are slipping. so i ask. tell. pray.
Find me.

Before the deeds.

Where are the spies now?
hurry, for my loves.
hurry, for my lovelies.
Hurry, beg my Lovely, Lovely Angels.

33

The phone rings midmorning, just before lunch. It's Mr. Alvarez calling for Antonio.

"He's not there?" Natalya asks.

"No, he's not."

"I don't know. He told me he was going to work this morning." Antonio lied to her, and Natalya experiences a flash of relief, relief that they are not sliding into the routine of living their lives without Alex. Not yet. She takes the cross on her neck between her fingers and slowly slides it back and forth along the chain. "Maybe he's out with the search parties?"

Mr. Alvarez sighs and begins with a tone of tired resolve. "I've tried, Natalya. I explained to corporate the best I could. I held out as long as possible. The only difference between holding out one more day is it will mean my job too. I have to let him go."

Natalya stops breathing as she pulls her necklace tight against the back of her neck.

Pleading does not help. Mr. Alvarez explains the ultimatum once again, explains what he told Antonio, what Antonio never told her. Natalya touches her belly, remembers standing in the mirror that morning, trying to see if she was showing. Mr. Alvarez apologizes again and again, exclaims his hands are tied and there's nothing left to do. One more day, she asks, but he says he has already given one more day too many times. There's nothing more to be said. He has to hire someone else.

Natalya hides out in her bedroom, knowing not to encounter Antonio's mother in the kitchen or she'll lose it and say something she'll regret. She is furious at Antonio, but at the same time understands his choice. Would she have expected anything different from him? She alternates between pacing the room and sitting on the edge of the bed, unable to stop sliding the cross on her neck back and forth along its chain. She wants to run away. She wants to disappear for a few hours like she did as a child, and find upon return, that everything she was worried about had blown over. Or maybe she could wake up to discover this was all a dream. She would rub her eyes in the dead of night and walk down the hall to find Alex lying in his top bunk. She would climb up with him, wake him with her motherly embrace, and contemplate just how vivid a dream it had been. She needs something, anything to get out of this predicament.

Natalya contemplates their situation and sees no way of staying afloat, which is all they've been doing so far. They will lose their insurance. With no income, they will have to make another drastic move, like max out another credit card or sell one of their beat-up cars. That will only prolong the inevitable. Antonio won't find a new job; no company will insure him with Katya's pre-existing condition. She will try to find work, but who would hire an expectant mother of five over some gum-chewing teenager? Even if she does find a job, would it even be close to enough? How will she make it through another pregnancy? Will the new baby be healthy?

Wrapped intrinsically around every one of her questions is the most important one. Will they find Alex?

She lies back on the bed and closes her eyes, finding herself so overly tired but unable to sleep.

34

Even though he only drank one O'Doul's, Steve opens his eyes with a headache that resembles a hangover. Discombobulated, turning throughout the night from all too vivid dreams, he wakes to the dread of an empty Saturday, an empty house with rooms that encapsulate the lost past. The phone rings and he looks at the caller ID to see if it is Detective Kruthers. Another Arizona call from Arielle's grandparents. Another shot to the gut, causing him to roll over and pull the pillows from the other half of the bed, the empty half, and squeeze.

He rises and showers, turning the water hot enough to redden his pale flesh. It feels good. He then wipes the steam from the mirror and studies the features looking back at him, wishing he could wipe the steam back on. He hasn't been eating and his face is gaunt, like a cancer patient wasting away from chemotherapy. His eyes are yellowed and bloodshot, while his pupils seem to have lost their normal blue, turning to a soulless gray. The man he looks at, who was once a husband and father, doesn't look fit to be either now. He thinks about the previous night, black clouds and bursting aggression, and massages his palms against his temples while scratching his fingernails into his scalp. Steve wants to push the thoughts from his mind but can't.

He steps outside to grab the paper. He shivers without his jacket, but the air's sharp freshness flushes out his stale lungs. Picking up the paper's blue bag, he looks up and down his calm, suburban block and wonders if everyone lives behind a similar façade. Perhaps he'll go for a jog.

He finds white shoes with green swooshes in the back of the third bedroom closet. They are too white, the creamy surface of potential wear that never happened. Steve ties them on and then places the sole of his right shoe against the toe of the left shoe and pushes, embedding dirt onto the bone white surface. He thinks about when he purchased these shoes, remembers picking them up at a sporting store while running errands for something else. He remembers wandering through the golf section, trying out the latest driver that was on display. On impulse he bought a pair of running shoes, then grabbed a can of tennis balls for April. This was just before the accident, and he hasn't exercised since.

He attempts to stretch, but stops when something pops, a dull crack emanating from somewhere near his hip socket. He walks out the front door, chooses a direction, and leaps into a long stride down the block.

He quickly remembers the problem he's always had with jogging. Regardless of his condition, he likes to run fast. And his current condition is quite poor, causing him to suck in thick breaths by the end of the block. The first stomach pain reveals itself before he has made one lap around the block, where Steve is thankful to find the sidewalk slanting downward toward his house.

He watches his house suspiciously and decides another lap will be good for him. Winded but trying to remain graceful, Steve manages this second lap before having to shove his fingers into his side, picking up the pace against the ache. In the past, a run like this would have been nothing, but now it strips his lungs of oxygen and ignites the muscles in his legs. He feels like a fool but does not want to stop. He wavers on the sidewalk, steps onto someone's lawn, and then veers back onto the concrete, extending his stride as he goes. No longer out for a jog, Steve sprints for another lap, determined to make it back home as he gasps for more oxygen.

Black splotches pierce through his eyesight, and within these shadows, he sees visions of his family: April's eyes and Arielle's curls. He pictures them at home, waiting for his return while he circles the block, unsure if he is running to them or from them. His thighs contract, his lungs suffocate, and his heart aches. Careening over the last stretch home, dry spittle crusts onto Steve's lips, but he has no breath to cough it out, no strength to swab it with his tongue.

Stumbling up his driveway, he finally stops at his doorstep, hunches over and holds his knees. His face fills with blood, a hot pressure boiling inside his cheeks and forehead. He heaves twice but nothing comes up.

Two Advil and a large glass of water later, he rests on the couch. The black splotches come and go whether he closes his eyes or not. Moments of rest fade in and out, but they feel more like lost consciousness than sleep. When Steve finally sits up, the clock on the family room mantel reads 11:10. His body purged, he feels relief having exchanged the slow tick of the clock for real pain and the quick slide of a few hours. He stretches again, re-pops his hip joint, and takes another shower.

Still slightly disoriented, Steve picks up the phone and scrolls through his caller ID. He dials the number marked ARIZONA and feels lightheaded all over again.

The other line answers but says nothing. Steve knows what the other person is thinking. No news is good news. "There aren't any updates," he assures, "nothing new."

"Thank God," Ruth exhales. Ruth Aberdeen. April's mother. Wiry blonde hair, full face, a woman of generous proportions with a calming smile. April never looked much like her mother, but they share the same whispery voice, and Steve is reminded of his wife every time he talks to Ruth. This is one of the reasons he stopped calling, preferring email to update them on Arielle. "So we're just waiting for a break?"

"Yes. That's all we can do."

"We've been watching the news, calling the authorities. Just piecing together as much as we can. And praying. Praying as much as we can."

"Good," Steve says, remembering another reason why he stopped calling them. The Aberdeen's religion never bothered Steve before. They went to church every Sunday, adult Sunday school, Bible study, and various church retreats throughout the year. They left Christian books lying around the house, kept all their radios tuned to the Christian Radio Network, and occasionally quoted the Bible.

Growing up with no religious influence whatsoever, Steve held a quaint affection toward the Aberdeen's views, a curious endearment to their religious outlook. But when Ruth gave her eulogy proclaiming April's death as God's will, he at once realized the large chasm between them. A curious endearment was not faith, and one either believed or did not believe. Since losing their only daughter, the Aberdeens believed even more, espousing their views in every conversation, while Steve only became more certain they were wrong.

"Why haven't you returned our calls?" Ruth asks.

Steve realizes he still has his headache. Black splotches still paint his vision. Through this haze, he needs to do the right thing. "Can you come out here?" he asks.

"Are you sure?"

"Yes."

"I've got the flight schedule right here," Ruth says without pause. "There's one tomorrow morning that gets us in at noon. I can send you the details."

"I'll pick you up." His headache shifts, like a change in cabin pressure. "I'll see you tomorrow."

35

In the second note, the culprit's cryptic message alluded to some sort of remorse, a hint that he understands the cruelty of his actions. If he really feels that way, then Terry has an emotion to prey on, an opportunity to agitate, and perhaps they can delay the perp's plans, if not convince him to abandon them altogether. Of course, this remorseful message was still packaged with another severed toe, which DNA tests revealed belongs to Arielle Cardell. Terry is not necessarily hopeful in this plan, but at least it's a plan.

He never had a specific reason for keeping the notes from the public in the first place. If anything, Terry followed the simple logic that the culprit wanted the messages to go public, wanted the attention, so holding back might disrupt his schemes and open him up to making a mistake.

But so far, this has been fruitless, and Terry is relieved when Agent Samperson decides to release the kidnapper's notes to the public, along with the fact that a pinky toe was delivered with each message. There will be renewed attention from the media, renewed support for the search parties, and better odds that someone who knows something might come forward. Not least of all, Terry simply doesn't like to lie and is tired of telling reporters that there are no new clues.

The stage has been set for almost two weeks, since the first press conference after the children went missing. The police lawn has been trampled to a muddy field, with news van tire tracks and foot traffic zigzagging between the walkways and park benches. Everyone gathers before the station's front steps, where at the top, a podium made of stained particleboard is propped, adorned with the usual cluster of microphones. Day turns to dusk, and one of the camera crews shines a spotlight from their van onto the front steps, completing the theatrics. Terry approaches the microphones and asks the same question a technician has just been repeating, "Can everyone hear me?"

Terry recaps the facts that were headlined in that morning's press release, the same facts interrupting TV screens across the U.S. The police have received two notes from the children's abductor. Both came packaged with one of the children's toes, first Emily Hughes' and then Arielle Cardell's. Both had the same traits, including the black outline that links them to the first case. Terry doesn't have to say it because the reporters will, but the theory that there was an accomplice in the original abduction is probably correct, making Art Morrell something of a celebrity. As Terry reads from his prepared statement, with the families and officers gathered at his side, reporters and camera crews watching with silent intensity, a sense of uncertainty washes over him. He scheduled this conference, set the time, contacted the families, and alerted the media, yet he senses that strings are being pulled. This is all part of the criminal's plan, and he is just another puppet on stage. A flick of the wrist, a tightening string, and everyone jumps to attention.

"This is the evidence sent to us. This is what the culprit knows we know, and therefore we're willing to release this aspect of our case. The rest of the facts, the other leads we have, will remain concealed for now. The reason for this press conference is to send a message. To let whoever is responsible know that the circle is tightening, and the best possible outcome for everyone, including him, is to see our children come home safely. That's what we're after, that's what is right, and that is what we hope the culprit can appreciate. I'll answer questions at the end, but would like to take a moment for the parents of these missing children to speak. Please hold all questions until they're done." With that, Terry looks back toward the crowd gathered just off stage, at the parents waiting anxiously. Today is devoted to their pleas for their children. If the culprit is really reaching out for a reason to hold back, Terry hopes they can provide one. He walks off stage and nods to Natalya as she takes a breath and walks to the podium.

Natalya looks around, nervously touching her belly with her fingertips, then self-consciously pulls away. She unfolds a piece of paper onto the podium.

"Family," she starts, looking up to see if people are listening, "was not a word I fully understood. I grew up an only child and lived a life of quiet dinners and empty rooms. But somehow, I met and married Antonio Collini. One of six children, twenty-six cousins, and extended family beyond count, the Collini family gatherings gave me a glimpse of family in action. They get together every holiday, filling a house with mothers and grandmothers, aunts and uncles, nieces and nephews all talking and shouting and running around in complete chaos. It was a lot for me at first, almost too much, but my husband brimmed with such excitement at every occasion, that I hesitantly went along with the chaos. Then we started having our own children, building our own version of that everyday Collini chaos. Every time I announced I was pregnant, Antonio's face lit up and he would spend nine months kissing my belly and asking me if I needed anything. The more I lived in that house, the more I learned what family really was."

"Then, when only a few months old, our daughter Katya got sick. Yellow skinned and in need of a liver transplant, we would visit her in the hospital, taking shifts from the waiting room because only so many people could fit in her room, gathering around her bed, holding her hand, comforting her. It was then I realized how important everyone is in a family, how miraculous each and every member is. Katya had a successful liver transplant this year and we go to sleep every night thankful for how well she's doing, praying there won't be any signs of organ rejection. We pray for her because she is an integral part of the Collini family."

Natalya never looks up, is too nervous to properly read emotion into the words she spent two days writing. But she stops here and closes her eyes and bites back the tears in order to finish. "And so is Alex. Without him, we all fall apart. Every day from here on out, for every one of us, will be darker. Every day has a hole and we know exactly why; we ache for that special child missing from our lives. Life can be tough. Life is tough. We can't keep up with Katya's medical bills, my husband just lost his job, and yet... and yet none of that matters. Alex is missing, he is in danger, and that is the only thing that matters. All I can ask is, please do not do this to us. Don't do anything to Alex, a boy who will have unconditional love and support from his vast family for the rest of his life. A boy who will know what family means without question, who won't understand anything but the love of a large family. Please let our Alex come home."

Still looking down, she folds up the paper and walks from the podium, where Antonio steps out and embraces her. He wipes the tears from his eyes as he squeezes her with all his might, presses his lips against the top of her head, kissing her for her words, her love.

Terry steps toward Steve Cardell, who stands next to an older couple he introduced as Arielle's grandparents. "Are you ready?" Terry asks.

Steve looks again at his notes, the message he spent all day constructing, and after listening to Natalya, realizes the mistake he has made. Rather than write a plea to their children's kidnapper, asking for the safe return of Arielle, Steve wrote a conviction. His speech says his daughter has a guardian angel, that her mother is watching over her, and that even if the worst happens, the two will be united. He is not sure if he truly believes it, but spending all day at his desk, staring at a family picture, the thought of Arielle and April reuniting was the only thought that comforted him. Standing here now on the police steps, Steve comprehends just how truly different his thinking is compared to the other families, how much they are pinning their hopes on an almost impossible outcome. He puts the speech back into his shirt pocket and tells Terry, "I'm sorry, but I don't think I can do it. Not today."

"Are you sure?"

"Yes. I'm sorry." Steve holds his palm against his pocket, holding the speech close, knowing it will be appropriate another day, perhaps when they confirm that Arielle and April truly are together. Perhaps he will read it at the service.

Terry gives Steve a sympathetic nod and turns toward Carrie Hughes. He notices that, for the first time, she is wearing make-up. Not a lot, but enough. She is dressed in beige slacks and a navy blouse. She has pulled her hair back, exposing more of her face, and though the bags under her eyes still loom large, she no longer looks distraught and lost, and instead just looks tired, like a mother tired of wondering where her daughter is.

Carrie walks to the podium and holds up a framed picture, the same picture that is circulating in most of the newspapers, television shots, and missing posters. Rather than just a close-up of Emily's face, this is the entire picture. The loop of a roller coaster juts up in the background and a stuffed giraffe rests in the comfort of her arms. "This is Emily Erin Hughes. She is in the sixth grade at Meadows Junior High. She plays soccer for the park district. She plays her radio loud, and when I open the door to her room, she is usually in front of the mirror singing into a microphone she made by taping all of our pens together. She doesn't like lima beans or brussel sprouts. She does like reading the Sunday paper with her dad, spreading out each section over the floor and lazily picking through them. She really only enjoys the funnies and Dear Abbey, but she'll pretend to read as long as he does. She likes the smell of his coffee but hates the taste."

"She used to be afraid of spiders, and though she claims she isn't anymore, prefers to point them out in the hopes that someone else will take care of them. She's doing well in school, but has trouble with math. She likes boys in her class, but doesn't like to talk about them, at least with us. She still watches cartoons Saturday mornings. Emily watches the cooking channel and says she wants to learn to cook but doesn't yet have the patience. She enjoys school, especially her friends, and tells her parents she loves them every day. She wants to be a veterinarian when she grows up because she loves animals and wants to make them better."

Carrie's eyes glisten and her voice begins to break. "Emily Erin Hughes is like most junior high girls. And just like most junior high girls, she is the most precious creature on this earth to her parents. She is young and she is eager to grow up. All I can do is ask, all I can do is plead, please let her grow up. Please let her come home. Please give us our daughter back."

Carrie holds the picture up for a moment more. She holds back her tears, holding onto the belief that what she has said makes sense, that everyone should be able to understand and agree with her. But before walking away, she cannot help but make one last request, a slight whisper that the microphones pick up, leaving a finishing emphasis to her words. "Please."

As she walks away, Terry waits, leaves the podium empty, letting the message soak in. For the first time since he met her, Terry senses the untapped strength within Carrie Hughes. Something has changed and exposed her growing will and force.

Terry hopes that if the abductor has any reservations, if there is the slightest chance he is holding back, even just delaying, that this press conference convinces him.

36

After the press conference, after watching Natalya and Carrie offer their heart-wrenching pleas, Terry had a renewed sense of optimism that things would turn out all right. They had to. But as the evening turned to night, his hope fades and he reverts back to the reality of the situation. Did he really think a plea from the parents was going to change the perp's mind? Did he really expect the kidnapper to show up at the station and turn himself in? Did he really think they would find the children unharmed after missing for so long?

At home and unable to sleep, Terry calls himself a fool one more time and twists the knob on his desk lamp, alternating the crisp white sheet of paper between light and shadow. He was supposed to be fishing this weekend, out on Lake Horn, one last trip before the winter. He was looking forward to this weekend, sitting in a boat, drinking beer, pulling in fish, and sleeping at his buddy's cabin. A simple escape. Little thinking, plenty to do. That's the way he likes it. That is what he takes pride in as a cop.

In Edgebrook, making arrests doesn't require any stupendous powers of deduction. There is never a need for a Sherlock Holmes, or even a Columbo. Terry is not a bloodhound, he is a working dog, and that is what Edgebrook needs. Work hard, work by the rules, and get the job done. The locals like him because of this straightforward tenacity as well as his honesty and fairness in every situation. There are laws, and if you break them, you are punished. Everyone knows that. Everyone accepts that.

But this case is so different. The criminal is flaunting his crimes, proud of his accomplishments. He has no respect for laws, neither those on the books nor those of human nature. He is devious and evil, and he is nothing like Terry has ever dealt with. Terry wonders again if he is right for the case, if the children would be in better hands if he were off fishing while someone like Agent Samperson, someone worldly, someone who understands the complexities of life, handled the case.

Tonight however, Terry's renewed vigor from the evening's press conference has broken down into despair, almost fear, and he uses that fear to review the facts one more time. His mind has dug deep ruts into the facts of the case, burrowed along the same paths leading nowhere, that he accepts there is nothing new for him to find. His mind is useless. He turns back to the beginning one more time, hoping a mental cog catches and creates some sort of momentum.

Terry starts with the first and simplest question, who is a suspect? He needs to think like Art Morell, at least once, and start with the idea that everyone is a suspect. Terry makes three columns across the blank page and scrawls a heading on each.

`Suspect`   `Motive`   `Crime`

What did Art Morrell say? Amongst his babblings, what simple idea caught Terry off guard? He said, if the motive were to write a book, to garner fame from this ordeal, then Terry should put his own name near the top. So that is exactly what he does, scribbling Me, then crossing it out and printing a more formal `Terrence Kruthers`. Under `Motive` he writes `Fame and Money`, and under `Crime` he writes `Kidnap three children. Cut off two pinky toes.`

Writing the last line, he shakes his head at the insanity of it all. Who cuts off a child's toe just to make some money? Who is that obsessed with fame? Definitely not someone who would rather be fishing. Only one name comes to mind, even though Terry questions if the man could truly do it. But Terry obligingly writes it down on the next open line under suspect. `Art Morrell`

The motive is the same as his. So is the crime. But as Terry studies the page, he realizes why this entry is such a departure from his normal thinking. The crime has always been kidnapping three children, but it also included molestation and probably murder.

What if the crime is just what they know and nothing else? Kidnap three children, cut off two toes, and that's it. These are serious crimes, but they are not rape. They are not murder.

Working back across the sheet, moving from Crime to Motive, Terry wonders if the motive is merely to accomplish what they know, kidnap three children and sever two of their toes. That's it. Working from there, Terry has to ask again, who would have that as a motive?

Art's book is back in the spotlight, as is Art himself. Edgebrook is on the map. Terry has gained momentary fame, although barely five minutes worth. What else? What else has changed? What did he learn today at the press conference?

Technically, nothing. He already knew the day's message. Family is important. Parents love their children and wish for their safety. Who doesn't know that? Yet why is he up again past midnight, making himself once more go over facts he already knows by heart? Why was there an almost awed silence in the police station after the conference, whispered shuffles as investigators moved about with intent, resolving anew to find the children?

Why had the town changed so much, with so many people volunteering to help? Why did nothing else matter? School productions were put on hold. The city council discussed nothing but the missing children. Every officer was working on this case, and yet all other crime had either stopped or become so trivial no one reported it.

Why did newspaper, magazine, and television crews camp out on the station's front lawn? Why did every newscast, every radio station, continually provide updates?

And why did everyone watch? Why were people across the nation tuning in, discussing it, attending vigils and sending their prayers?

Children went missing all the time. A horribly sad fact, but true. What was so different about this case? It couldn't just be Art's book. It couldn't just be that there was a connection to an old case. There had to be something else.

In the bottom right corner of the page, Terry writes out Hope. He then underlines it three times. Is that the difference? Because the children escaped in the prior case, because they survived the abduction and came home, did people suddenly have hope it could happen again?

Hope

Is that the word he has been looking for? Is that the spark this case provides, the reason there is so much interest? Yes and no, Terry thinks. He would have said yes a week ago, but he reads what people are saying in newspapers and blogs. And while still hopeful, there is a feeling that the children have been gone too long to return unharmed. Not impossible, but unlikely, and the national hope is fading fast. But the interest is still there. Why?

Perhaps it is now real to them. It may have started just because it was interesting with three children abducted at once. This interest only grew with *The Spying Toes* link. And now, a morbid curiosity rises as people learn about the families, read the perpetrator's notes, and discover the horror of the severed toes. These are all hooks, pulling people into this case rather than the hundreds of other abductions. This story has meaning to people, and now they care.

Trying to find the right word, Terry writes Realization under the motive column, but it doesn't quite capture what he wants. He crosses it out and puts down Personalization, but that isn't correct either. He then writes two lines:

```
To Give Meaning
To Make People Care
```

He studies the words and realizes it isn't just how people feel about the case, it is how they feel about everything. The town is suddenly warmer, closer, and more concerned about one another. Edgebrook's residents care for each other, their families, and their children in a way they didn't before the abductions.

Terry thinks about his weekly phone call home, just a few hours ago. He droned on to his mother about how badly he needed to solve this case, how frustrated he was by the lack of a breakthrough. Then, when he was done, unprompted and with more feeling than he had in years, he finished the call by saying, "I love you." Normally he said it with an obligatory tone, skipping the "I" and just finishing with a quickly mumbled, "Love you." This time he said it deliberately and his mother replied, "I love you too, Terrence."

Something has changed, even within himself.

Who would understand? Who knew this would happen?

A name comes to him and it feels wrong. Terry revolts at the possibility, but following Art's advice to be complete and go with the craziest ideas, he writes it down in the Suspect column. As he does, as he sees the name on paper, he experiences a momentary sense of revelation. Maybe, just maybe, it's possible.

But how can he find out? He can't suggest the name as a suspect; it's more ludicrous than one of Art Morell's novels. Terry rubs his temples, and as feverishly as his thoughts are running, he knows if he puts his head down he will fall asleep at his desk. In the morning, if he reads this piece of paper with the clarity of rest and a cup of coffee, he will crumple it up and throw it away. No, he will shred it.

Terry forces himself up and tries to keep himself on the right side of sleepy consciousness. He drives to the station and enters, traversing the eerie quiet of 2:00 A.M. He goes to the storage room and grabs the GPS transmitter from a back shelf. A sales rep gave a presentation on the device, explaining how they could place it under a car and it would communicate its GPS coordinates, allowing them to know where the car was at all times without physically tailing it. Everyone agreed it was a good idea before realizing that their department never tailed cars except the occasional drunk pulling out of Nellie's on a Saturday night. The device was boxed away and forgotten, unused until now.

In Terry's sleep-deprived stupor, driven by the idea that he has to do something, that the case will not be solved on its current course, Terry takes the GPS unit without signing it out. He reads the instructions, tracking his own position as he drives through Edgebrook, and spots the car he wants waiting conveniently outside in the driveway.

Terry knows this is illegal without a search warrant. He knows that if he's caught he won't be able to explain his intentions. He'll be taken off the case, probably suspended, and possibly fired.

Looking around the empty suburban street, Terry lays down on his back, inches himself under the rear bumper, and clamps the GPS unit out of sight.

Something has to be done. Something out of the ordinary. Terry is convinced of that, if little else, and now he can go home and sleep.

37

Carrie raises the cup of coffee to her nose, closes her eyes and inhales. She has not had coffee in years. It's a dark roast, Jim's favorite, and she enjoys the stiff aroma, the swirls of steam, and the brazen heat against her face. She sips delicately from the cup, careful not to burn herself. This is a good moment, she thinks. Sipping her coffee once more, she clasps it in her hands and watches the leaves blow outside the kitchen window. She knows this is a good moment.

Moments like this will no longer be tied to the physical events around her. Instead, the little yellow pills, and her body's reaction to them, will dictate her motivations, her good moods and bad moods, her energy and her desires. This, according to the doctor, will be life, medicated.

It might have sounded scary had she cared, were she not so frightened of her status quo. But now, sipping coffee and feeling a bit like her old self again, she can't be anything but grateful for the yellow tablets. She will do as she is told, writing down her moods, monitoring the effect of each pill and charting it over time, learning to predict her body's reaction like any other periodic event: the rising and setting of the sun, the passing of each season, and whether she felt like crying or smiling.

Over time, she will come to hate the swings. That is what Dr. Henry told her. Over time, they will try to get the doses just right, the reactions just right, so that she can maintain a steady-state existence. "Functional" was the term the doctor used. That word stood out, and as clinical as he tried to make it sound, from where she has been, "functional" sounds like a wonderful place to be. And to actually have good moments, like now, is more than she could have hoped for.

Carrie sips slowly, allowing the coffee to turn cold. She pours out the last few drops, and rather than place her cup in the sink, she rinses it out and puts it in the dishwasher. Seeing that the dishwasher is empty, that one lonely cup rests inside, she takes it back to the sink, adds a dab of soap and scrubs the cup clean. She then pulls out a dishtowel, wipes it dry and puts it away. She wipes down the sides of the sink and rinses the sponge. The industriousness of each motion creates a sense of accomplishment.

Finished, she heads upstairs, and rather than turn down the hallway toward the master bedroom, enters Emily's room. She has been here recently, since Emily went missing, but that was during a bad moment. She looked around confused, as if she had taken a turn onto the wrong road late at night, her headlights exposing a place never seen before. The room seemed foreign and she left. But now she looks around the room and thinks, this is my daughter's room. This is Emily's room. The photo collages on the walls, the necklaces and hair ties sprawled across the dresser, the white bear playing the drums on her nightstand. The alarm clock covered by stickers of the planets, the book *Girls Rule* folded open next to it. The dolphin comforter, the pictures from Cedar Point, and the silver karaoke machine... so many things. This is Emily's room, and the crushing downside of being normal hits Carrie in two waves.

The first wave is for herself and the realization that she may lose, may have already lost, her only daughter. In a way, she already felt like she had lost everything, like the world were slipping from her grasp, and Emily's abduction was just one more component of that loss. But now, as the rest of the world comes into focus, Emily's abduction becomes more intense, more acute. Emily is gone and may never come home. Carrie sits on the bed, brushes the pillowcases with her hand, pushes the creases on the bedspread away from her, and sobs. What will she do without her Emily?

Then the second wave hits, the wave for Emily. How lost is she? How frightened is she? How much does she wish, above all, to be here in her room again, to sleep soundly in her own bed and to have her life back? How much will she miss in life? Even if she does come home, how scarred will her outlook be, how lonesome and sorrowful will her life be beneath the heavy weight that nothing will ever be the same? Carrie clutches the bedspread at her sides, slowly pulling its edges out from beneath the mattress, trying to say her child's name, trying to tell her she loves her and that she is sorry, but unable to because her sobs steal every breath.

This is part of a good moment. This is what good moments will feel like. This is real. This is life. This is unbearable.

38

St Mchls Hsp

Natalya reads the name on the caller ID and feels momentarily disorientated, like missing a stair step. St. Michael's Hospital. She has seen this name flash on the caller ID a hundred times. Calls from the hospital. Updates from the numerous tests they put Katya through. Doctors calling with their uncertain diagnosis, until finally they determined she had a liver disease. She can't remember ever receiving a call from this number and hearing good news.

"Gioia!"

"What?" Antonio's mother responds from down the hall.

"Where's Katya?"

"Right here."

"You're sure!"

"Yes. Why? Who's on the phone?"

With Katya's safety confirmed, Natalya lifts the receiver off the cradle. "Hello?"

"Mrs. Collini?"

"Yes?"

"Hi, this is Andrew Torsburg, from Saint Michael's Hospital. I am an executive administrator and member of the board here at the hospital."

"What's going on?"

"We recently received a call about your current standing with the hospital."

Natalya places her feet on the floor and braces for support. It is not her worst fear, Katya is all right, no word on Alex, but still, Antonio lost his job a few days ago. They haven't even discussed it.

"Already?" she asks, incredulously. Were they canceling his insurance already? Did the hospital's accounting arm, the one that sent them crushing bills every month, somehow know their payments were about to dry up completely?

"Already what?"

Natalya has not spoken to Antonio about their situation, has not put words to their plight, and is not about to now. She holds her breath and wonders how long the silence can last.

"Mrs. Collini? Already what?"

"Nothing. Never mind."

"All right. As I was saying, we recently received a call, from one of our most generous benefactors."

"Yes."

"This person has a strong relationship with Saint Michaels, and cares deeply, not only about the hospital, but about all of its patients. I guess you could say, he thinks of Saint Michaels Hospital as part of his family."

"Part of his family," Natalya repeats, unsure of where this is going.

"In fact, without this benefactor's assistance, we would have never been able to start the new oncology unit that opened this year. Have you heard about it?"

"I think so." Natalya remembers all the bulldozers and cranes outside Katya's window. The time the parking lot was closed. The construction signs and yellow tape. She seems to remember a large billboard near the entrance, boasting about the new Edward T. Couris Oncology Unit, while her one-year-old daughter lay in a room upstairs suffering liver failure. "Why?"

"Oh yes, my apologies. I understand you are going through a lot, so I'll get to the point. Anyway, with your approval, our benefactor would like to assist with your current outstanding medical bills."

"What do you mean assist?"

"They would like to pay off your current debt, as well as help with future fees in relation to your daughter's condition."

Natalya reaches for the cross on her neck.

"Mrs. Collini?"

"What was that? I don't think I heard you correctly?"

"I said, this benefactor of Saint Michael's would like to pay off your current medical bills, all related to the treatments of Katya Collini. They would like to help clean the slate, so to say, and even help with her future bills, at least what your insurance will not cover. Now, they don't mean to presume anything, and naturally don't mean to impose…"

"Why?" Natalya asks incredulously, rising and walking down the hallway, peeking around the corner to see Katya staring up at a singing purple dinosaur on the TV, clapping her hands out of rhythm to the song.

"Why? Well, for starters, this person understands you are in a very difficult situation, a most horrible nightmare, and though this won't help directly, our patron wanted to help in whatever way he could, even if it's just giving you one less thing to worry about. Like I said, I'm certain you have more serious concerns right now, so the hope is that this helps a little."

"Does he really mean all of it? Does he know how much we owe?"

The voice on the other end laughs. "Not exactly. I mean, we don't just release that information without your approval, but I can assure you that it won't be a problem."

Returning to her bedroom and closing the door behind her, Natalya comes clean. "My husband just lost his job. We're going to lose our insurance."

"Oh my. I'm very sorry. Our friend will have to take that into consideration, but from what I've seen, when he finds a cause worth helping, he can be most generous."

"I don't know what to say."

"Well," Andrew says, "there's going to be quite a lot of paperwork. Although I'm sure our mutual friend would not mind paying everything outright, there are ways to make everything tax deductible. So you'll have to meet with a lawyer and fill out all the paperwork. We'll prepare everything beforehand, so you'll simply come to the hospital and sign the forms. I know that probably sounds like a large undertaking right now, so we'll set it up, and if you're not ready, we'll just put it on hold. The bottom line is you won't pay another dime toward Katya's medical costs."

"I still don't know what to say."

"That's all right, Mrs. Collini. My understanding is that..."

"Wait! I mean to say thank you! I can say that much, thank you, thank you, but I don't know, I'm speechless. Thank you!"

"It's not me, Mrs. Collini. And though this generous patron would like to remain anonymous, there is a simple way to thank him."

"There is?" Alarms go off as she sits back down.

"It's not much. Simply, if St. Michael's Hospital is brought up again, be sure to say good things. As I mentioned, this benefactor has already contributed a lot to St. Michael's, and he would like it to be thought of as not just a hospital, but as a pillar of care in our community."

"Yes, of course. Gladly," Natalya says. "Have I...? Have I ever said anything bad? I hope I..."

"No, no, Mrs. Collini. I'm just saying, for example, like today's article in *Time*, it would be a nice gesture to let them know that Saint Michael's is helping. I mean, that came out wrong. This is not a payoff or anything like that. You do not have to do anything in return, but like yesterday's press conference, when you said your medical bills were forcing you into bankruptcy, that doesn't reflect well on the hospital..."

Yesterday's press conference? Natalya hardly said anything at all, and she doesn't remember mentioning St. Michaels. And today's article in *Time*? It must just be hitting newsstands, but Natalya has no idea what it says. "Of course," she repeats. Whatever it takes. She is ready to tattoo 'I Love St. Michaels' on her forehead, if that's what they want. All she can do is mutter "thank you" over and over, and as Andrew Torsburg ends the conversation, she watches the words 'St Mchls Hsp' disappear from the caller ID, turning to emptiness, and she wonders if it was a mirage. Or a prank.

She picks up the phone again, and rather than dial the number he has given her, calls the number she has memorized for the pediatric ward, asking for an administrator of the hospital, an Andrew Torsburg. The receptionist doesn't know him, but transfers her to another desk, where she is transferred again, and then put on hold. Natalya's mind turns pessimistic as she waits. How many other families have trouble affording their medical bills? Who just goes around paying them off, for nothing in return? How many phone calls have started in earnest about the abduction, until they realized it was a reporter trying to get a story. How many times had they...?

"Hello. This is Andrew Torsburg."

Natalya hears the steady voice she was just talking to, the tone of a man who gets things done, who doesn't seem surprised when miracles happen.

"This is Natalya Collini."

"Yes, Natalya, do you have some more questions?"

"I was wondering," she starts, looking around her bedroom with concern that she is about to look silly, scatter-brained at the least, but knowing she has to do it for her own surety. "Did we just talk?"

"Yes. Yes we did."

"Okay, that's all. I just... thank you. I just wanted to say thank you again."

"Actually, one thing I forgot, or I wasn't quite sure how to say, but I hope everything turns out for the best with your son. I hope he comes home."

"Thank you."

Natalya puts on her shoes, grabs a jacket from the hall closet, and tells Gioia she'll be right back, closing the door without answering the litany of questions. She gets into the station wagon and heads to town. This is not enough, as Antonio still lost his job, but it is a good start. It will help their odds of finding other work. It is something.

Turning onto Main Street, she parks at the far end in order to keep her distance from City Hall and the police station, and specifically the carnival of reporters on the front lawn. She keeps her head down as she steps through the Book Nook's red awning and veers straight to the magazine rack.

Time magazine is on the front row, where the cover displays a patchwork of leaves, delicate and dry, spread across a forest floor. In the middle, cut through the leaves, is the outline of a footprint. Superimposed over the footprint is a single question mark. Further to the right, near the bottom, Natalya reads the headline, "*The Spying Toes: A Sequel?*" She checks the price, opens her wallet, and grabs two copies, one for everyone to read through, and another to hold onto. She thinks about this second copy and questions if she really wants another reminder, something to stumble across at the bottom of a box that will bring back the worst moment of her life. 'Where's Alex, momma?' She puts the second copy back, pays the cashier, ignores his glances of recognition, and heads back to her car.

Flipping the magazine's pages, she finds one long article describing the details of the old case and the new one, comparing similarities and dissecting differences. Graphic overlays fill the pages, showing the number of children kidnapped each year along with the odds of different outcomes. Found Alive. Found Dead. Never Found. She has seen similar statistics in the paper and tries to avoid them. She isn't playing odds. There is only one outcome, and that is all that matters. Near the end of the article, she finds insets on each of the three families. Natalya goes straight to "The Collinis."

"Antonio and Natalya Collini are an old world family, a large clan that watches over and protects itself. During our interview, three of the Collini children were present, two uncles and their wives, as well as the family's matriarch, Gioia Collini. They all tromped through the small house, engaged in overlapping conversations, while Antonio and Natalya tried to answer my questions amidst the bustle. Antonio held their daughter Katya in his lap, picking toys off the ground to distract her, while Natalya stacked them in neat piles at the base of the couch, keeping some sort of order. When Gioia enters with a wooden spoon so I can try her bolognese sauce, the picture is complete for the Italian-American cliché."

Natalya stops reading, recollecting that afternoon when the man from *Time* arrived, a quiet but watchful man, and how nice they tried to be to him, how they welcomed him into their home as best they could. She wonders if while leaving, as he thanked them for their hospitality, he already knew he would paint them with such a simple, cloddish brush stroke? An "Italian-American cliché". The problem though, is that it's true. Natalya has always been aware of their cliché existence, but she has never really put words to the idea, vocally or internally, and to see it in national print aggravates her. Over the years, she has given in with a grinding acquiescence, a slow acceptance. The Collinis are one big spaghetti-eating family. Antonio, with his curly black locks and the Italian horn around his neck, who likes to sit at the table and laugh while playing ignorant to what happens around him; would he even get mad at this article? Or would he shrug it off, laugh, and belt out a verse from "That's Amore"?

Natalya contemplates the arc that got her here, how she thought his Italian mannerisms were endearing, how she let his familial customs take hold while letting pass the strict ways of her Polish and Russian family. Once they were married, she realized she had no right to ask him to change. The one thing she did put her foot down on was the opening in Ohio. She wanted the move. Not only did it seem like a good opportunity, it got Antonio out from under the control of his mother. That was Natalya's lone act of defiance, and that was what brought them to Edgebrook, unwittingly settling down in the home of *The Spying Toes*. She knows none of this is her fault, but if she never pushed for that move…?

"But the Collinis are not new to tragedy. Their young daughter Katya has spent both years of her life in and out of the hospital, undergoing tests and treatments until last spring, when she was diagnosed with a degenerative liver disease. After waiting unsuccessfully for a donor, Natalya had a portion of her liver cut out and transplanted into their baby girl, the one with uncharacteristically blond curls. So far, the surgery has been a success, but complications are normal for the first year, a dark cloud they haven't made their way out of yet. And with a lifetime prescription for anti-rejection medication, they will live their lives burdened with the anxiety that rejection could occur at any time."

Natalya nods at the truth of this anxiety. The journalist did not mention that it is an anxiety they can do nothing about, an anxiety that is better left unsaid, unwritten, in the hope that it subsides over time and slips into the crevices of daily life.

"With this newest tragedy, the Collinis ramble about their house, grasping at trivialities for their distraction, discussing the kids' bus ride to school or whether there is too much garlic in the sauce, using all of their virtue to keep smiles on their faces. Even though the Collinis can be described as cliché, they are a cliché of a family that will support one another, a family with an unwavering strength of togetherness that will hold tight no matter the outcome."

Natalya rereads these last sentences and feels slightly placated. She hopes this "strength of togetherness" will see them through, although she wishes the reporter understood how empty the house is, just how large the hole is without Alex.

Natalya closes the magazine, flips it onto the passenger seat and drives home, preparing for the first question from her mother-in-law. She is not disappointed either and sighs when she hears, "Where have you been?"

"Out."

"Doing what?"

"Thinking."

Gioia's brow wrinkles to this response. "What's this about Antonio's job?"

"I don't know," Natalya lies, closing her eyes. "Why?"

"His boss, Mr. Alvio or Alverezzi or I'm not sure…"

"He called? What did he say?"

"He said something about corporate changing their mind. Something about publicity. He said Antonio wouldn't lose his job."

"Lose his job?" Natalya asks, trying to look confused as she bites her grin.

"That's what I said. How could he lose his job if he hasn't even been going?"

"That is strange."

"What's going on, Natalya?"

Natalya pauses, feeling gratitude for the magazine she has slid into her jacket.

"Did Antonio lose his job? Answer me, Natalya. What's going on?"

"I don't know. I'm going to take a nap now. I'm tired."

"You've been taking a lot of naps. A lot. Do you always sleep this much?"

"It's just stress." Natalya turns toward the back bedroom and smirks to herself, smirks at the cliché of the nagging mother-in-law.

She retreats, lies down with the magazine still in hand, and closes her eyes to indulge in a moment of relief. Antonio has his job back, and Katya's medical bills have been paid. Her second and third biggest worries, gone. She wonders if she can allow herself to enjoy this momentary good fortune, even with Alex still missing. Yes, she tells herself, but only for a moment.

39

Harry and Ruth Aberdeen keep their matching luggage in the guest bedroom, unsure of how much run of the house they have. They are guests, and though Steve has never made them feel like they were imposing, he has never made them feel welcome. They are April's parents, Arielle's grandparents, and without those bonds, what is there? They are here because of Arielle, and Steve is accommodating that.

Over dinner, Steve explains everything he knows. He covers the timeline, from the Friday morning Arielle asked if she could sleep over at Emily's house, to this morning when he picked them up at the airport. He tells them all the details about the toes and the notes that came with them. They hold back their emotions, trying to take everything in and still be objective. Steve goes over the theories offered by the police, the correlations with the previous case, the search parties and the church vigils. They ask what time the Baptist church is open and if they have daily services.

Afterwards, after all of their questions and all of his answers, after Ruth clears the table and Harry makes coffee, they sit in silence. It is into this silence that Steve utters, "I'm thinking of remodeling the craft room."

Ruth and Harry exchange glances. They know the room. Off the kitchen, before the mudroom. The door is always open a crack, just enough to look in but never enough to enter. It is where April nursed Arielle, knitted her baby booties and crocheted her snuggly. April built a mobile for the crib and made a photo journal of their early years. She was never an expert at any one craft but dabbled competently in whatever caught her fancy. She enjoyed it, and that was why they dedicated a room to her hobbies. A craft room. April's craft room.

"What are you going to do with it?" Ruth asks. When she can, when she knows she's alone in the house, she likes to step into the room and absorb the pictures, the smells, the presence. It's the closest she can come to April. She has no idea Harry does the same thing.

"I was thinking of making it a study room for Arielle. That desk in her room is too small. I don't think she has enough space."

"Why not just get her a bigger desk?"

"Her room's too small already. And I think it's good to have a place of her own, to study without distraction. No TV, no phone, just a place to do her schoolwork."

"When were you thinking of doing this?" Harry asks.

"I was thinking tomorrow."

Harry takes off his glasses, rubs his eyes, and puts them back on. He picks up a napkin and folds it. A bead of sweat forms on the crown of his balding head.

"What will Arielle think?" Ruth asks.

"She knows her desk isn't working out. She complains about it all the time."

"I mean, what will she think of not having her mother's room anymore?"

"That's part of the point too. I think it's always been... different for Arielle."

"Different?"

"Strange. Almost eerie, to be honest. We never go in that room. We never talk about it. Rather than having things out in the open to remember April, it's like we're keeping them tucked away, hidden. Does that make sense?"

"Yes," Ruth says, "but don't you think she will appreciate it when she's older? When she has more questions about her mother?"

"I'm not throwing anything out. I figure we'll box it up and put it in the basement. Then when she wants to, we can go through it together, and I can explain everything to her."

"Oh."

"I would rather put up more pictures, more mementos of April around the house, than keep one room closed off like a museum exhibit. I think the house has always been too cold, I think it has always been sad, because of that room, and I don't want that for Arielle anymore."

"I think we've just..." Ruth starts, speaking for both of them, "we've just wanted to keep everything we can about April around, try to keep it as it was. But if it's not best for Arielle, then I understand. If you think this is right. ..."

"I do."

The yellow plastic bag behind the sewing machine is the most difficult for Steve. It contains four rolls of felt, all the same size, all different colors.

A mauve, an orange, a leafy green, and a tepid yellow. The colors do not match and probably were not meant to. The receipt is still in the bag and April probably would have held the rolls up to whatever project she was starting, figuring out what she liked best, and returning the rest. She did this a lot. The receipt is dated April 17th. One week after her birthday. Three days before the accident. Steve has no idea what these felt rolls were going to make and never will.

They pack everything else into boxes, marking them and stacking them in the basement. Steve and Harry clutch opposite sides of the sewing machine and lug it down stairs while Ruth holds the doors. They decide, for now, to keep the rocking chair upstairs. They have thrown nothing out, just boxed and moved everything, all except this plastic bag of unused felt rolls. It would be easy to throw it in a box, squeeze it against something fragile and claim it for packing material, but Steve wants to remain practical. It is junk and needs to be disposed of. April's projects are no more. He needs to move on.

The room is empty and he should throw these felt rolls away.

The idea of moving on has lingered in his thoughts for the past year, but he had no impetus to act on. Over the past two weeks, every day that Arielle remained missing he grew more certain this was the right thing to do. His thoughts crept to the Columbus Museum of Art. Although April confined her crafts to sewing, knitting and the like, she always had an appreciation for paintings. So about once a year she would mention a new exhibit she saw in the paper, casually say that it sounded interesting and how long it would be on display. Within a few weeks they would rise early on a Saturday morning, drive to Columbus, and make a day of it.

They would meander through the new exhibit, April studying and commenting on what she liked and disliked, and when they left, someone always stood by the exit handing out a brochure of upcoming exhibits. They never had two exhibits running simultaneously. That would be too much trouble, too much to deal with. Steve understands. Maintaining two exhibits is too much to cope with. And so, when a particular display was through, they would take it down, box it up, and begin preparing for the next exhibit.

And so, Steve finds himself having wandered into Arielle's room while holding the plastic bag of felt rolls that will never take the form of whatever April was planning. He carefully sets it into the garbage can by Arielle's desk, never to be emptied. He looks around, trying to understand how this is the snapshot of his daughter's room that will persist. When the concept becomes too heavy, when he needs air, he steps into the hallway and closes the door, leaving just enough space to look in but not enough to enter.

40

Jim can't sleep, not that he expects to nowadays. He knows Carrie is awake too, releasing an occasional sigh as she rolls over, burying her face in the pillow in the hopes that suffocation will bring sleep, only to release an escaping gasp.

Jim first met with the psychologist the day after the press conference, insisting on seeing someone different than whom Carrie saw. She was a nice enough woman with plain features and an accepting presence, and she nodded her head in a way that seemed to invite Jim to open up and tell her everything.

"I haven't been a good husband," he admitted, studying her measured reaction, trying to peel through the layers of her muted judgment. Right now, he has her sympathy. She understands how Carrie's depression must have been difficult on him and she probably worries that he's blaming himself. But he wonders how quickly that sympathy will falter if he admits to the affair. "I mean, I watched her change, watched her struggle, and never did anything about it, never even asked her how she was doing."

"This is hard on everyone involved. Depression is not an affliction that affects one person, but like all diseases, affects everyone in their lives, especially those that care the deepest."

Jim wanted to tell her why he couldn't mention the affair. He wanted to tell her how, when they first started dating in college, one of Jim's roommates had just been caught cheating on his girlfriend and was trying to woo her back. He told Carrie the story as they eavesdropped through his bedroom wall, listening to his roommate plead over the phone. Jim wanted to tell the psychologist what Carrie said to him, without worry or accusation, but with a simple resolve, "You know, if you ever cheat on me, I'm gone." Jim knew she meant it, and always would.

The other Carrie, the one that had crept into their house the past few years, the depressed woman who showed no joy, probably would not have cared. She would have accepted any situation, would have accepted everything as her own fault. But as glimpses of the old Carrie emerge, determined and forthright, he feels a growing fear in telling her. She will not understand and she will not accept. He is sure of that. And so, lying in bed, he holds back one truth, and with that secret, finds himself unable to open up his fears about Emily, his inconsolable worry that he may never see her again.

From the darkness that wraps their masquerade of sleep, Carrie calls out his name.

"Yes."

She says nothing for a long time, but with each night passing so slowly, they have grown accustomed to these stretches, embraced them with a burdened ownership. "Do you blame me?" she finally asks.

"Blame you?"

"Yes."

Jim puzzles over the question, unsure of what she's asking, certain it is important.

"I used to walk Emily over to Arielle's," she explains, "I used to call the Cardells when she stayed over, to make sure everything was all right. If I had done either of those things, if I was more involved with Emily's life, like a normal mother..."

Jim watches the shadows from the oak outside swaying in the bedroom, projected onto the ceiling by moonlight. He gathers the weight of the question and ponders the implications of his response. How long has she wondered this? Has she always blamed herself? He cannot turn to look at her but senses Carrie watches the same overhead entanglement of boughs, expecting the worst judgment possible to befall a mother.

"Carrie, " he starts, realizing it is not enough, and sternly repeats for emphasis, "Carrie! I do not blame you. I do not blame you in the slightest bit!"

Carrie waits, letting the echoes and the intensity of his words fade, before responding. "I do."

"You what?"

"I blame myself."

"You did nothing wrong."

"If I were a better mother, if I did what I was supposed to..."

"How could you have prevented this? Someone took Emily. Someone abducted her. We can't watch her all the time. We can't lock her in her room."

"But if I..."

"Carrie, there's nothing you could have done to avoid this. It wasn't your fault."

"I'm sure..."

"We don't even know what happened. They got off the bus. They went to the park and into the woods. You can go to those woods almost any time and you'll find children playing by themselves. This is not your fault."

"I just..."

"You just what?"

Carrie rolls to her side, away from Jim. "I just wish I were a better mother."

Jim's mouth opens but the words stick. He closes his mouth and thinks, before finally uttering, "Emily loves you."

Jims waits, waits for her to say something, but nothing happens and a strong gust blows outside. He wonders if he has failed Carrie again, not told her what she needs to hear, until he feels a light touch against the side of his leg, the circular caress of her ring finger. His hand reaches down and embraces hers, palm against palm, fingers clasped, and they both squeeze tight.

41

Lovely, a tiny, Texas, panhandle town, sees unusually high mail volume, most of which is not meant for its residents. After the first message came through its doors, federal agents thoroughly searched the postal facility, but uncovered nothing. The FBI did not predict the perp would send another message in the same manner, and therefore missed the opportunity to obtain the package sent to Art before it was restamped, before more hands had touched it. They were not going to miss a third opportunity. An officer now remained in Lovely full time, monitoring every package and noting its final destination, studying it for anything suspicious.

Which is why no one noticed the small package that arrived in Peace, Indiana. Just like in Lovely, a postal employee opened the package to find another package inside along with instructions for its express overnight delivery. It is unusual to find cash inside to pay for the shipping charges rather than the usual check, but not unheard of. "Peace" is stamped in the top-right corner and the package is sent on its way without anyone noticing the final forwarding address, a Detective Terrence Kruthers of Edgebrook, Ohio.

But the police department still screens all incoming mail, and the little brown package tied with a red cloth ribbon does not go unnoticed. Terry meets the forensic team in their trailer as they prepare to surgically open the package. Since the newspapers have printed how the first toes arrived by mail, he knows there is a good chance this is a hoax. When one of the technicians unwraps it and then opens the cardboard box inside, out slides a small black velvet box, and though there is nothing distinguishable about it, Terry knows it is identical to the first two.

Using two pointed metal rods, a technician pries open the jewelry box, and the implications are immediate. This is not a hoax. A small pinky toe, painted in the same red, the nail outlined with eyeliner, stands serenely on end. The severed side is tucked into the slot meant for the band of a ring, hidden from view, and the toe looks eerily like a parlor trick, as if someone were hiding beneath the table and had pushed his toe through the slot, about to wiggle his digit to everyone's shock.

"It's fresh," one of the technicians says, trying to remain professional.

But Terry understands the implication. The owner of this toe was alive recently and might still be. The children might still be alive.

Like before, a sheet of paper is folded inside the cardboard box and a technician grasps it with needle nose pliers and pulls it out. As a professional, he is careful not to touch the box, as he does not want to contaminate it. As a human being, he is even more careful not to touch the toe.

When the note comes out, another object trapped behind the note pops out with it, emitting a beep before landing on the examining table. A sealed plastic trinket, not much larger than a business card, lands on the counter. A loop of wire hangs from one end and its purpose becomes immediately apparent.

They don't recognize the device from the eight LCD squares, displaying 05:59:59:99. But as the bottom two numbers start racing down, they realize it's a small counter, marking hours, minutes, seconds and hundredths of a second, with the bottom numbers wheeling down to 00 again and again at a furious pace. The device counts off 6 seconds before anyone even moves. The technician on the other side of the table unfolds the note, hoping it will tell them what finality the plastic device counts toward.

you win.
you win and I win.
you win most compelling and I win most compelled.
you win because you get them back.
I win because I am human.

But. but. but.
What an ugly condition we humans are?
I give up, I retire, I touch the sunset red
But I still cringe at the blemish.
I am still angered.
Once
That's all it takes. Once to be once.
So for my gift of parting,
I want the one who got away.

That is the offer, that is the trade.
One for three. Three for one. All for one.

Andy Alone.
Andy Unfollowed.
Andy Unnoticed.

Andy begins at 38.11484° -80.600609°
Andy ends at 38.13962° -80.559238°

Time heals all wounds. It does not right all wrongs. We were
wronged. We seek restitution. We seek revenge.

At 06:00:00:00 I offer
  Three for one
At 00:00:00:00 I offer
  Nothing

    Terry studies the timer: 05:56:25:00. The last digits count down a
hundred hundredths of a second, then another hundred, then a hundred
more. The numbers blur together and provide no useful information except
to indicate how quickly time passes. Ten seconds pass while Terry watches
the simple timer. The note gives them six hours, and they are now down to
5 hours, 54 minutes and 58 seconds. 57... 56... 55...

42

"Any word?" Agent Samperson asks during a lull, his voice emanating from the black speakerphone inside Conference Room A at the Edgebrook Police Department.

"He should be here any minute," Terry says. He looks around the conference room one more time, contemplating that the case is coming to a conclusion and these are the people that will see it through. Agent Sebold heads up the FBI SWAT team that is waiting outside. Agent Dietrich is the tech specialist in charge of surveillance, monitoring and tracking the final showdown. Officers Manzie and Taylor will help coordinate Edgebrook's police efforts, although they remain quiet and subordinate to the FBI, who appear much better prepared for the upcoming scenario.

Baumgardner sits in a corner. He will remain at the station, working with the press to keep this final mission as quiet as possible. Finally, on the speakerphone, Agent Samperson and his colleagues provide guidance from a conference room in their Columbus headquarters.

Terry shuffles through his papers one more time, rereading the latest note from the perp. "Let's go through the scenarios one more time, see if there's anything we missed."

"The kidnapper sent us a note," Agent Sebold starts in, irritated by the repetition. "He wants to trade the children for Andy Frempt, the kid that got away thirty years ago. If he doesn't get Andy at the coordinates provided within the specified time limit, he will kill the children. So we're going to bug Andy, send him in, and apprehend the perp at the transaction point."

Terry swallows. Normally, he would operate in the same straight-forward manner as Agent Sebold. But straight-forward detective work has gotten him nowhere. Once again they're just following the perp's notes, following instructions. And Terry's one chance at doing some real work, stealing the department's GPS tracking device and putting it on a car in the middle of the night, has provided no information. Terry has recorded his suspect's movements and found he drove around Edgebrook just like anyone else would, never going anywhere out of the ordinary, never going into the forest where the children were abducted. And with this latest note, Terry is now certain his one attempt at detective work was wrong. He won't get another chance.

"I assume the perpetrator expects us to bug Andy," Terry states. "He's been one step ahead of us so far. Why will this time be different?"

"I don't know," Agent Sebold says.

"We can't speculate," Agent Samperson chimes in.

"But I think we should. Do you think he's going to harm him?"

Agent Sebold folds his hands on the table. "To be honest, yes, I assume that's his intention. He wants revenge. But in what manner and how quickly, that determines our window of opportunity."

"That's it?" Terry says. "We're hoping the perp attacks Andy slowly, draws out his revenge so we have time…"

The conference room door clicks, turns from the other side, and everyone looks up to solemnly watch Andy Frempt's head lean in, wide eyed as he looks at all the unfamiliar faces staring at him. There is a moment of silence as everyone in the room wonders if Andy heard anything.

Terry jumps up and says, "Thank you for coming."

"Sure. Didn't have much of a choice. They said it was an emergency," Andy says, "so I just got in the police car. My truck is still parked on Wabash." Andy is still in his postal uniform and holds up the mail sack around his shoulder as evidence of how quickly he left his route.

"I'll take that for you," Terry says, reaching for the mail sack.

"That's all right. I'll just hold on to it and finish up when we're through."

Terry diverts his eyes from Andy, disagreeing with silence, to which Andy asks, "What?"

Terry pulls out a chair at the end of the table and unfolds a copy of the perpetrator's note before it. Everyone in the room remains still as Andy sits and reads and rereads the note.

When he finally looks up, Terry adds, "There was another toe. We think it's Alex Collini's."

Andy closes his eyes and shakes his head, exhaling. He slides the mail sack from his shoulder and hands it to Terry. "So what do we do?"

"Time is critical, so I'm going to do a quick rundown. First off, the toe was in good condition, meaning the owner was alive when it was severed. So we have good reason to be hopeful that the children are still alive."

"What does he want?"

Ryan Scoville

"After the second note, it seemed like the kidnapper might be experiencing some sort of remorse. This note seems to be a continuation of that thinking. With this note it seems like he may have reconsidered his whole plan, that he may let them go home."

"In exchange for me?" Andy asks.

"Yes. That seems to be the offer."

"That was more than thirty years ago! I was seven! Why would he still care?"

"I don't know."

"I mean I was a child. I was… I was just trying to get away. That's it. And now he wants to kill me, just for running away!"

"We don't know that he wants to kill you."

Andy pulls the note before him and reads, "'We were wronged. We seek restitution. We seek revenge.' This guy has no problem cutting off children's toes. What do you think he's going to do to someone he's been obsessing over for thirty years? Do you think I'm getting a damn pedicure?"

Terry shares Andy's concern but knows this is not the time for sympathy. This is the time for convincing. "We just don't know Andy, but here's the thing, if he really wanted to kill you, why not sneak up and do it stealthily, come after you while you were home alone, or while you're on your route?"

"You mean just drive by and shoot me?"

"Yes. It would be so much simpler than sending a note to the police and asking them to deliver you."

"Because the psycho probably wants to do something more elaborate, torture me first, make it slow."

"We are not going to let that happen."

"Just like you were not going to let anything happen to them? They're still missing, and they're having their toes cut off, one by one. It doesn't seem like you have a lot of control over the situation."

Terry purses his lips with pained acknowledgement. Everyone in the room is waiting, letting the exchange happen, and concentrating on how to proceed once Andy agrees to be the bait. It's up to Terry to convince him. But what can he say to convince a man to sacrifice his life? Instead, he knows it will be easier to just assume consent and carry on, hoping Andy won't have the time to ponder the immensity of the situation. "Those numbers on the note are GPS coordinates. We're narrowing down the exact positions, but basically, the first location is where you will start. It's by Tate Park. The other coordinate is further into Busey woods. We don't quite know where yet, but it's about three miles from the first coordinate."

"And how am I supposed to find it?"

"You'll have a GPS device with you. Simply follow the readout and it will take you to your destination."

"My final destination?"

"The second numbers," Terry says, ignoring Andy's remark, "are in reference to a timer that came with the note. It began a six hour countdown when we opened the package."

"Six hours? So how much time do we have left?"

"Three and a half hours. The timer will run out just after 6:12 PM."

"And this timer, how did it start?"

"When we pulled the note out."

"So how does the kidnapper know it started? I mean, why not pretend we never even got this note, the package, or the toe. Why don't we see what happens then?"

"We thought of that, but the counter had a small wire loop hanging off of it, connected to an encased computer chip which is powered by the battery. We have to assume it's some sort of transmitter, signaling the perpetrator as to when the countdown began. We don't know for sure, but the technicians claim there's no way they'll have it figured out before the timer expires. It could have sent out a signal, but it could also be a decoy. We just have to assume the worst, that he knows the counter is running."

"Great. Is there any way to stop it?"

"It probably doesn't matter. All the perp needs to know is when it started. From there he can figure out when it will stop. Right now we're going on the assumption that the deadline is real."

"So is that it? You're going to send me off alone, hope the children come back, and consider it a success? Is that a fair trade?"

"You are going to be alone, carrying a handheld GPS unit to the destination coordinates, but we're also going to have a tracking device and a wire on you. That will allow us to know exactly where you are and what's going on. We'll have every officer in Edgebrook as well as an FBI SWAT team waiting in the wings, ready to move in."

"You're going to follow me? It says 'Andy alone.'"

"That's the challenge. The final coordinates are deep within the forest without any paths or landmarks. There's no real way for us to get close to the destination without risk of exposing ourselves. But we will be close. Officers will be nearby on ATVs and mountain bikes, which means from the moment the signal is given our guys will arrive in minutes."

"So from the time any problems start, I have to somehow stay alive for five minutes, defenseless against some psychopath?"

"Like you just said, he probably doesn't want to kill you outright. He could have done that on his own. He probably has something else planned."

"So now that's a good thing? Hopefully he just tortures me a little, maybe I only lose a few toes, before the cavalry arrives?"

"Andy."

"And you don't think he'll expect the police to follow me? You don't think he'll assume that?"

"You'll have another advantage too."

"What?"

"Have you ever fired a weapon before?"

"Never in my life."

"Well, the note never said you could not be armed. If you get into trouble, we figure you can get a shot off. You don't have to shoot the perp, just shoot in the air as a distraction, then hide for cover. We'll be there as quickly as possible."

"So you're leaving this up to me? I'm my own protection."

"No, Andy, giving you a weapon is part of your protection, but we're all here for you. We're all part of your protection."

Andy rereads the note and looks around the room. The FBI agent with the box of gadgets is laying them out on the table: wires, bugs, tracking devices, and very clearly on the side, a small black pistol.

"So what's to stop me from saying no and walking out that door?"

"Absolutely nothing."

"I need a moment," Andy says, standing up, "Just give me a minute."

Terry stands to protest but only watches Andy exit. He looks at the others in the conference room, questioning what to do next, but everyone diverts their eyes, letting the responsibility of convincing Andy rest solely on his shoulders.

"This isn't going right," Agent Samperson says from the intercom. "You need to be more convincing."

"Convincing? How?"

"Tell him he has the opportunity to save the lives of three children. That he can be a hero one more time. Those are the facts you need to emphasize. All this talk about what the perp could do isn't important. What's important is the lives of those three children."

"I think he is more than aware of what's at stake," Terry says. "Here's how I see it and let me know where I'm wrong. We have made absolutely no progress on this case ourselves. Besides tracking a credit card to a dog, we have not uncovered a single break. Everything, and I mean everything, has been set up and played out by the perpetrator. This is just one more act and we're following his script. You think the perp doesn't know we're going to wire him? You think he won't be prepared for Andy to have a gun?" Terry raises his head toward the door, motioning for Baumgardner to look outside and make sure Andy isn't listening in. With an affirming nod, Terry continues, "We know the perp wants Andy, and that he's offered to trade the three children for him. But we're gift wrapping him, delivering him exactly as asked, and there's absolutely no assurance we'll ever see any of those children."

"If you have a better plan I'd like to hear it. Otherwise, these are the risks we have to take."

"But we're not really risking anything, compared to Andy. What do you think the smartest move is? If you had three kids locked up in a place no one could find, would it be easier to kill them there, or go through the trouble of returning them home?"

"He doesn't have to return them, per se, just let us know where they're being kept. If it were somewhere in the forest, like before, he just needs to give us a GPS coordinate and then disappear."

"And risk that the children might have seen his face, or that a fingerprint or strand of hair was left behind? Why?"

"It's all we've got."

"I know! That's what pisses me off so much. We've got no choice."

Baumgardner's head appears in the doorway and he nods to let everyone know Andy is returning.

Andy quietly enters and returns to his seat. He carefully lays out three sheets of paper on the table and stares at them for almost a minute, his hands clasped in front of his chest almost as if he were praying. He studies the three smiling faces looking back from the missing posters he pulled from the hallway bulletin board. Andy eventually looks up and says to no one in particular, "I'm in."

43

Terry watches Andy in the passenger seat and wonders what must be going through his mind. They head down a tree-lined street, past row houses and a gas station. They pass an open field with decaying tree stumps and an old country house, one of the oldest in Edgebrook. Andy has lived in this town his whole life, passed these markers for years, and made the map of his existence fit within the map of Edgebrook. Terry looks outside with passing consideration, aware of his personal assumption that he will see these houses and fields again. He wonders how Andy views them.

"I don't want to die," Andy says aloud, staring out the window.

Terry is unsure how to respond. Agent Samperson would give him a hurrah-hurrah speech, tell him how he is doing the right thing, how he is about to save the lives of three children, tell him how many officers and agents are right behind him, how many years of experience they have and how everything is going as planned. But of course, none of this is their plan. They're about to drop Andy at the doorstep of the dragon's cave and say good luck, while everyone else tiptoes back and waits. Andy's confession does not need a reply; none of us wants to die.

"It was so much easier when I wasn't involved, reading about it in the paper, watching for updates on TV. I could say how sorry I felt for them, how much I would like to help, if I could. But now..."

Terry can only offer a cliché response. "You're doing the right thing."

"I know. I mean, I don't think there really was any choice. The funny thing is, the last time I was the so-called hero, all I did was run. I didn't even try to save Sue or Beth, I just got the hell out of there. Nobody ever mentions that. And what if the police got there a minute later? He would have killed Sue. And given another minute, he would have killed Beth. How's that for being a hero?"

"You were seven.

"They were trapped on the forest floor, right next to me, and I never said a word, I just ran. I've thought about that, thought quite a bit about it. What if? Maybe this is my chance for redemption? Maybe this is another chance to go back into the woods and do it right."

"Do you believe that?"

"I don't know what I believe. But I'd rather think there's a purpose. It's easier to think there's some sort of fate at work, because if I'm just up against some manipulative psychopath, what chance do I really have?"

Terry nods, having seen too many accidents on the job, too much loss, to believe in fate or second chances. But if this is the stimulus that gets Andy going, he will support it. "Maybe it is, Andy. Maybe this is an opportunity to truly be the hero you want to be."

"The thing is, I don't ever remember asking to be a hero."

The van pulls into the parking lot of Tate Park. The tennis court's nets have been taken down. The basketball court is empty. The sand beneath the playground equipment is cold and hard. Winter approaches, Terry thinks, as they step out of the van. He watches Andy walk in a circle, monitoring the changes on the GPS display, watching the digital compass turn. Andy loosely fingers the pistol hidden in his pocket, now with the safety off. He looks to Terry, his eyes shallow but questioning, hoping for some last command, some sort of reprieve, anything to get him out of this.

Terry mumbles "Good luck," but the words fall hollow in the crisp air.

Andy's mouth opens, about to say something in return, and then he turns, looks at the GPS unit, and begins walking. He goes a few feet before stopping and turning around. "If this turns out like the kidnapper says, if he really returns the children but I don't make it… I hope they realize it. I hope they appreciate the gift of life. Not that I've given it to them. It's a gift we all have. But I hope they appreciate it." With that, Andy turns and walks with determination toward his fate, a lone figure crossing the empty park, a slight breeze blowing from the west. The GPS unit's latitude and longitude alter themselves with every few steps, taking Andy to the softball back stop on the far side, then behind it to a small opening in the tree line, and finally onto a path that leads into the heart of Busey Woods. As Andy disappears, Terry comprehends with a heavy weight just how empty this whole plan is, how they are sending Andy in as a sacrifice, and no matter how much they talk of backup agents and SWAT teams, they are just surrendering Andy to the kidnapper, hoping he keeps his word.

Terry pulls out of the parking lot and drives three blocks over onto a nearby suburban cul-de-sac. The van that followed them most of the way to Tate Park is conspicuously waiting. Terry opens the sliding door and steps inside, where Agent Dietrich, a.k.a. the gadget guy, watches a monitor and calmly speaks into a closed channel transmitter. "5100 meters," he says, stating exactly how far Andy is from his destination. Terry checks his watch. They are more than an hour and a half ahead of the deadline, but Andy needs to traverse a little over three miles into the forest. He isn't running, and it will be slow going in the fading light, but he should make it easily.

The entire Edgebrook police force, as well as officers from surrounding towns and an FBI swat team, are waiting patiently at various access points to the forest. They are waiting for the signal to converge on the same coordinates Andy is now walking toward, but they have the sound relief that someone else has to make that call, tell them when to move in.

"4500 meters," Agent Dietrich says.

That responsibility lies with Terry. If he sends them in too early, they could lose the children. If he sends them in too late, they could lose Andy. Worst case, they could lose them all. Terry isn't even sure what information he should base his decision on.

"4000 meters."

Andy has a tracking device, broadcasting his location, which Agent Dietrich is reading aloud. But what good is that? When he arrives at the destination, will the perp be there waiting, or will he wait until the deadline? Maybe he won't show up at all and instead provide directions to a new location.

"3500 meters."

Andy is also bugged, a small microphone sewn into his collar leading to a transmitter in the back of his shirt, broadcasting his thick breath and the rustle of wind through the trees. They advised Andy not to talk into the microphone unless there was a reason, so the perp wouldn't suspect it was there. Terry puts most of his hope on the microphone. If there is any discussion, a pronouncement by the perpetrator, or even an acknowledgement by Andy of the perp's presence, Terry can send the SWAT team in. Until then, the plan is to wait.

"3000 meters."

The sound of Andy's steady breath is amplified through the van's speakers. Terry watches Agent Dietrich, who checks the readout of Andy's location, marks it onto a map, calculates the distance to where he is going, and reads it into the microphone. Agent Dietrich seems oblivious to the staggered breaths around them, able to put aside the fact that they are following a man, and concentrating on the numbers.

"2500 meters."

That is how Terry likes to work. Straightforward and simple, he asks the mechanical questions, connects the dots, and gets things done. On past cases that unfolded in a crucible of emotions, when a wife was yelling obscenities at her husband or a child was crying, Terry remained calm, separating the heart from the mind, and progressed in a systematic manner. This self-control has always been a point of pride.

"2000 meters."

This time Terry struggles to remain level-headed. The whole case is on the verge of concluding. Whether it will be remembered with sorrow and dismay, or relief and celebration, they will probably know before the day is over. The rest of his career, the rest of his life, as well as so many other's lives, will stand on today's outcome.

"1500 meters."

The countdown progresses as Terry clutches the van door, deeply aware he is at the heart of mission control, yet filled with the now familiar doubt that he is not controlling anything.

"1450 meters."

Terry is stirred by the realization that this is going down without anyone's knowledge. The news vans are still parked on the police department lawn, certain something is taking place as they watched the police and FBI roll out, but directly ordered not to follow the departing police cruisers. The Collinis, Hughes, and Steve Cardell are going through the worried motions they have developed over the past weeks, just as unaware that they are near the end as they were unaware that Friday afternoon, when their children disappeared, that the first chapter was beginning.

"1470 meters."

Terry pauses and looks at the other markings that Agent Dietrich has carefully listed. "Isn't that further than the last one?"

"Yes."

"Why would he do that?"

"He may have run into a creek he has to go around. Or maybe an elevation, like a butte or rock face. You really can't draw a straight line on the map and expect him to follow it. He's been zigzagging to some degree all along."

"I guess. Where's he headed now?"

"Still moving laterally. About 1460 meters."

"Okay."

"This better not be a long creek or anything, as that could significantly hurt his arrival time."

"He's stopped," Agent Dietrich says.

"Stopped? Why?"

"He's probably thinking, figuring out how to get where he's going. Those GPS units aren't easy to follow. He's done a good job so far. Give him a minute."

Terry gives him a minute. Then another and another. "Well?"

"Nothing. He's not moving."

The speakers continue to relay Andy's calm breaths as they wait, listening. "Anything?"

"He's still not moving."

"I wish he'd say something."

"We told him not to," Agent Dietrich reminds Terry.

"He can talk to himself. 'How do I get around this river?', or something like that."

"We told him not to."

Five silent minutes pass but nothing happens. "We've got to do something. Something has to happen."

As he finishes, a loud swoosh punctures the calm, as if the air were being sucked out of the van. The microphone is amplifying Andy's spontaneous intake of breath, followed by a long pause. His breathing resumes, but with short pants, as if Andy were hyperventilating. Terry closes his eyes, concentrating on the sounds of Andy's hidden microphone, listening for a voice or a noise that gives some indication as to what is happening, but the steady short breaths only scurry on.

"1490 meters."

"What?"

"1520. He's moving further away. Fast. He's moving laterally to the target location, around it."

"What the hell?"

"1540 meters."

"Where's he going?"

"1540 meters. He seems to have stopped again."

Terry opens his eyes and looks at the display in front of Dietrich. The numbers are no longer moving. Terry grabs the radio transmitter and waits, ready to transmit the command for everyone to move in, but he has no idea what is happening. He knows storming Andy's position prematurely could be fatal. But so could waiting.

The location readout flips blindingly through a few numbers and then settles onto a bold NS. Agent Dietrich begins twisting knobs furiously.

"What does that mean?"

"No signal."

"No signal? How could that happen?"

"It happens in urban landscapes, interference from other RF signals. Usually that just throws off the numbers, but sometimes you lose it completely. But in the woods, I don't know. Maybe if he went into a cave or something, but he wasn't even moving. I don't know what would cause this."

"Well something's causing it."

"I know. But he's not there. I can't get a signal anymore."

"Could he have turned it off?"

"Yeah but, the switch is inside the battery compartment. You need a screwdriver just to open it. It's not easy. It's not meant to switch on and off."

A shock wave emanates through the speakers and everyone in the van jumps. There is a deep roar like a motor starting up which then cuts to silence.

"What was that?"

"We just lost the mic feed."

Terry studies the puzzled gaze of Agent Dietrich as he presses the radio's transmit button and shouts, "Move in! All units move in!"

44

Every reporter at the station knew something was going on, the commotion, the officers that rushed Andy Frempt in and, a while later, the way everyone rushed out. Furthermore, they knew the case was breaking just by the way no one would answer their questions, purposely diverting their attention from the media, avoiding the uncomfortable lie of denial.

And when officer Baumgardner got their attention with an announcement that everyone with the media had to remain at the station, the consensus was the case would be closed before the day was over. Of course, no one could order the media not to do their job, to stay put while news broke elsewhere, but after enough protest, the trump card was played. Yes, they had received contact from the perpetrator, but he had been very specific that the media should not be present. If anyone left and followed the departing squad cars and FBI vans, they would be jeopardizing the lives of the children. The reporters debated if this were true, knowing they were powerless to do anything without being certain, swearing what they would do if Baumgardner were lying. But they followed orders and remained on the station lawn, gathering in the ready for the right time.

Martin Young, the reporter who followed the original case thirty years ago and had blogged about what it meant to him, due to his unique viewpoint, was now covering the case for *The New York Times*. He receives the first call. "Do you want to know what the ruckus is all about?" a mysterious voice asks, mechanically altered into a deep baritone. "Do you want to see the final act? Might I say, everyone's been so good to me. To deliver young Andy with nary a trace, another bird for my collection. I have the children, and just added their only hope of salvation. Like trading cards. What fun, what fun, what bubble gum. Are you having fun, Martin? But while the blind play hide and seek, I hide where they will never find. Ghosts in the graveyard, we hide and wait. Simon says, Simon asks, do you want to know where?"

When the call is over, Martin calmly steps into the van of his paper's affiliate station and whispers directions. Everyone watches as the van's engine turns over and it carefully pulls out and off the station's lawn. Then another reporter's cell phone rings and the message repeats. Then another. And another.

45

Terry's team consists of Agent Dietrich, two more FBI agents, and two Edgebrook officers. They move the slowest of all the teams, using Agent Dietrich's notes to retrace Andy's steps rather than just converge on the final coordinates. From the moment they stopped receiving a signal from Andy's GPS unit, followed by the loud burst of a revving motor and then silence as his microphone turned off, chaos reigned over the operation.

Terry's frenzied command for all teams to move in raised everyone's adrenaline at the cost of execution. At each park and trail that led into the forest, an officer was supposed to stay behind to catch anyone leaving. But after Terry commanded everyone in, everyone followed the order, literally. Once Terry realized the blunder, he ordered the officers who were supposed to stay behind to return to their watch point. But without their own GPS devices, two of them got lost while backtracking.

And as everyone converged, Terry realized that they were all moving toward the final coordinates in the note, not the actual location where Andy went missing. He needed to redirect half of his personnel, especially the SWAT team, to head toward Andy's disappearing point in case the perp was there. He wanted the rest of the agents to move toward the note's final coordinates, in case the children were there or there is some sort of clue. But after changing the orders, the two teams ran into each other inside the forest.

The FBI agents continued with the orders, but the Edgebrook officers lit up Terry's receiver asking why they didn't get new orders. Some decide to follow the FBI agents, and Terry has to stop, regain everyone's attention and explain the situation, wasting valuable time.

As the lead teams begin arriving at their destinations, they report back exactly as Terry expected. Nothing. No signs of struggle, no signs of conflict, no signs of anything. Terry orders them to spread out, but he knows exactly what the situation is. Andy Frempt has disappeared from under their noses without a trace.

As he nears the location of Andy's disappearance, the inept lunacy of the situation takes hold. Men with drawn weapons are traipsing about the forest, flashlights zigzagging back and forth, all the while running into each other like Lotto balls. They carry on like this for almost an hour, everyone searching for clues while coming to the same realization that they will not find anything.

Agent Sebold gives orders to his SWAT team, approaches Terry, and says bluntly, "There's nothing here."

"I know."

"We missed him."

"I know. But what else can we do. Have your men keep looking."

"I'm just saying the perpetrator expected us and somehow made a clean break. Even the dogs can't pick up a scent from the point we lost his GPS signal."

"I know."

"So I don't think we're going to find anything else."

"I know that!" Terry shouts. "I know we lost him. I know we fucked up again. But we're going to keep looking until the sun goes down, and then all day tomorrow and the day after that."

"You're in charge."

Terry bends down, hunches over his knees, and clenches his fists. Did they just kill Andy Frempt? He tries to figure out what their next move will be, but has nothing.

His phone rings and he recognizes the number as that of Agent Samperson. Samperson had been patched into all the radio transmissions, kept up to date every step of the way. He can also transmit onto their frequency, although everyone will hear it. This must be something just for Terry to hear.

He presses the cell phone to his ear and cups it with his other hand to block out the chaos of the situation. As he listens, Terry learns how the perpetrator has been contacting the media, one by one, and alerting them to another location. As Samperson explains, Terry realizes how much sense it makes. Never trust the police to not follow someone. Never give them the benefit of the doubt. Just assume that they'll pull back far enough for you to slip the bait off the hook.

Then choose the best setting for the show and call in the cameras.

46

The community center sits on the far end of an open stretch of land. A single street, Short Street, deviates its way from one of Edgebrook's major north-south roads, Yackley Avenue, and across this open land to the community center. The three entities, the winding road, the plot of land, and the community center, have been with Edgebrook for as long as anyone can remember, and as the town grew, so did the three.

The community center was once nothing more than an auditorium with an adjoining office. The auditorium was used for town meetings, school plays, and events and productions organized by Edgebrook's various social clubs. At some point a simple swimming pool was dug in the back, only to expand into an official water park over the years. Water slides, wading pools, water fountains and volleyball courts sprouted up as the pool's fence was repeatedly torn down and rebuilt further out. When the pool first opened, only one lifeguard was required. Now the Edgebrook Community Pool, between the additional custodians and concession workers, employs nearly seventy-five people during the summer months.

Around the pools, long rows of lawn chairs were occasionally bombarded by stray tennis balls lobbed from the adjacent tennis courts. A concrete courtyard stretched out from the parking lot where picnic benches lined the meandering walkways. Old men sat in the shade of a gazebo and waited for their turn on the shuffleboard courts.

Short Street, running the half mile to the community center, was transformed from a thin stretch of pavement into an opulent boulevard. Mums sprouted from brick potters, while light poles curved up from the ground, their electric lights modeled like antique gaslights. The brick walkway on each side of the street was widened so that whole families could pass each other, side by side. And if they cared, they could bend down to the occasional copper brick and read the name of a Community Center contributor along with their contribution rank.

The open plot of land, originally just a flat clearing of little use, now has two man-made ponds, their excavated dirt used to build a hill nestled between their banks. Paths curl around the ponds without purpose, circling back upon one another for those who want to walk without going anywhere. Trees were planted in clusters across manicured lawns that have been the site of innumerable picnics, kite-flying expeditions, and the occasional game of frisbee golf.

Closer to the Community Center, the grounds evolve into a sports complex. Four baseball diamonds face away from each other like the points on a rose compass. Further down is Rice Championship Field, which has professional-style dugouts, twenty rows of bleachers behind them, and an announcer's booth. This is where every Little League, high school, and summer softball league's championship game has been played for as long as anyone can remember. The latest addition, which opened last summer, is a skateboard park, a complex of curving ramps and reinforced rails. And all around, more soccer fields are wedged in year after year.

The Edgebrook Community Center is the town's centerpiece, the reason everyone within an hour's drive knows how to get to Edgebrook. The Fourth of July Festival is the largest, September's Keepataw Days has the most popular bands, and the Winter Wonderland is the most extravagant.

Terry's car turns onto Short Street, and he looks out onto the Community Center ponds encircled by twisting paths, completely void of people. A cool breeze ripples across the water's surface. The Center looks deserted.

Terry reads today's date on the Center's marquee, followed by ANNUAL PARTY – CNTR CLOSED. He knows about the Center's annual party, held for all the summertime staff. A few years back they were called in because some of the lifeguards, still in high school, snuck alcohol into the event and somebody got sick. But what he remembers now is that, for whatever reason, they never actually threw the party at the Community Center. Today is one of the only days of the year where the Center is closed and empty. The perfect location for a showdown.

Terry pulls into the main parking lot, crosshatched with media vans, none of which has managed to park within the designated spots. Terry wishes the media weren't here and momentarily ponders writing tickets. He maneuvers to the far end of the lot, away from the media, creating an area for only the police and FBI, allowing them to plan without reporters writing down, recording, and broadcasting their every word.

Baumgardner is waiting, pacing helplessly, and expresses his relief when he spots Terry. "Finally!"

"What's the situation?" Terry asks.

"They all got calls from the kidnapper. He told them to come here, but it's closed and locked up, so besides a few peeks through the windows, nothing."

"So we don't even know if the perp's here?"

"He is." Baumgardner reaches into his pocket, pulls out an envelope, and hands it to Terry. "That Martin Young guy was the first one to get here and said he found this at the main entrance."

Welcome to my debut,
My Opening Night Finale

My eyes.
My eyes are everywhere.
Wait, and all shall resolve.
Act, and there shall be retribution.

"Shit, shit, shit!" Terry exclaims, handing the sheet back to Baumgardner, who is unsure what to do with it. "I am so sick of this psychotic bullshit."

"So what do we do?"

"I don't know."

The second van, comprised of the FBI SWAT team, is gathering supplies, and will arrive shortly. Their strategy has changed from a forest infiltration to an enclosed structure surround, possibly with negotiations, and an eventual siege. It helps that the area of assault is now much smaller, but that also means the perp can monitor outside movement much more easily. At least this situation is something the FBI simulates more often than the previous one, sending an inexperienced civilian into an unmapped forest. Terry feels nauseous when he thinks about it, how they lost Andy, how they gave him up.

Terry starts toward the news vans to gather any information they might have, when he notices a silver sedan parked along Short Street. He changes direction and heads to the car, eyeing two figures in the front seat. The window rolls down to reveal two college-aged kids in baseball caps and long-sleeved t-shirts, looking at Terry innocently. A smart phone is propped on the dash, streaming live video from the Community Center.

"Is there a problem, officer?" the driver asks, reminding Terry of the numerous pull-overs he has taken part in, as if they were caught speeding. As if this were any other day and speeding were important.

"What are you doing here?"

"We saw the report on TV. I live down the street, and we just thought we'd come over."

Terry looks back across the parking lot to the Community Center, a tan brick structure with large open windows along the first floor. The auditorium rises up behind, and two waterslides can be seen rising from behind. But the windows, as far away as they are, worry Terry. For all he knows, for all that has happened, the perp might as well be a sure-shot sniper too. "It's too dangerous to be here."

"What about all those TV people?" the driver asks. "They're all the way up there. Is it too dangerous for them?"

Terry would like to move them too, but knows that is not going to happen. "They're professionals. This is part of their job."

"So we should be able to stay too."

"Reporters know how to protect themselves, stay out of the way. It's part of their job."

At this comment, the kid in the passenger seat knocks the driver in the arm. He grabs the phone and holds it for Terry to watch. "What about that guy?"

"Live on Five" flashes across the bottom of the screen, and a local news personality is standing on the Community Center's lawn, not more than fifty yards from the Center's bay windows, out in the open. A much easier target than these two kids in their car.

Terry straightens up and looks toward the Center's parking lot. What is happening dawns on him immediately. Gathered beneath the parking lot lights are three distinct groups. One area has paramedics and fire trucks, professionals waiting patiently if they are needed. The next group consists of the news vans, pure commotion as they all maneuver for the best shot to capture the showdown, the best angle to portray it in. Finally there are the police and FBI. The SWAT team vans just arrived, and the agents exit them like clowns from a miniature car. Spread across the parking lot, this has become a three-ring circus.

"All right, how about this? Back up about fifty yards, to that tree over there, and promise you'll stay in the car, all right?"

"Yeah, sure."

"If anything happens and this road gets congested, and we need the fire trucks or ambulances to get through, I want you completely out of the way. I want you off the road, on the grass."

"Sure."

Terry stands up straight and sighs. This is not supposed to be entertainment. He knocks his palm against the top of the car. "Get going now," he says. The engine turns and the car veers backwards, swerving as the boy tries to keep it on the road's edge. This is not supposed to be entertainment, he thinks again, heading toward the media-filled parking lot.

Another car comes slowly down Short Street, an old station wagon, and Terry knows it does not belong to the police or the media. Another spectator. He walks in front of its path on the street and holds up his hand. The car stops next to him and Natalya sticks her head out the window while

Antonio leans over from the driver's side.

"Detective Kruthers! What's going on?"

"We're not sure."

"What about Alex? Where's Alex?"

"We don't know."

"Is he in there? Please tell me, Detective."

"I'm sorry Natalya, but I just don't know right now. We received a message from the kidnapper today, and we're basing everything off that."

Natalya looks to Antonio and then bites her lip. "Was there another toe?"

Terry's face betrays him before he can speak.

"Is it Alex's?" Natalya asks, already knowing the answer.

"We don't have DNA tests back, but it's the same blood type. We believe it is Alex's."

"Why? Why would someone do that to a little boy!" Antonio shouts.

"I don't know."

"Are they," Natalya asks, her voice shaking, "Are they in there?"

"We don't know. That's what we've been lead to believe, but there's no real evidence so we just don't know."

"What are you going to do?"

"We're evaluating the situation for now. I need to get back to the team."

"Of course. Please do everything you can."

"I will."

"I know you are. But please. I don't know what we'd do without Alex."

Terry does not know what to say. "I need to get back. Can you stay out of sight from the center? Park behind the police van over there and stay in your car. If Alex is in there, and he gets access to a window, I don't want him to see his parents and act in a way that might put him at risk. Okay?"

"Okay."

"Thank you. And remember, we're doing everything in our power."

"We know."

Terry watches the station wagon dutifully roll behind the police vans as he contemplates his words of strength, how they are doing everything in their power. He doubts the Collinis even believe that amounts to much anymore.

As he walks back, Terry thinks again of the circus. The Collinis are part of the high-wire act, balancing above, looking down on everyone and everyone looking up at them with clenched fists, hoping, praying. One misstep and they lose everything. So what does that make Andy Frempt? The analogy comes easily, the man who puts his head into the lion's mouth. The man who volunteers to risk it all. The news vans and FBI SWAT vans are parked like lumbering elephants. The journalists and newscasters move around like the beautiful women in sequins, waving their cupped hands as they usher in each act. The police are the clowns, running around, acting distinctly silly at every turn. And Terry is the head clown. He is sure of that one.

But the show must go on and the show must end.

So who is unaccounted for? P.T. Barnum. The ringleader. Speaking into the microphone with dazzling bravado, stepping aside to narrate each act, running the show and determining how it will end. Terry is sick of it.

As he enters the gaggle of officers and agents, Terry realizes he has lost control. The SWAT team has spent much more time training for situations like this, surrounding an urban structure, possibly with hostages inside. They are making plans, determining how to gather more information and figuring out how to mediate. Terry finds himself answering the questions of an FBI negotiator, while the Edgebrook officers are delicately being told to wait patiently, or even worse, move back and do crowd control.

For the first time, Terry finds he can distance himself from the case. For the first time he can watch and reflect on how little control they have without directly owning the guilt. They have followed the script, blindly obeyed the perpetrator's will, and now the conclusion almost feels like a curiosity; not that Terry doesn't care, but he is curious how the perp plans to remain one step ahead.

How can a single man, with up to four hostages, stop twelve FBI agents, with all of their training, high tech gadgets, and lethal weaponry? He can't. And with simple clarity, Terry realizes there can only be one of two outcomes. The first is that the kidnapper has already killed everyone or is about to. They'll find five bodies on the auditorium's stage. That is the one outcome the SWAT team cannot stop. But how could that be the point? The perp has been too controlling, too directed with every step to end with a senseless murder-suicide. That conclusion doesn't feel right. That can't be the final action from the man who sent those notes, who willfully severed the pinky toes from three children and sent them to the police, making sure they passed through the towns of Lovely and Peace. Those actions are the taunt of someone who plans on winning.

So what is the other possibility? Terry arrives at the only answer he can. The perpetrator is not inside. The children, and possibly Andy Frempt, might be in the Community Center, dead or alive, but Terry is suddenly sure that the perp is not there. He may be watching on TV, watching safely from afar, and there is nothing they can do. But Terry has to do something and in a moment of desperation locates Baumgardner watching beside a police cruiser.

"So what do we do now?" Baumgardner asks.

"You're in charge now."

"What?"

"You're in charge."

"What do you mean?"

"I mean, you are in charge of handling this case, as far as the Edgebrook Police Department is concerned. The FBI should be handling most tactics from here, so I don't think it matters, but as of right now, I'm giving my authority to you."

"What's going on, Terry?"

"Nothing."

"Nothing? Why am I in charge? Where are you going?"

"Don't worry about me. I'll be in touch when I can."

"Tell me what's going on, Terry."

"Don't worry."

"You have to tell me."

"See. You're already giving orders. You're meant to do this." With that, Terry turns and walks away, getting into his car and locking the doors so that Baumgardner, who has followed him with a string of questions, is left knocking on the window.

As Terry pulls away from the lit stage, driving back up Short Street, he sees how many cars have gathered; rows of spectators spread out across the park's lawns, waiting and watching. The silver sedan is parked at the front as the two college boys have taken control and are now directing spectators onto the lawn. As they usher in the audience, Terry wonders how soon until the final act begins.

47

Living in Edgebrook, one always hears about its continuing growth, the ever-expanding subdivisions and strip malls appearing in what used to be an empty field or an old cluster of trees. Most people accept the growth. Generally, the newest owner, with the newest house on the newest block, complains the loudest about the next row of houses zoned for his back yard, oblivious to the fact that his house was just built in someone else's backyard. The major complaints among long-term residents are the overflowing classrooms and the lagging development of intersections, from yield signs to stop signs to traffic lights, always a step behind what is necessary. Residents who have witnessed much of the growth, residents like Terry Kruthers, think of Edgebrook as a budding metropolis.

But one look at a map reveals just how much open land remains. There is the southern flood plain, the Harper farms to the west, two expansive forest preserves on the north side of town, and of course to the east, Busey Woods. This transfer from town to forest did not occur along a distinct line, like the edged wall around someone's garden. Instead, the forest has long fingers that still protrude deep into Edgebrook.

It is along one of these fingers Terry marks GPS coordinates, the same GPS unit he borrowed from the department and placed onto his suspect's car, which without a warrant, Terry knows is highly illegal. But as long as it is there, he spent the open moments of the past week marking down the suspect's coordinates, keeping watch from a distance. As of yesterday, the coordinates showed where any innocent person would go, through various locations around Edgebrook. Terry didn't know them all, but the suspect wasn't driving into the forest and wasn't sneaking out in the middle of the night. There was nothing suspicious going on and nothing that seemed worth following up on. The mysterious point his suspect stopped at almost every day did not seem mysterious at all, just another point within the town's borders. When Terry looks for it on a map, he sees that Main Street was only a few inches away. Ogden Movie Theaters, flanked by a Starbucks and a Hallmark store, were less than a thumbnail's distance. The Edgebrook Community Center was also not far off, a fact that had little relevance yesterday.

Terry looks at the map one more time and sees this spot is alongside one of the forest's fingers that reaches into Edgebrook, near its very tip. Further east, at the base of the finger, is the Edgebrook Community Center. One could hike the short distance through the woods and never be spotted.

As Terry turns onto the side street shown on his map, he realizes just how this point appears to be near the middle of town on a map but manages to feel like the middle of nowhere as he drives up to it. A tattered brick house situates itself at the corner, a faded yellow Dead End sign in its lawn. Terry drives past the house and up the narrow road, tree branches reaching in from both sides. On the map, this is less than a mile from the Brookdale mall. On the road, this is a densely wooded area, one of the forest's thick fingers, reaching in, clawing. Terry could park his car here and make his way on foot into the forest, and from there he could go anywhere related to the case. Where the children first entered Busey Woods. Where the search parties have been combing for weeks. Where Andy disappeared earlier today. Where Andy disappeared thirty years ago.

Terry tops the gently rising slope and sees the road fall before him, trees crowding all around. There are no houses, no lights, and Terry instinctively takes the car's headlight switch between his fingers, about to illuminate the depths around him, then thinks better and releases the knob. Instead, he pulls the car to the side of the road and eases to a stop.

With only a few wooded hills between him and the Community Center, Terry has to guess exactly which direction it lies in. His only marker is the sun's trailing glow of red, setting in the west, illuminating the cluster of tree branches around him. He wonders what is taking place at the Community Center. This whole ordeal could be ending right now and he wouldn't know, while someone in Florida or California could turn on his TV and catch a live feed.

Terry walks down the gravel road, staying on the edges where the grass has crept in, and makes out the end of the road and the start of a driveway. A house emerges from the trees, two stories of weathered brick and worn shutters with a weathered wrap-around porch supported by circular columns. Yellow and brown leaves gather in the house's crevices. The trees dwindle across an overgrown lawn patched with weeds. Terry turns, looking back up the road, and squints to catch a shaft of light reflect off the grill of his car. He is alone, and when he turns back, his fingers slide against his holstered gun, reminding himself how farfetched the idea is that brought him here.

This is probably the home of someone who has done nothing wrong, and obviously, prefers not to have visitors. So how will it look if Terry is caught tiptoeing around, peeking into windows?

But he can't knock on the door and ask if anyone's home. His whole premise is that the perpetrator might be here, and based on that hunch he needs to stay out of sight. If he's wrong, he'll deal with the consequences. Terry remains behind the tree line, keeping an eye on the front bay window, all the windows, as he circles the house.

He passes the wraparound porch, the empty garden bed beyond it, and finds himself in the back of the house. A large shed, about the size of a two-car garage, sits on the far side of the backyard. The metal structure has a flat roof, a long sliding panel that is probably a door, and a small side window covered with newspaper. Were it not so angular, so plain, he might mistake it for a guesthouse.

Terry follows the yard's outer edge, moving slowly so as not to make a distraction. He is keenly aware how visible he is to anyone peering out from the house, and just how hidden they are to him. As he ducks behind the shed, out of view for a moment, he stops and collects himself. Most likely, the case is already over. The children have been found, dead or alive, Andy Frempt's fate has also been sealed, and the perpetrator has gotten away, again. He asks himself the question he has repeatedly been asking himself since he left the Community Center. What the hell is he doing?

As he turns the corner, he finds a partial answer. A small motorcycle is propped against the wall. Inspecting it, he realizes it is more of a mountain bike with a small motor rigged to the axle. A metal plate is fastened onto the seat, extending backwards so that it can hold two people. But most importantly, the tires are wet with mud and fallen leaves, which means someone recently rode it through the forest. Terry jumps back behind the shed, out of view, and debates what to do next.

He peeks around at the house again, glares at the solemn windows, and tries to discern shapes or movements from within their black depths. Terry slowly inches around the shed, his back pressed against its rippling metal, when a sudden low thump resonates from within. His legs lock as his eyes dart from side to side. Someone is inside. He unbuttons his holster and draws his gun.

Terry breathes deeply, cognizant of the fact that, on the job, he has drawn his gun only a handful of times and has never fired it. He steps around the shed, now ignoring the house that gazes down on him, and stands next to the shed's sliding door, noticing a hinged handle meant to be pulled open with a large sweeping motion. At the base of the door, a metal chain lies in the grass with an open lock on one end. Terry puts his left hand against the door's handle and rests his right hand over his forearm, holding the gun directly towards the door's entrance. With a stern push the door gives just enough for Terry to slide into the darkness. As he does, his vision goes black while his eyes adjust.

He breathes in and his nostrils ignite with a burnt chemical smell, a thick acid stench that seems to have replaced the air. There is no color inside, only light and dark, silhouettes of an unformed scene. A noise emanates from the far wall, a swoosh of liquid, and Terry points his gun toward the sound. There, against the wall, is the silhouette of a man standing over a long, circular basin that runs across the back wall, carefully dumping the contents from a potato sack. He only pours a little at a time, after which he sets the bag down, grabs a metal ore, and mixes. Terry internally counts to three and then forces himself to shout out, "Freeze!" He holds the gun with both hands, but his finger is not on the trigger.

48

Steve arrived at the funeral home early. It was part of his responsibilities as the husband of the deceased. Arielle was still at home and April's parents would bring her later. He was there to greet everyone, and everyone came. It seemed like anyone April had ever crossed paths with was in that line, which eventually wrapped through the funeral home, out the door and into the parking lot. People shook his hand and claimed some shared activity he could hardly remember, a thin strand connecting them to years past. "Thank you for coming," was all he whispered, nodding, accepting a hug and a passing condolence. The people just kept coming while he kept greeting. Only when he broke away for a moment, to use the restroom, did he look outside.

The funeral home parking lot was full, as were the adjacent parking lots. No one directed traffic, so there was a mass of cars trying to enter and exit. Yet with so much disorder everyone showed a courteous patience, cars idling, as they allowed one another to pass, waiting with the heavy quiet that wraps grief. No one shouted. No one accelerated to try and make an opening. Something more important had transpired, and waiting in a crowded parking lot did not seem so bad.

Steve works his way down Short Street toward the Community Center, maneuvering through the patchwork of parked cars, parking lights illuminating the way, and he thinks of April's funeral. Déjà vu. These are the only conditions in which he has seen so many people gathered calmly, patiently watching, and collectively trying to understand. People he doesn't know, people he'll never know, are here to share in his worry and anticipation, to say it means something to them.

Is that all he is now? A lesson, a reminder on how awful life can be? Is he the patron saint of misery?

An officer stops Steve's car, recognizes him, and directs him to an area

215

behind two ambulances. The parents of the other children are already gathered there. Steve pulls off the lot and onto the Community Center lawn, away from the commotion. He gets out of his car and walks to the appointed spot, receiving hugs from Natalya and Carrie, handshakes from Antonio and Jim.

"They're still making plans," Jim says, "preparing to go in."

"What do they think they're going to find?"

"Nobody knows," Natalya says.

"It was supposed to happen a while ago," Jim continues. "They were going to storm the building, but the night janitor just showed up. They're drawing out floor plans with him, determining the locations of all the doors and emergency exits, as well as the windows and anything else that might be useful."

"And then what?"

"Then they go in."

"What are the ambulances for?"

Everyone looks at them, as if they just noticed the red and white vehicles parked next to them. "I assume they'll take the children to the hospital," Natalya says, "no matter what condition they're in."

"No matter what condition?" Steve asks.

"Even if nothing's wrong," Antonio responds, "just to be safe."

"Just to be safe," Steve repeats. "And what are we supposed to do?"

"Wait," Natalya says. "We're just waiting, hoping and praying."

With that, Steve turns away from them and walks toward the edge of the parking lot.

"Where are you going?"

"Over here," Steve responds, pointing to the curb, "to sit."

"We're supposed to stay behind the ambulances. In case the kidnapper tries to shoot his way out."

"Let him," Steve responds, lowering himself to the curb. He could care less about himself, but as he sits and watches the other parents, he does feel empathy for them, for what they are about to go through and the pain they will have to endure. He pities that they might end up like him.

49

Behind the ambulances, Jim wraps his arms around Carrie and holds her tight. He sways ever so little as he whispers to himself, over and over, "Please, please, please…"

Carrie listens and rubs his arm, clutching at his hand and squeezing.

Natalya recites prayers, ones she learned as a child. She makes up her own. She begs. She pleads. Antonio joins in, but occasionally, with taut lips and narrow eyes, assures her, "Alex is coming home tonight."

50

"Freeze!" Terry shouts again.

The figure drops the oar and falls to his knees, while Terry's gun remains trained on him. "Oh God!" he shouts. "Thank God you're here. He just... just... fell in...."

"Stand up! Slowly. And keep your hands up!"

The figure rises, extending his hands above his head, and turns. Terry finds himself standing face to face with Andy Frempt. "Detective! Thank God, you're here. Thank you! Where are the children?"

"Stop!" Terry yells, unsure of what Andy should really stop doing, his hands in the air in cooperation. Terry wants everything to stop; he needs to think.

"It's me, Detective. Andy."

That much is apparent. Andy is still wearing his postal uniform, as if this were part of his route, as if this were any other day. "What's going on?"

"It just... He brought me here, he said he was going to kill me, and then, I pushed him, and he fell into... that." Andy nods toward the metal basin, the basin he had just been mixing, its surface swirled into a frothy paste.

"Who?"

"The kidnapper. He brought me here." Andy's chest rises and falls in deep breaths. "I was so scared."

"What did you pour in there? What were you mixing?"

Andy's mouth opens, searching for a word.

"What were you pouring in there?"

"What are you talking about?"

"From that bag!" Terry shouts, briefly pointing with his gun toward the large rucksack, now empty, slumped onto itself, resting beside the basin.

"Detective... Terry... I don't know what... you must be mistaken."

"I'm not mistaken. I saw you pouring from that sack and then mixing it

218

with that oar. That's what I saw and I want you to explain what you were doing."

Andy Frempt's hands slowly drop. Terry shouts for him to put them back up, but Andy seems to slip into another world, submerged beneath his own thoughts, oblivious to Detective Kruthers, oblivious to the gun pointed at him, oblivious to everything.

When he seems to regain some semblance of recognition, he turns square toward Terry, staring intently at the detective, his jowls hardened and his stance resolute. Andy closes his eyes, looks up to the ceiling, and swallows. When he looks back at Terry, his eyes narrow and he looks despondent and lost.

"What did you just swallow?"

Andy sighs. "Determination. In pill form. But let me ask you, who else knows you're here?"

"The FBI is just outside," Terry lies.

"The FBI SWAT team?"

"Yes."

"So you're telling me there's a whole SWAT team outside, and they thought the best plan was to send you in?"

"Yes!"

"Really. Why would they do that?"

"Because I know you."

"You don't know me at all."

"Put your hands up!" Terry shouts, realizing they are now resting at Andy's sides again.

"No, I will not put my hands up. I am not a threat. I just want to talk. If you feel the need to shoot me for that, then so be it. So once again who knows you're here?"

"The entire department."

Andy scowls. "You're lying again. I guess it doesn't matter though. We don't have much time, so I'll plead my case and let you be the judge. Are you ready to listen?"

"Listen to what? Where are the children?"

"Patience, Detective, I'll get to that."

"Who's house is this? Where's the owner?" Terry asks, wondering if there is another victim in this whole mess.

"There you go again with more questions. I'll answer that one since it's irrelevant. Alan Fields owns the house. His only connection to the story is that he's spent the past month in Salt Lake City, visiting his grandkids. His mail's on hold through the New Year. He's involved as a matter of convenience, an empty house in the right location. That's not the right line of questioning, detective, but like I said, I'll explain everything if you let me."

"Then explain."

Andy looks around, and for the first time Terry notices the strange contraptions around the room. At first glance, they look like nautilus equipment found in any gym. With another look, Terry identifies shackles and cuffs, ropes and buckles in compromising positions, and he realizes they are either for masochistic pleasures or pure torture.

"Where are the children?" Terry asks.

"They're on the other side," Andy says, pointing to a door's outline in a wall that partitions the shed. "They're fine. They can go home tonight. They'll just have to wait a few more minutes until I finish my story. Do you mind if I sit?" Andy asks, turning towards one of the benches.

"Don't move!" Terry yells helplessly, knowing he will only shoot if he thinks he or the children are in immediate danger, not at the slow movements of an Edgebrook mailman, no matter what the circumstances.

"Much better," Andy says, lowering himself onto a bench. A metal pole rises on one end, holding a leather strap tied to a hand crank. The bench has brackets along it for holding something, or someone, down. "I'm not quite sure how much time we have, so I better talk quickly. As such, I'd appreciate if you don't interrupt unless there's something you don't understand."

"I don't understand any of this!" Terry confesses.

"Good. It's better when I explain it, when I tell the story. Let me step back, closer to the beginning, to *The Spying Toes*, or just after *The Spying Toes* incident. We spent three days in the hospital. Sue's foot was sewn up, we slept and were fed, regained our strength and our stamina. After that..."

"How did you know?" Terry interrupts.

"Know what?"

"About the toes. The nail polish and the eyeliner? You never saw them that way." Even though he planted the GPS on Andy's car, Terry still can't believe he has anything to do with the children's disappearance.

"Oh, that?" Andy smirks. "He told me. He sat down next to me and told me exactly what he did, how he polished them, what they looked like, and why. He told me how lovely they were to him. I think he wanted a friend, someone to understand, and so he told me everything."

Terry's thoughts wrap around this response, mulling over the simple solution to the mystery.

"So after that," Andy continues, "when we were released from the hospital and were no longer interviewed by the police, after the parade and the celebrations and after everything was supposed to go back to normal, we quickly realized that Edgebrook changed. To put it melodramatically, everyone loved their children a little more, appreciated their lot in life, and all around, everyone just seemed happy, joyous. They considered themselves lucky, blessed to have narrowly escaped the type of tragedy so many communities never do. As for Beth and Sue, they became the apple of their families' eyes. The darlings of the entire town. Every moment with them was considered a blessing, and we all knew it. It sounds corny when I say it, but Edgebrook was truly an amazing place back then. I guess I don't have to go into detail though. You'll find out soon enough."

"And you?" Terry asks, reformulating the theories he had written down late one night.

Andy smiles in acknowledgement. "And me? I was a hero. I was the hero."

"The hero of Edgebrook."

"Yes, yes, I was the hero. But let's keep this moving. Time passed. It always does. We grew up, went to high school, other things became important, but to some degree, we still remembered. We still appreciated. Ten years passed and people still remembered. Sue, Beth and I were still living reminders of lessons learned."

"What lessons were those?"

"Come on detective, let's not be naïve. The lesson of significance. The lesson of meaning in your life. Love your neighbor. Love your family. Cherish what's important. Live life to the fullest. Carpe Diem. All that stuff. The lessons we've heard a million times over but never seem to grasp. The ones we nod our heads in agreement to, yet can't seem to fit between the small distractions that grow like weeds and eventually take over our lives until we find we have everything we want except the happiness we expect. We don't understand how to appreciate it."

"So kidnapping three kids and cutting off their pinky toes will make everyone happy?"

"You'll see what I mean. You might not feel it yourself, because of this," Andy says, pointing between himself and the detective, "because you know the truth, but if things play out like I plan, you'll see."

"And how are things going to play out? I know you're guilty."

"Patience, detective, just a little more patience. Moving on, we finally reached that age where we left our little haven and went off to college. I went to Ohio State for two months before dropping out. The problem was, outside of Edgebrook, I was a nobody, or to be more precise, I was just like everyone else, which was unacceptable after having spent most of my life as a someone, a hero. So I came home, moved back into my room in my parent's house and got a part-time job at the post office, which became full time and eventually a career. I liked the post office because it gave me a chance to see the people of Edgebrook every day, to still be a hero. At the time, it seemed like an important thing."

Andy's eyes look upward as he thinks through the story, moving where he needs to go. "Let's see. More time passed. People forgot a little more every day, moved away, moved on. I got less and less attention, but I was still a hero at home, still praised for something I did when I was seven years old. We still had the newspaper clippings and magazine articles framed on the walls. And I took it in like sunlight on the face. I at least had that much."

"So what does this have to do with the children?"

"First my mother passed. Stomach cancer. Dad went three years later. Heart attack. I found myself alone in the room I grew up in, alone in the house I was raised in and alone in the town I saved. I felt left behind and forgotten, and rather than attempt to move forward, I wanted to hold onto the past. Those were dark days, and I did what any troubled, lonely person with no hope of reclaiming lost glory might do. I put down a half bottle of aspirin and a full bottle of Beam and tried to end it all."

With tired arms, Terry lowers his gun but still grips it tightly. "When was this?" he asks.

"Almost three years ago. It was a half-hearted attempt, to say the least. I puked up most of what I swallowed, lay in bed for two days, and woke up wondering what to do next. But when I was lying there, thinking I was dying, I had the solace that my life had not been a complete waste. I had made a difference, no matter how long ago it was. I had saved people.

"And what people they were. What people they are. Sue and Beth are the most endearing, kind, blessed women I have ever met. We still keep in touch, and I've visited them both. Where they live, almost no one knows of the ordeal they went through. Sue even has a prosthetic toe so she can wear sandals and open-toed shoes. But they remember, they know how close they were to losing everything, and because of that, they've created lives that are so full of love, of appreciation, that they've touched almost everyone they've come into contact with. I remember walking with Sue down the main street of her town. People would come up and hug her, say how good it was to see her, and want to stand there and talk all day. They are so inspired by her, not because of what she went through, but because of who she is. It's truly amazing. She's just one of those people who understands. One of those people you wish you could be like."

"Because of you?"

"Not because of me, but because of what happened. Both Sue and Beth have confided in me, without any prodding, that in a way they are thankful for what happened, that it made them better people. Although they'd deny it, they both claimed that if they had to do it over, with the same outcome, they would. So when I lay there on the bathroom floor, smelling my own vomit as it dried on the porcelain, the idea that had been shoved so deeply into my subconscious finally came free and for the first time I didn't reject it with disgust. Why not do it again? Why not help some children appreciate every day of the rest of their lives? Why not help some families realize just how lucky they are to have each other? Why not help an entire town gain their own miracle that they could draw upon for inspiration? I don't think I ever dreamed it would become this big, a national story like this, but why not give the world a story to latch on to, a story that ends with, "They lived happily ever after?"'"

Terry can't speak as he tries to comprehend Andy's claim that this will help people. He compares that against the irrefutable fact that this is a crime, a despicable crime against small children. He can't reconcile the two thoughts and is unwilling to try.

"Think about when you've finished reading a book that inspires you, or watched a powerful movie. You have that surreal moment where you think the course of your life has changed. You've gained wisdom and perspective that you think will alter every day, forever after. Don't tell me it's never happened. But you put the book down or walk out of the theater and realize you have to make dinner but the dishes aren't clean. You're behind on paying bills. You have to go to work the next day and you complain about your job. Your car's out of gas and due for an oil change. You get busy. The vision fades and you fall back into your same old routines. You lose that inspiration and slide back into your old interpretations of life." Andy's eyes roll to the side as he places his hand against the bench for support. "Whoa."

"What was that?" Terry says, raising his gun, but Andy ignores him, regaining his composure and continuing.

"I'm providing meaning where there was none. Take Arielle's dad. He was never home and never cared for his daughter. Work, work, work. Or Mrs. Hughes. She would come out now and then and I would say hi and ask her about her day, just polite small talk. She would look at me like she didn't understand a word I was saying. These people had no meaning in their lives. And it's not because they didn't have reason, with their beautiful children and their beautiful homes; it's because they didn't know how to interpret it. They didn't know how to ingest, how to incorporate meaning into their lives. But this act, this act is the catalyst for change. This act will show them how to live by teaching them just how to appreciate the value of their lives."

"It will show them how to live?"

"Yes. I mean, look at Mrs. Hughes at the last press conference, stoic and righteous as she described her daughter. She is not the same woman of a month ago. She has changed."

Terry listens but can't get past one irrefutable, indefensible act. "You cut off their toes."

"The hardest thing I've ever done. I drugged their food, just to make them sleepy, and then applied a local anesthetic. I made sure to keep the wound clean and bandaged it properly. I took the utmost care."

"You," Terry repeats slowly for emphasis, "cut off their toes."

"I had to! I debated that one for so long, but I just had to. If they came back unharmed, people might think they were never really in danger to begin with. They've had food and shelter, they haven't been molested, they haven't been threatened or abused. I needed something to prove the danger. By symbolically altering them the same way Sue was, I thought I could solidify how lucky they are to survive."

"Symbolically altering them? Symbolically? You cut off their toes!"

"I know!" Andy yells, exasperated. "Just like Sue, they will have a reminder of how lucky they are to be alive. And isn't that worth it? They didn't feel a thing, they weren't tortured, not really. Most people have all ten toes, and spend each day complaining about work and bills and whatever other minutiae they want to complain about. Wouldn't you rather be lifted from that burden at the expense of one pinky toe? Don't you think the trade is worth it?"

"The trade? You never offered them a trade. You kidnapped them and cut off their toes!"

Andy shakes his head. "So ignorant, so bullheaded. Just like everyone else, you don't think you need a catalyst, vainly declaring you can do it on your own. But you're wrong. You need the jolt. Have you ever driven tired late at night, telling yourself over and over to stay awake? You think that's all it takes, repeating that mantra, but it doesn't work. Not until you close your eyes for too long and you open them to find yourself veering to the side of the road or worse yet, to the honk of oncoming traffic; that's when you wake up. That's when your heart beats and your mind understands. It takes a real lesson to fully understand. Look around, look how many people let their lives fall apart, claiming the whole time that they can pull things back together. They never do. They never do because they can't. They can't without a reason. An impetus. An event to teach them how to find meaning in their lives, how to interpret their lives."

Terry holds tight to the facts; Andy kidnapped three children and cut off a pinky toe from each one. That's all that happened and everything else is crazy talk. "I want to see them."

"Just a few more minutes," Andy says. "Look, they're fine. They're a bit scared and tired. They want to go home. But they're fine. They eat and sleep. I couldn't let them be too comfortable, but they're going to be fine. They've been kept in a room for a few weeks. Yes, they've missed their friends and family, there's been some crying, but they're going to recover."

"Let them out!"

"Hold on. I'm not finished with my story. I haven't told you how it ends."

"It ends with your arrest."

"Detective," Andy smirks, "that's not really a possibility. Please let me finish. You can either shoot me or listen."

Terry doesn't respond, looking at his gun again, pointing it toward Andy before lowering it again.

"Back to the families. Mrs. Hughes was a wreck. Arielle's dad was never there. Never. And as for the Collini's, I didn't investigate them beforehand. I was only going to take the girls, but when I came across Alex that night, the opportunity to help another family presented itself. So I took it. And it so nicely kept the comparisons in line with the previous abduction, with *The Spying Toes*. That worked out very nicely."

"You're sick."

"Beyond the families, Edgebrook will also be changed for years. Trust me, I know. And how many people across the country are following every article, watching every TV update? Millions. If their safe return provides joy to millions of people, if only for a few weeks, even a few days…"

"Somehow you're claiming to be a saint when you're really a monster."

"That's a reasonable assessment, at first look. I mean, I was repulsed by the idea for so long. I still am. But did you see that last press conference? Did you see what a better person Mrs. Hughes is for this? Did you see the love of the Collinis? Wait until they get their children back. Wait until they can hug them and hold onto a miracle."

"You're wrong."

Andy sways and grabs onto the bench again. "Fine. This is going nowhere." He looks around the room and says, "I don't have long, I need a better way. I need to convince you."

Terry is convinced this is just an elaborate attempt at justification. He needs to arrest Andy and bring the children home. He needs to follow through on his job. But he can't help spinning through Andy's arguments, looking for holes. "You know there's a problem."

"What problem?"

"You. You were one of the children saved. You were a product of this awakening that you say is supposed to change everyone's life, yet look what's become of you."

"Detective," Andy says, ashamed. "I was not a rescued innocent. I was the hero. I was at the front of the parade, given the key to the city, literally and figuratively, and I came out believing I was something special. Rather than appreciating life as a gift, I only appreciated myself. I became vain. I mean, carry it forward, why do you think I'm trying to save everyone again? It takes a lot of vanity to believe you can help so many people, that you know what's right. I accept that. But to your point, the difference is this time none of the children will be the hero. They will all be rescued innocents, just like Sue and Beth."

"And who was supposed to save them?"

"Yes," Andy sighs, "there was a side benefit for me. But it doesn't look like that's going to happen."

"What side benefit?"

"Let me complete the picture. Had you not entered when you did, here's the way it would have gone down, as simple as can be. A man abducts three children, the same man who was an accomplice to the first abduction, just as Art Morrell conjectured. He takes them here, where as you can see, there are all sorts of devices for him to hurt the children. But in the end, he realizes he has recreated the act more out of revenge than out of any desire to harm the children. So he convinces the police to give him the one that got away, me, where he takes me by gunpoint and brings me here. He plans, for his final act, to kill us all and dump us into this acid bath, whereby our bodies decompose into an untraceable slush and he escapes. But as he's about to kill me, I put up a struggle and push him in instead. The kidnapper dies. I save the children, and triumphantly return them to their families while the media captures everything."

"So you're the hero. Again."

"Yes."

"But what about this imaginary perpetrator? Where's his body?"

"Let it be known that a human falling into an acid bath leaves the same chemical soup as any other mammal of similar size. I've already mixed in the correct measure of a pig carcass for the forensics teams to think one person fell in. So our mythical kidnapper is already gone and no one can prove otherwise."

"You've surely left some other evidence, something to identify you as the abductor."

"You've had weeks to find a slip-up and never did. But even if there were some piece of evidence that doesn't match the crime, if something did evade my years of planning, how hard do you think the police will investigate it? With the villain dead and everyone home safely, with everything wrapped up so nicely, will the police really try to find an alternate scenario? Of course not. The story's too good to look for another ending. Would they really suspect me, the hero of Edgebrook?"

"The hero," Terry says, "you would be the hero again, just like you always wanted."

"That's correct, I'd be the hero. And I know what you're thinking, Detective. That's my motive. That's why I did all this, to return the children and be their savior once again. And you're somewhat right. I certainly looked forward to having the recognition again. But remember, this all began when I tried to kill myself. And before I ever started down this path I promised myself that I would follow through if it would help the children and their families, if it would help the cause."

"Follow through with what?"

"With suicide."

"Suicide? How does that help anything?"

Andy stands and shuffles toward the basin. He bends over and picks up the empty bag and drops it in. A low sizzle emanates as the acid consumes the bag, breaking it apart at the molecular level. Andy then reaches up to a bar screwed into the wooden planks overhead. He steps onto the basin's edge and hoists himself up, placing his feet on each side for balance. He stares Terry in the eyes before looking down at the acid bath below him. His hand momentarily slips from the overhead bar and Andy jerks as he regrips. "It's just a minor change in the story. The kidnapper takes me here, I put up a struggle, and rather than just him falling into the acid, we both go in. You come in right after, find the children and bring them home, and everyone lives happily ever after. Everyone but me. But when you think about it, one innocent casualty really cements the gravity of the situation. It really drives the point home. This may just be for the best."

"You're serious?"

Andy grins softly. "Dead serious."

"You're not going to just fall in…"

"As I said, I already have my courage. I swallowed it. A little poison pill that will be my demise anyway. A nice warm feeling. All over."

Terry studies the frothy liquid beneath Andy, emitting the pungent chemical smell that stings his nose and throat. The thought of entering it alive, of decomposing while still alive, is more than he can handle. "Why not just let the pill…? Why not let the pill do it?"

"A tempting idea. A very tempting idea. But does that make sense? The kidnapper brought me here to this acid bath, only to feed me a poison pill? No, this is the only way. That's why I'm up here, about to swerve into oncoming traffic so that others can learn."

Terry raises his gun and points it at Andy, "Step down!"

Andy just laughs. "What are you going to do? Shoot me?" The words slur as Andy blinks repeatedly, fighting the shutdown his body is experiencing.

Terry grasps how little time there is. He needs time; he needs to sort this out. He points the gun at Andy again, closes one eye and looks down its sight. "Step down from there!" Terry repeats, realizing he is the one with the gun and is absolutely powerless.

"You're missing the important point, why I told you this story. There is going to be a decision, your decision, as to the final outcome. You have a choice. You can tell everyone that I'm the kidnapper, that there never was an accomplice to the original abduction and that the children's lives were never at risk. If you do that, they'll never appreciate this gift. If they were really never in danger, then they have no reason to be thankful for their escape. This will just be some crazy memory that didn't mean anything. You can't let that happen."

"I'm going to tell the truth."

"You're willing to ruin their lives, let them return to their freefall? You're going to tell them they were never in any danger and this was all one big hoax?"

"I won't be your accomplice."

"You didn't kidnap the children. You didn't write the letters. You didn't cut off the toes. You've only done your job. You'll get the children home safely; you'll know the true culprit is dead. Everything will have worked out. Everything will be wrapped up nicely. But you have the power to make this either some crazy ruse or a truly life-altering experience. It's your choice."

"I will not be part of this."

"You already are a part. You have to make a decision one way or another."

"I will tell the truth."

"Detective, you don't have to make up a lie. Just say you showed up too late and didn't see anything. Say you don't know what happened. That's all you have to do. I've left plenty of clues, signs of a struggle, signs that there was another person. Let them piece it together and come to their own conclusion. Just don't ruin this, Detective. Please!" The last word echoes in the shed as Andy's features slack, but he resolutely stares at Terry as a tear runs down his face.

"Don't make this all for nothing. It's come so far, worked out so perfectly. I know I'm right. I know it!" Rather than succumb to the poison, Andy seems to be growing stronger, his conviction overpowering the drug that is shutting down his body.

"You're mad!"

"This isn't about me! That's what you've got to understand. In a few minutes I'll be dead. Whether I'm sane or not is pointless. But how people interpret this, how they move forward and live their lives, that's what's important. You have the power to control it. You have the choice."

"You're mad!"

"I can't beg anymore. You're just being so stubborn, so damn pig-headed. You don't want to believe any good can come out of this and won't give it a chance. Open your eyes! Give it a chance! Just watch the children re-unite with their families and then decide! Please. That's all I ask."

"Mad."

"Fine. I know that having strong convictions does not mean you are justified in your actions, that just because I believe in something, you should too. But I'm hoping this act shows just how sure I am, that it convinces you to at least open your mind. This is purely for you. The pill hasn't overpowered me yet, not like I'd want it too. I think I should have another ten, twenty minutes before I really go numb. I can still think. I can still feel." Andy swivels sideways over the basin.

"What are you doing?"

Andy does not respond. He concentrates on his balanced movements, talking aloud to himself. "May this act be enough to save those families. May this act be enough for redemption. May this convince you." Andy lowers himself, his hands and feet clutching the sides of the basin as he straddles the chemical broth. He inches his hands further out, holding himself upright, his arms shaking.

"Andy! No!"

"May this sacrifice be enough," Andy says, face-to-face with the foamy burn. "God help me." He closes his eyes, inhales one last deep breath, and then releases.

Terry's first reaction is to move forward, to try and save him, but as Andy drops into the basin, he immediately thrashes, unleashing gurgled screams. There is no saving him. Terry instead turns and runs out the shed door, fleeing the chemical's release into the air, the horrific sounds of sloshing.

Outside, Terry falls to the ground. He gasps for breath but only inhales the toxic burn, making him shudder at the thought of what Andy is going through. This is madness, complete and total madness. He almost wishes he had never come here, never placed the tracking device beneath Andy's car, never discovered the truth. He almost wishes Andy had gotten away with his plan, that Terry could be another spectator, standing forlornly outside the Community Center, rejoicing as Andy brings the children home.

Terry stands and paces, taking in deep breaths of air to expunge the smell. The sun has set and darkness surrounds him, and he wonders how everything came to this, how this could possibly be the ending. He knows the children are still trapped inside, and reenters the shed, keeping the foamy basin to the edge of his vision, making sure there are no movements. He cannot look directly at the monstrous end that befell Andy Frempt and instead concentrates on the shed's dividing partition.

Thin brown paper lines the wall, holding back the fluffy layer of yellow soundproofing, the bright color protruding in tufts along the floor and ceiling, as well as a rectangle in the middle. The blanket of soundproofing easily pulls away to reveal a metal door with slide bolts holding it shut. At the bottom is a hinged door, probably for pushing food in and out of the room. Terry slides open the bolts and pulls on the simple ring handle, putting his hand on the adjacent wall for leverage. The door is thicker than Terry expects, indicating how trapped the prisoners are, as well as how much work Andy has put into this plan. With a few strong tugs, the door opens and Terry peers inside. The floor is cement, and his eyes make out three white mats lined up in the corner. A simple nightlight shines above them, highlighting trays of food stacked haphazardly atop one another. Besides that, the room looks empty.

A tiny gasp comes from behind the door, followed by a, "Shhh!"

"Emily," Terry calls out stepping through the door and into the room. "Arielle. Alex." They say nothing. "My name is Detective Terrence Kruthers. I'm with the Edgebrook Police Department. I'm here to take you home."

"Home?" a girl's voice asks, followed by another sharp hush.

"It's all right," Terry says. "You're safe."

"Where's your uniform?" Alex asks.

Terry realizes how visible he is, that the children must be in the other corner, watching him. His eyes have only started to adjust to the dim light while the children's eyes have been adjusting for weeks.

"I'm a detective. I don't wear a uniform."

"Then where's your backup?"

"Are you all right?" Terry asks, squinting to make out the three forms huddled in the corner. "Can you walk or do you need help? As the children form into view, he first sees the white bandages around each child's legs. "I promise you," he says, speaking slow and direct, "I am here to help. I am here to take you home to your parents. Can you walk?"

"Yes, if I can go home."

The children look thinner, their skin no longer the ruddy complexion of youth, but overall they seem healthy and their expressions are hopeful. They watch his every move, assessing Terry through the darkness, determining if their nightmare is finally ending. They are the same children from the pictures, wearing the same clothes described over and over, and Terry holds out his hands and waits for them to approach him.

Emily and Arielle hold hands, while Alex stands by their side. "I want to go home," Arielle says.

"He looks okay," Emily confides.

"Show us your badge," Alex commands.

Terry pulls it from his jacket pocket. "See," he says. "Here's my driver's license, my credit cards."

"I don't know," Alex says.

"Look," Terry says, surprised by the children's distrust, "you can stay here, but I am going outside, and whoever wants to come with, can."

"I'm going," Arielle says, while the other two look at each other for agreement.

With that, Terry leans back and looks out the door, stares directly at the basin to determine what became of Andy. He could not look for himself, but with the responsibility of the children, with the possibility of an image that will haunt their dreams, he is able to view Andy's fate. The foam is thick, having bubbled over the sides and through a drain in the floor. The foam is red, blood red, but there is no trace of human form. The acid has stripped apart all life, leaving nothing more than a chemical broth.

He turns to find them standing in line behind him, Emily, Arielle and

Alex, all eager to leave their prison. He leads them in single file across the shed and into the cool night air. They breathe deeply, looking around in bewilderment while holding hands, keeping enough distance between themselves and Terry to show they don't fully trust him. They hardly limp at all, as if their bandages were just oversized, white sneakers.

"Are you ready?" Terry turns and asks. "Are you ready to go home?"

Night has fallen on the Community Center, but artificial lights glare all around, from the camera crews, from the hundreds of cars parked in the distance, and from the overhead parking lot lights around the Center itself. More lights line the surrounding walkway and its perimeter. Even the stadium spotlights of Championship Field have been turned on, illuminating the empty ball field in the distance. It is out there, past first base, the home team dugout, and the bleachers behind them, atop a ridge lined with trees, that the silhouette of a man and three children emerge.

They hold hands: Emily, Arielle, Terry and Alex. They walk slowly and awkwardly, and when Terry grasps the enormity of the situation, the field full of cars with people watching, the camera crews, police cars, and ambulances, all gathered outside the Community Center, he stops, lowers himself to a knee and gathers the children around him. "These people are here to rescue you."

"From what?" Alex asks.

"They're going to take you home."

"I know how to get home from here," he says, "It's that way."

Terry smiles at the boy's resilience. "You're right. But they've been out looking for you. They really want to make sure you get home."

As he talks, Terry hears the commotion begin. He's not sure how they've been identified from this distance, perhaps by one of the FBI agents with binoculars, or by one of the parents who could spot their child from any distance, but once verified, the secret cannot be kept.

The center of focus quickly shifts from the Community Center. Points of light flash in their direction, blinding them to the advancing throng of the media, police, FBI, and paramedics. The spectators exit their cars and join together forming another crowd. Shouts of amazement and jubilation ring out, while some plead for everyone to slow down, but the masses press on.

"It's all right," Terry repeats to the children, leading them to Championship Field's home plate and then gathering them behind him for protection. He prepares for the oncoming deluge and can't help but feel anxious himself. There is so much commotion bearing down on them and Terry wonders what he'll do or say. The crowd bears down, then stops on its own, halting just a few short yards from them. Most of the people are on-lookers, coming close enough to watch, close enough to feel part of the rescue, but not close enough to help.

The voices grow quieter, whisperings back and forth, when a single voice calls out, "Alex!"

At this, the boy jumps out from behind Terry, searching the faces. Antonio breaks through the crowd, pulling Natalya behind him, and they rush to Alex.

"Momma!" Alex screams out, leaping into Natalya's arms.

Natalya wails Alex's name over and over as she lifts him up, unable to hold back, squeezing him tight while Antonio's arms wrap them both even tighter. They kiss the boy on his head and face, asking if he is all right but not allowing him to answer, determining his response by his smile.

The surrounding crowd tightens in on them. Terry watches; his eyes sweep back and forth across the many faces, the cameras and the commotion, taking in the scene, oblivious that everyone is watching him. He is dimly aware that paramedics are now with the two girls, agents are pushing everyone back, and someone is asking him questions, but he can't make out the words.

Another break in the crowd occurs, a woman screaming, determined to be heard over the din, makes her way through. Emily sits beside a paramedic, who is trying to read her pulse and assess her condition. Emily pulls her wrist out from beneath the paramedic's two fingers, pushes herself up with her good leg, and though the paramedic tries to contain her, she leaps into her mother's arms. "Oh baby!" Carrie yells, tears streaming down her face as she pets the back of Emily's head, cups her cheeks in her hands, and lavishes her with kisses. Jim stands beside them, unable yet to cry, unable yet to do anything. With an open, dumb grin across his face, the tall wave of emotions swell within and he is aware that he is about to be overcome by total relief and total joy.

Terry still doesn't speak. Someone continues asking him questions as a bright light shines in his face. A reporter stands beside the camera and speaks into his microphone. Terry recognizes him, the same reporter that slipped Terry his business card, who told Terry he should write a book no matter the outcome. He wears a designer suit, his hair is slicked back, not a strand out of place, and he has the tonal good looks of a movie star. But as Terry's eyes adjust to the light, he sees the man's eyes are glistening, near tears. A police officer approaches and pushes the reporter back, who concedes his space, no longer edging his way to the front, no longer slipping his card into jacket pockets.

Antonio and Natalya stand by as a paramedic examines Alex. They each hold one of Alex's hands, unable to let go. Antonio will carry him to the ambulance. They will ride with him to the hospital. They will stay the night, leaving his room only when the doctors force them to the wait outside.

Arielle has her pulse taken as she answers another paramedic's questions. She watches Emily, still in her mother's embrace, as Jim is finally overcome, blubbering incoherently when he is given the chance to hold his daughter. Carrie leans over, takes Arielle's hand and asks her if she is all right. Arielle grins. When Carrie releases her hand and steps back, Arielle sees her father standing before her.

He studies her, confusion drawn across his face. "You're alive?" Steve questions, before dropping to his knees. Arielle walks to him and puts her arms around his neck, burying his face within her black curls. "You're alive!"

"Yes, daddy."

Steve lifts his arms and slowly closes them around Arielle, fearful that she won't be there when they come together. But as his arms wrap around his girl's slender frame and he feels her breath, his girl who looks so much like her mother, he calls out again, "You're alive!"

"Yes, daddy," she says, embarrassed that he is stating the obvious.

"Thank you," Steve cries, holding her out to look her over again, brushing the curls back that have fallen over her eyes. He pulls her tight and embraces her again. "Thank you, April. Thank you, thank you, thank you. Thank you for watching over her."

Terry makes a full revolution, witnessing the reunion and taking it in. All the children are safe. They are reunited with their families. They can go home. The ordeal is over.

"Are you all right?" Baumgardner repeats.

Terry nods, knowing he is about to be asked what happened. Terry replays the truth in his mind. There was not an accomplice in the original case. Andy Frempt abducted the children and he always planned on releasing them. When he cut their toes off, he used anesthetics so they would not feel any pain. He sanitized the wounds, sewed them up and put on a cast for protection. He never tortured them in any other way. He never molested them. The truth is that the children were never in mortal danger and they were always coming home tonight. They weren't really saved because there was nothing to save them from. That is the truth.

"What happened?" Baumgardner asks.

"Where's the perp?" another voice barks, Agent Sebold. "Did he get away?"

Terry inhales and chooses his words carefully. "The perpetrator is dead."

"You're certain?"

"I'm positive."

"How did he die?" Agent Sebold asks.

"Acid."

"Acid?"

"Yes, an acid bath."

"Why would there be an acid bath?" Baumgardner asks.

Terry says nothing.

"To dispose of bodies," Agent Sebold answers, "that's why. An acid bath can break down a body and not leave any DNA evidence. That's how the sick perp planned on disposing of the bodies."

"What about Andy?" Sebold asks.

"Yeah," Baumgardner says, looking around. "Where's Andy?"

Terry looks at Baumgardner and states the truth. "He's dead too."

"What? Dead? What happened? Did the perp...?"

Terry takes one last look around. He looks at the children, held close by their families, red faced with tears flowing. He looks at the reporters capturing the scene and broadcasting it across the country. Throngs of people stand in the periphery, the people of Edgebrook wrapped in each other's arms, smiling, crying, and quietly celebrating.

"What happened?"

Without fully acknowledging what he is doing, Terry responds, "He died trying to save the children."

"Did the perp kill Andy?"

"He died trying to save the children," Terry repeats.

"Trying to save them?" Baumgardner asks, "They are safe. He saved them." Baumgardner listens to his own words and repeats loudly so others can here, "Andy Frempt saved the children!"

Terry ignores the follow-up questions from Baumgardner and Agent Sebold, lowers his gaze, and works his way into the crowd. With head down, few people recognize him as they concentrate on the children's return, and he eventually emerges alone on the back side of the crowd, heading toward the Community Center. Terry inhales and mutters to himself, "I hope so. I hope he saved the children. I hope he somehow saved us all."

ABOUT THE AUTHOR

This is Ryan Scoville's first novel. He currently resides in Illinois with his wife, three children and Bernese Mountain Dog.

Made in the USA
Lexington, KY
25 March 2014